The Life of Gronsky

BILL ENGLESON

tellwell

Tellwell Talent
www.tellwell.ca

ISBN
978-0-2288-8842-0 (Hardcover)
978-0-2288-8841-3 (Paperback)
978-0-2288-8843-7 (eBook)

"In a way, people like her, those who wield a pen, can be dangerous. At once a suspicion of fakery springs to mind — that such a Person is not him—or herself, but an eye that is constantly watching, and whatever it sees changes into sentences; in the process it strips reality of its most essential quality—its inexpressibility."

Olga Tokarczuk, Drive Your Plow
Over The Bones of The Dead

Acknowledgement/Preface

The Life of Gronsky was initially written for two separate writing experiences. The first third was created for the 2021 3-Day Novel Contest. This was my first ever attempt at devoting seventy-two hours non-stop at anything. Confession: I did take a few breaks…and I slept well.

At the end of the weekend, I had a novella.

I shared it with my most loyal reader, Mary McDonough.

She wanted more of Gronsky.

Come November, I signed up for my first NaNoWriMo engagement. Its very simple premise is to write fifty thousand words in November.

My loyal reader, Mary, seemed to enjoy the expansion of Gronsky's world.

Since then, beta reader Bette Kosmolak, a member of the Comox Valley Writer's Society, has offered important information to help finalize the book. Scenes set in Winnipeg needed her keen eye.

Editor/writer Amy Reiswig performed a stellar professional edit that vastly improved my more egregious grammatical and narrative missteps.

I would also like to thank authors Terry Fallis, Stephen Miller and Merrilee Robson for graciously reading the manuscript and offering succinct blurb-worthy comments.

Labour Day Weekend, New Westminster, 2021.

Friday Morning, September 3rd

There it was. The first lie. The first fiction. It wasn't morning. It was evening. Friday evening. Gronsky had thought he might stay up past midnight and at least knock out a few words, get started, set the stage, do something. But it was around ten thirty, and he was starting to fade. The wine, he supposed. Yeah. The wine. And there was nothing better than a good night's sleep. Everyone knew that.

When it had been Friday morning, he had sat on his porch. It was a little past seven. He was sipping his coffee, hot, tongue burning hot even with the 2%. Traffic was moving. The sounds of the day beginning were humming in the air. It was a little wet. Rain had finally arrived. He was pleased about that. Wet earth. We all needed damp soil. Grass was going to grow a bit now. There hadn't been much lawn to cut this past summer. Droughts were useful for something.

Gronsky called it a porch, this thing that he was sitting on, but what his mother had insisted was a porch was what he preferred to call a veranda. She would have none of it. "Airs, Gilbert. No one appreciates a little boy putting on airs." So, porch it was. Veranda had been one of his first big words. He loved the way it had rolled off Miss Hastings tongue. VERRRRR RANNNN DAAA. Magic. He had been in grade three. She was young, Miranda Hastings was. As young as an adult could be. She'd laughed when she rhymed Miranda with Veranda. "Try it, yourself," she'd said. Not veranda but Gilbert. But it was disappointing. "Gilbert" offered few rhyming options then. Or now. None really, other than filbert. And Gronsky was hopeless. There were no fun rhymes to be had there.

But Gronsky hadn't cared about rhymes all that much. He had had such a crush on Miranda Hastings that first day. And it grew during the weeks, the months that followed. The way her red lips formed words, smiled like he and she had a secret no one else knew.

But she was gone in a year. "These young teachers," his mother had clacked her tongue. "All they want is a man. Security. They'll find out."

She'd be over eighty now, Gronsky thought. Miss Hastings. Miranda Veranda. Whatever the name of the man she married, he never knew. Or if he did, it had faded. He remembered how crushed he was though. What his crush on her had come to.

Still, he wished her well. He would always have veranda.

He sat there Friday morning, wondering if he could pull off a novel in three days, something he'd never even come close to before. He'd had only a few hours to sign up.

He was no spring chicken, no clichéd early fowl, but it was a challenge that he thought he needed to take, and there was nothing like the present. Time was moving along. The last few years he had started to write things. Trivial things. Notes about his life. Then one day he discovered flash fiction. It was like a new world had opened. Stories told in miniature. At first, he grabbed little incidents from his days, thoughts, puny tales, and shaped them, went online, and posted them. There were a ton of sites that encouraged writers. They'd come and go, and he would play as often as he wished. He knew he was self-taught, but that didn't mean he hadn't learned from other writers. He wasn't even sure that he thought of himself as a writer. What he did was similar to doing crosswords. His mother had enjoyed doing crossword puzzles, and, in truth, it *was* like writing, filling in the blanks, one-word stories at a time.

Three Days preyed on his mind. Three whole days. A mental list of pros and cons flashed before his eyes. On the pro side, he didn't have a lot to do. No obligations. No social engagements. Covid had been useful that way. You could be a hermit and still be a responsible and engaged citizen. Gronsky believed that he had just the right number of social contacts. He was in control of his life. Granted, it was mostly an inner social life, but it worked for him.

The con side was a tad more daunting. He had habits. One was watching the US Open. Any tennis contest, really. The past few years had seen a wonderful array of Canadian professional tennis players, and Gronsky felt a patriotic obligation to catch as many of their matches as he could. Why, he wondered, did the three-day novel writing contest have to fall smack dab in the middle of a two-week feast of tennis? It wasn't logical. Forget logic. It just wasn't right. But there it was. Could he do both? Watch tennis for hours at a time AND write a novel. Gronsky fist pumped and yelled, YEAH! He then signed up. He was in. Fifty bucks. Sixteen sixty-six a day. Cheap at half the price.

Even with those extra two pennies.

Morning, September 4th

Gronsky had gotten a good seven hours' sleep. Only a little tossing and turning. A few sirens had wailed in the night, and he supposed they had upset the tranquility of his slumber, but the bodies of city dwellers adjusted to those ever-present sounds. He certainly had. And sirens in the night, especially in the night, as distressing as they were, they were also somehow comforting sounds. It meant attending incidents that needed attending. Saving lives. Hopefully, saving lives. Lives were always at risk. Age was a risk. Every minute of life was a risk. Maybe that was why he was going to write this time-compressed novel. He was running out of time.

He got up at seven, made coffee, grabbed some yogurt and fruit, went to his den, sat down at his word processor, TV at his back ready for tennis at eight, and started pounding out words. In a number of his tiny flash fiction pieces, he'd given birth – that was what it was – to Jimmy the Slider Watkins, Private Eye. Watkins would carry the load of this novel. What to call it. He didn't have a title. *The Big Sleep* was taken. *The Little Snooze* seemed stupid. Gronsky always wrote titles. He needed a title. *THE LAST BREATH*. Yeah, he thought, that would do.

Chapter One, The Last Breath

The first thing I noticed about her was her ankle. Believe me, it had been years since a well-turned ankle had grabbed me by the eyeballs.

"Mr. Watkins," she asked, right leg stepping in from the hallway. I noticed the ankle and the leg and then she was fully in the office, and I was willing to admit the obvious: "James Watkins, Private Enquiries at your service."

I told her to take a seat. She followed instructions. I appreciated that. So rare these days. "And what might your name be?" I asked, rather sloppily.

"Do I have to tell you?"

I understood that some folks required a level of comfort before they exposed themselves. "No, that'll keep. For a while. How can I help you?"

It would turn out to be one of the oldest stories in the book.

Mid-morning, September 4th

Gronsky stopped at that point. He wondered why it was one of the oldest stories in the book. What book? Every detective book he'd read. That book. He took a breather, and his attention was drawn to Bianca Andreescu's match. She was a set and two games up on her third-round opponent. Last night, and the night before, four Canadians had won amazing matches. Most amazing had been the soon to be nineteen-year-old Leylah Annie Fernandez. She would in fact turn nineteen on Labour Day, the last day of this three-day novel writing deal. Gronsky was amused by the coincidence, what he thought of as a coincidence. Surely this spoke to the symbiotic relationship between rapid writing and tennis.

There was a knock at his den door.

"Gilbert? You in there?"

Gronsky got up and opened the door. "Morning, Miriam. Kind of tied up. Remember?" He didn't want to sound short with Miriam, but it likely came across that way.

Miriam O'Malley was one of Gronsky's two tenants. A soon-to-retire librarian at the local public library, she had lived in Gronsky's renovated triplex for about ten years. Occasionally, they had been intimate. Very occasionally.

"Oh, that novel thing?" Miriam said.

"Yes. I've just started with it. Is there something the matter?"

"Your TV is on."

"It's a writing aid, Miriam."

As he said that, there was a yell from the television. Gronsky glanced over and saw that Andreescu had just won her match.

"Not very efficient, Gilbert. I would think that quite a distraction."

He held his tongue, did not say, "Not as much as you, Miriam." Instead, he said, "It helps me focus."

She shook her head. "Okay. Different strokes."

Gronsky avoided the word stroke, did not like to hear it, even in the context Miriam had used it. His mother had died of a stroke. As did his father. He expected to go out the same way.

"So, Miriam, what did you want?"

"Oh, sorry. Sam and I were going to cook Thai tonight and we wondered if you wanted to join us. Actually, he's cooking and I'm the scullery maid." Sam was Gronsky's other house-tenant, Sam Simmons, who worked in International Development and was frequently away, either in Ottawa or overseas. When he was at home, he loved to cook and tell stories of his travels. They always seemed to be the same story, just set in slightly various locations.

Gronsky weighed his options. He liked to eat. He didn't like to cook. Gronsky hadn't travelled much so he more or less enjoyed Sam's tales and genuinely liked his food.

He would need fuel. It would steal into his creative time, but he might die if he didn't eat properly. He loved spicy Thai food. That was the clincher.

"Sounds good," he finally said. "I might have to just eat and run. Back here. That okay?"

Miriam nodded that it was, and they settled on seven p.m.

Gronsky shut the door and returned to the task at hand. Tennis continued. Sakkari and Kvitova. Both were impressive players. Talent will out, he thought, and fell quickly back into his tale.

Chapter One cont., The Last Breath

"I think my husband is in trouble," she continued. "Serious trouble."

I watched her closely for a bit. Not in a creepy way. My way. I sound like a certain ex-New York Governor, don't I? Anyways, she had red hair, my favourite hue other than blonde and brunette, was in her mid-thirties, give or take ten years the way some well-cared for women can look. You can never tell. Even a raconteur like me has trouble. Years of watching women and I was still in the dark.

"What sort of serious trouble?" I plunged in.

I knew she wanted to tell me, but she was also playing her cards pretty much close to her bumptious breasts, or at least that was how I imagined them.

"Can I trust you?"

"That's the name of the game. Private enquiries. My word is my...do I need to say it?"

She almost offered a smile. I almost said, "Bond, Jimmy Bond." But thankfully didn't. Another thing best left unsaid.

"I guess I have to. Trust you, I mean?"

"It can't be that hard. You came to me. You have the problem..."

"My husband has the problem..." she attempted to equivocate.

"He may have a problem, but you have him, right?"

Another attempt at a smile.

"Is that a problem?" she asked.

I am no good at double entendres, so I let it slide. We could get into that quagmire later.

"Look, now that we have parried some, time to add some nitty gritty. Like I asked before, what serious trouble are we talking about?"

"He exports equipment used in catastrophic events. Earthquakes and the like. It's not a big company but with global warming and all the disasters happening, he needed to expand. For some reason, his partner went to offshore funding sources. He thought it would be cheaper to finance…"

"And found out it wasn't?"

"Yes. Now they…the money people…are squeezing him and his partner."

"Squeezing how?"

"Harry Stokely, my husband's partner…they are…holding him… somewhere until Gerry comes up with a million."

"Dollars?"

"Yes."

Almost small potatoes these days, I thought. Not that I had anywhere near that many spuds.

"Here might be where we talk turkey. I get $150.00 an hour, ten hours in advance, and the key thing…I need to know your name…and his name. Before we go any further."

"Claudette Conway," she confessed. "Gerald…Gerry is my husband. Would e-transfer do?"

I said it would. She made the payment right there. I loved this modern technology. And the red hair.

And the folding money.

"At some point," I said, the police will need to be involved."

"Is that necessary? Gerry doesn't really want to involve them."

"He knows you are hiring some help?"

"No. He said he'd handle it. We fought about it. It's been two days."

"So, he's missing as well?"

Late Morning, September 4th

Sakkari won the first set. Gronsky turned to the tube to watch a few minutes. There was an intensity on the court that easily impressed a couch potato, especially between Sakkari, a muscular young Greek, and the Czech, Kvitova – an equally if not more impressive player. Aside from her talent, Kvitova was also a victim of a terrible assault over Christmas 2016, when she was stabbed in her dominant left hand by an intruder. Potentially career ending, in six months she was back playing.

By ten thirty Sakkari had beaten Kvitova. Gronsky decided that it was time for a longer break. A few minutes anyways. Sakkari was being interviewed post match. She admitted that she used a lot of hairspray to keep her long hair immobilized on the top of her head. Gronsky muttered that he did not need to know that. Post match interviews in any sport were often mundane, repetitive. The injection of hairspray was a new one for him.

Gronsky went into his kitchen and poured another cup of coffee. It needed a microwave blast. He added the 2% and went out onto his porch. Veranda. It was a cloudy morning, not cold, but there was a slight sense of chill in the air. It was on its way, autumn, winter, sorrow. The forecast for the weekend was still for rain. It was a good day to be inside. Gronsky thought that this sort of weather, dour, dark, was likely conducive to writing a thriller. He wasn't sure about that, but instinctively he felt that storm shadows, grey skies, the portend of torrents, all of it enhanced his grimmer personality. Not that he was a stern man. He quite liked a good laugh, occasionally even offering a joke. But a surlier disposition flowed in him. There was no denying that.

As he sipped his coffee, he did what he often did in random reflective moments: reviewed his life. Selective snippets of course, the same old ones, for there were practically no new ones to speak of. This was a sad fact of aging. One of many sad facts, if he was being honest. He supposed that he was as honest as anyone cared to be.

Truth was, there was little new to discover when he did engage in this casual diversion. He supposed that the act of creation, of writing, inspired such voyages into the past. He allowed that perhaps Miriam's knock at the door, the dinner invitation, the possible hint of some later familiarity spurred this particular venture. Miriam was not a passionate woman, but she was open to sharing her bed from time to time, and Gronsky was available, flexible in an arthritic way, and not particularly demanding. In fact, she had been his tenant for some years before they had initially stumbled, literally stumbled, into bed.

She had received word that her brother, Vincent, had passed away in Edmonton, and she would be flying there in the morning to be with his widow and their adult children. She was sad and wanted to talk about Vincent, remember their childhood growing up on a farm, the harshness of their life, a controlling father, a weepy mother, Vincent's rebellion, her own meekness, a younger sister's withdrawal inward. Gronsky had offered a hug of commiseration, and that had quietly, surprisingly led to an intimate moment. Gronsky had offered to stay, but Miriam sent him back to his quarters. In the morning, he drove her to the airport, they shook hands, and she was gone for two weeks. When she returned, he thought, well, that was that. It wasn't. Every few months, Miriam would initiate closeness, and Gronsky felt obliged to respond. Not much was ever spoken about their infrequent liaisons, and that too suited them both.

As he thought about Miriam, he naturally thought about his marriage to Stella Fishbine. His only marriage. A disastrous effort. That had been decades ago, 1967. Decades. The 1960s were a strange time, particularly for a straightlaced fellow like Gronsky. He thought of himself that way. Possibly it was the influence of his mother. She had been widowed quite young, and Gilbert was her only issue. That is how she talked about him. Her issue. He'd been raised in this very house, which he had later invested heavily in to create three self-contained suites. His of course was the largest, but the other two, one on each floor of the three-story Georgian, were pristine. In his mother's day, *his* early days, it had been simply a boarding house. Room and board. Not much else. In 1966 a group of students moved into the house next door. In the vernacular of the day, hippies. Ten or fifteen people at a time lived there. There were noise complaints to the city. Eventually a sort of truce was reached; his mother softened, or maybe she just got worn out. In any case, one day Gronsky met a new resident,

Stella Fishbine. She had recently moved there from Oregon. Gronsky was smitten.

Stella was intoxicating. In months she was pregnant. Marriage was inevitable. Gronsky got a job at a local paper mill, and they rented an apartment on the hillside looking over the river. Robert Gronsky, a healthy eight-pounder and change, was born in April 1968. A year later Dawn Gronsky, a whopping nine-pounder, came into their life. By 1970 dissention overtook the marriage, and Stella took the kids and left with one Jacob Loewen for parts unknown. Shattered and angry, Gronsky moved back with his mother. He harboured the thought that Stella might keep in touch with her former commune mates next door. It was a longshot that never bore fruit.

Gronsky noticed that his coffee was also finished and so returned to the den and *The Last Breath*.

Chapter Two, The Last Breath

Part of me knew that I should step away from the Conway case. There were enough indicators to suggest that it was far more than I was equipped to handle. I preferred and was skilled at domestics, cheating husband, floozy wives, runaway offspring – your average socially explosive situations that required a smart hand, a good camera, a sense of humour, and a willingness not to risk life and limb.

I liked my life and all of my limbs, and Claudette Conway and her compromised hubby were knocking on big trouble's door.

I got Claudette's particulars, the home, and business addresses for the Conways and the Stokelys, their phone numbers, a picture of Gerry and the works, and suggested she go home and wait.

"Wait for what?" she asked.

"Maybe a call from me. Harry Stokely married?"

"Divorced. He has a …"

"Partner?"

"I was going to say lover. I don't know his name. He's pretty new."

"Good information," I said, not that it was.

After Claudette left, I did a Google search of all the parties. CS Imports was there and also photos of both owners. I sensed that I might need some extra eyes on the case. Phil Gains was a friend I occasionally subcontracted with. Phil was old school, even older schooled than I was. He only took smaller jobs, and surveillance was his specialty.

I called Phil, asked him to check out the business and, if possible, try and keep an eye on Claudette. It wasn't that I didn't trust my new client. It was more…I didn't trust my new client.

Hypocrisy sometimes saves your life.

Afternoon, September 4th

Gronsky looked at the time. Noon. Hunger pangs. Another seven hours before the Thai dinner. He decided it was a suitable time for a sandwich break. Food always before dishonor. A first set tiebreaker between Djokovic and Nishikori was just ending. The Japanese player was victorious. An interesting turn of tennis events.

Aside from some routines, Gronsky had fairly flexible eating habits. Leftovers, should he have any, were as desirable as not. They were familiar, like old memories. A meal partially eaten one day would serve him well the next. All very practical. By the same token, he was not averse to eating something new. His mother had not been a spare the rod and spoil the child mother. "Eat what's on your plate," was her down-to-earth mantra. She had been raised that way and expected Gilbert to be the same. There were no food allergies when she was growing up. Food was fuel. His brief eating life with Stella and their two progeny was mostly along the same lines. Stella refused on principle, it being a time of liberation, to cook for him. She did breast feed both children and took care of their nutritional needs. Gerber's and such. Gronsky had to fend for himself. Stella did expect him to feed her. "I look after them. You look after me." Gronsky accepted her dictates but not without a little grumbling. When Stella left with Jacob and his children, he comforted himself somewhat by realizing that she had been planning her marital abdication all along. He had reported her disappearance to the police, and they did a cursory investigation, but it led nowhere. They discovered a good reason for it leading nowhere. Stella Fishbine was not Stella Fishbine. Her identification, passport, and birth certificate belonged to the real Stella Fishbine who still lived in Salem Oregon with her hubby and three kids. "No wonder I couldn't find that stuff," the real Stella told authorities when contacted.

As the only photographs Gronsky had of his un-wife, the fake Stella, and his two real kids, had been carted away when fake Stella up and disappeared, that part of Gronsky's life lacked meaningful documentation.

His mother did encourage him to search further, as she was just beginning to feel grandmotherly. However, it turned out that even Jacob Loewen was a pseudonym and all traces of the quartet – his beautiful offspring, non-existent wife, and her fake-named lover – were history.

Gronsky reluctantly gave up any thought of finding any of them.

He dwelled on these irreconcilable losses over lunch, which consisted of a leftover sausage, sliced onion, and gouda cheese sandwich with a side plate of charred broccoli. Oh, and a few garlic stuffed olives. Returning to his den, tennis was still afoot. Djokovic had taken the second set. The men would be at it a while.

Gronsky spent a few moments idling watching the ball being sent back and forth over the net, and occasionally into the net. The top seeds usually won. Sometimes they didn't. Therein was the true excitement: underdog victories. Gronsky himself was an occasional sporting underdog. He had recently taken up pickleball, a fine activity for those with even a modicum of mobility. If he had not taken up three-day novel arms, he might well have sought out a game. He had once said, in an especially vigorous moment, that "pickleball is life to me." But so was pizza. Gronsky often made stuff up.

Back to *The Last Breath* he went.

Chapter Two cont., The Last Breath.

With Phil busy checking out his two assignments, CS Imports and Claudette Conway, I drove over to the Stokely house and parked half a block down. It was a quiet neighbourhood on the east side of the city. I hoped I wasn't sticking out, but it was midday and there was little street activity. That could work against my stealth, but I looked harmless enough and hoped I wouldn't be there for more than half an hour. As it was, I struck paydirt. A car pulled up in front of Stokely's house and two gentlemen exited. One looked about forty and the other was somewhat younger. Neither looked particularly intimidating. They went to the front door, apparently had a key, and went in. That seemed good enough for me. I turned the engine on, put the car in gear, and drove up the street, pulling in just behind them. I got out, walked up to the door, and knocked.

The older of the two came to the door. "Can I help you?" he asked. Immediately, that put me on the defensive. I hadn't actually worked out my next lines. Detecting is sometimes adlibbing. I have a nice smile and people often comment on my warm presence. In the morning in the bathroom mirror, I don't often see it. Thank Christ others do. So I smiled and said, "Jimmy Watkins. Happened to be in the neighbourhood and thought I'd look up my old buddy, Harry. He home?"

Right away, the shoe was on the other foot. Either these guys knew Harry and might wonder why they had never heard of Jimmy Watkins, or they would fake it, give me some line that would essentially say, 'not home right now,' which would then bring up the point of who they were and what were they doing at Harry's house.

Older Gentleman looked back into the house and asked the younger one, who was not in my line of sight, "Peter, do we know when Harry might be back? Not today, right?" The other man's voice then answered. "Tomorrow…the next day. Hard to say."

"Too bad," I said. "Any way of contacting old Harry? I'd hate to be passing through and not touch base. It's been a while."

"Sorry," said Older Gentleman, "he's…incommunicado. You know, looking for a little privacy."

I almost left it at that but did give Older Gentleman a burner phone number I use and said, "if you can, give old Harry this number."

Older Gent wisely took the number, smiled almost as sweetly as I could, and we parted. I noted their license plate number, got in my car, and drove away. I then brilliantly circled the block and parked a full block behind them. And waited.

Late Afternoon, September 4th

Gronsky was feeling the need of a pee break. And some libation. *The Last Breath* was writing itself, but even at that, it was exhausting work. Never having written more than a five-hundred-word story, he was finding it challenging to maintain the tension to keep the narrative flowing. Even sitting at the keyboard was putting a strain on his antique parts.

He switched to another tennis channel to catch the fourth set between the entertaining thirty-five-year-old Frenchman, Gael Monfils, and twenty-year-old Italian young gun, Jannik Sinner who seemed poised to end his opponent's US Open hopes.

Gronsky went to the bathroom and quickly returned to watch the end of the set. He favored neither party. Often he was content to enjoy the process no matter who won. Sometimes that even applied when Canadians were playing. Though Gronsky had never travelled outside of North America, he thought of himself as a man of the world. Tennis certainly was one of the great universal sports, as players from countries big and small travelled the earth playing tournaments. Covid had shuttered that wonderful activity for a time, but the sport seemed to have rebounded without two many viral hitches.

As Gronsky thought about Covid and tennis, he wondered if perhaps it might be time to travel to places he had only heard about. He was not impecunious, and time was moving on. Portugal attracted him. He didn't know why. It just sounded like it would be worth at least one visit. Greece had a similar attraction. And Thailand. Even Iceland, though he absolutely despised the cold.

Forget Iceland, he thought. That might be a mistake. Mexico would be better. As he formed a mental list of where he might go, he had to allow that the world was a dangerous place. He was not an adventurous man. He had to live with the guilt of permitting whoever Stella Fishbine really was to take his seed, have his children, and then pilfer them far away to wherever she had landed. What sort of man would permit that, would not spend the rest of his days seeking them, finding them, protecting them?

As these awkward matters of self doubt swarmed Gronsky, the crowd on television let out a humongous roar. Monfils had fought back from what seemed like a fourth set defeat to take the set. It would now go to a fifth and deciding encounter. The entertaining older player had revived himself. All things were possible in tennis. The young overwhelming the experienced, the veteran announcing that he or she was still viable. Gronsky knew he should get back to *The Last Breath,* but the excitement he felt for Monfils was palpable and he deemed it worthy of a few more minutes of respect. He sought out another watery libation and some fruit and settled in to the fifth set.

As he did, he thought about Miriam's imminent retirement. Though she hadn't talked all that much about it, she did seem excited to be entering a new phase of her life. Gronsky knew that people who retired often decided to travel, to see parts of the world that they had never had the time to visit – or, in his case, the inclination. For the first time, he considered the possibility of he and Miriam travelling together. Though he wasn't sure that they had shared interests. In fact, he was a little unclear what interests beyond work she actually had, though that was likely because he often didn't pay close attention to her either in the bedroom or out, beyond his gentlemanly efforts at giving and receiving a reasonable measure of pleasure. He vowed to pay more attention to what she talked about. Tonight's dinner would afford him an excellent opportunity.

More tennis hoots and hollers refocused Gronsky to the screen, and he saw that Monfils was having a tough go of it. A simple overhead smash failed to succeed. Gronsky's heart slipped a notch. Was the young gun going to be victorious? Did it matter?

Yes, he declared. Of course, it mattered. Not as much as some things – food on the table, a warm bed – but it was worth something.

Gronsky noticed that he was having a very thoughtful day. While not at all sure whether he would complete the three-day novel excursion, he was venturing into small tributaries of interest that might prove just as fruitful as authoring a book. The fifth set between Monfils and Sinner was getting close to the end. He needed to watch it as well as return to *The Last Breath*. So much pressure, he thought. So many competing pleasures.

Chapter Three, The Last Breath

While I waited for Older and Younger Gents to depart the Stokely house, I gave Phil a call. I wasn't expecting much progress, but any information would help. He answered on the third ring.

"Hey, Jimmy, you turning into a task master?"

"Only if it would move your butt faster, Phil."

"Then don't waste your time. You know I only got one speed."

"Yeah, slow and steady."

Later Afternoon, September 4th

Just as Gronsky wrote "slow and steady, Sinner put the kibosh on Monfil's journey at the US Open this year. The young gun proved victorious.

In that moment of pause, Gronsky decided to have a shower and refresh himself. Writing a novel was no cause to work up a sweat, and he had a dinner date in a few hours.

He was mostly an afternoon shower guy. Always had been, though there were exceptions. While he disliked being wet in the morning, evenings of romantic embrace sometimes required a morning scrubbing. Afternoon showers were by far his preferred thing, especially if afterwards you could sit outside in the afternoon sun. Drink a beer. All clean and refreshed. That wouldn't happen today. It was a day he was quite content to stay indoors.

On the television, Gronsky overheard tennis commentators mentioning all of the support services tennis players had. Massage therapists, dieticians, nannies. Maybe not nannies. Dog walkers, apparently. Gronsky, even with the refreshing shower he had just had, was feeling the pain, the weighty tug of his old muscles, dormant things today that were strained from sitting in front of the word processor. He wasn't particularly envious of the services available to tennis players, at the US Open level. Still, he felt his muscles and tendons were starting to regret that they had more than forty-eight more hours of this creative torture.

He was delaying the obvious. He returned to *The Last Breath*.

Chapter Three cont., The Last Breath

"That's right," said Phil. "You get what you pay for. Slow, steady, and on the money."

"What have you found, Phil?"

"CS Imports is shut tighter than a constipated scotch terrier. Mail piling up. Checked with some nearby businesses. They said they haven't seen anyone in days. Maybe even weeks."

"And Mrs. Conway?"

"Headed over there now. Want to join me?"

"Other fish frying. I'll check back with you in an hour."

"Fine. Over and out."

"It's a phone, Phil. Not a walkie talkie."

"Whaddayaknow. Could have fooled me. Ciao, junior."

Phil rang off and I called a contact at Motor Vehicle. Lucy Chenille picked up, and we kibbitzed for a few moments. Every enquiry agent worth his salt had to have contacts like Lucy. The world needed information, and an agent especially needed help getting it. A few years earlier, Lucy's grandmother had been the victim of a hit and run. The police had done their due diligence, but the case went cold. Lucy's father had hired me to look into it. It took a year before I tracked down the repair shop that had worked on the murder car, a blue Subaru. It was one of my better moments. From that day forward, Lucy was in my pocket and was much appreciated.

I gave her the Two Gent's licence number and in a nanosecond, she got back to me with the owners curriculum vitae.

It was a company car. Gelbart Holdings. It didn't ring a bell, and Google had nothing to offer except an address on the opposite side of town. I beat a path there and found myself ensconced in one of those two-story business complexes that people use to hide whatever they are doing from prying eyes. My prying eyes were stimulated.

Evening, September 4th

Gronsky's ears perked up as he heard the next US Open match was about to begin with Canadian star, Denis Shapovalov.

He was already sensing that *The Last Breath* was needing some rejuvenation, that his plot line needed a transfusion. More to the point, he was reaching a level of creative exhaustion with which he was unfamiliar. He'd never immersed himself in such a demanding project. It had been fun up to now and he didn't want to lose that pleasure quotient. He knew he was close to a third of his minimum target, word wise. This offered some satisfaction as well as a challenge. How far could he go?

Gronsky decided to enjoy the tennis match and then join Miriam and Sam for dinner. That sounded immensely civilized.

Alas, the star Canadian fell. Gronsky could live with that. There were still a few Canucks alive and well in the tournament; there was still sporting hope for his country. Those things mattered in the same way that the life of an ant mattered. Gronsky believed he had his priorities fairly straight… one never really knew. It was all guess work.

Just before dinner, he caught the tail end of a fine tennis match in which Shelby Rogers, a veteran American player, miraculously beat the Number one player in the world, Ash Barty. Rogers had previously lost to Barty six times. During the post match interview, Rogers was a delight. Real, personable, authentic and a credit to her profession.

At seven, Gronsky joined Sam and Miriam in Sam's suite. Essentially a penthouse, it was spacious, albeit with slopping roof lines, and was blessed with a magnificent view of the cityscape and the river.

Gronsky had brought both a Pinot Noir and a Chablis to satisfy everyone's tastes.

"Glad you could get away from your writing adventure, Gil. How's it going?" Sam asked.

Gronsky had prepared a number of possible answers to this question, one he expected would be asked.

He offered a smile. A Gronsky smile. Adequate but not smirking. "Sam, it has been a challenging day. You ever tried to write a novel?"

"Thesis," Sam replied.

"How many words?"

"Forty thousand or thereabouts."

"Over what period of time?"

"Eight months…give or take."

"So, today I managed about seven thousand words. Or will before I hit the hay," said Gronsky.

"But no facts? No research?."

"Ah, Sam. My life has been my research. Writers need to know themselves."

As Gronsky pontificated, he was snickering as well. He has thrilled to be pompous. Pomposity was a hoot.

"Totally agree. But seriously, Gil, facts are facts. Fiction, fiction is any old thing you write."

Gronsky did not like these sorts of debates. And he didn't really want to aggravate Sam. At least not until he had eaten.

"Totally agree. You can't beat facts. Fiction is almost a harder slog. You not only have to make it up, but you also need to make it sound, I don't know, factual. At least what I'm writing."

"You two," chimed in Miriam. "I'm famished. What's on the menu Sam? It smells delicious."

Gronsky was ready to put on the feedbag. Eating was preferable to debating.

"Good idea," said Sam, "we have a few dishes…vegetarian for Miriam's benefit. Let's bring them all out and dig in."

It was a satisfying meal. They started with Som Tum, a very tasty papaya salad filled with garlic, lime and tamarind juice with tomatoes, papaya, and peanuts. Then a basic but satisfying noodle-festooned Pad Thai, and something Sam called Gang Jay, a vegetarian curry with plenty of tofu. These were accompanied by a tasty side dish of corn fritters in a spicy dipping sauce.

During dinner, they discussed Covid's impact on them. Sam's international travel had been truncated, and even his inter-provincial journeys had been limited. He acknowledged that he was fortunate to have family resources as well as his own and had not been much affected. So, no real adventures to relate. Miriam was unionized and had not been touched at all in terms of work, except for all the times public libraries were closed. Gronsky, being retired, a property owner, and a semi-recluse (except for his fluctuating weather dependent pickleball activities) barely noticed Covid, apart from the agony in his community and in the world.

With his admittedly inelegant social skills, Gronsky changed the course of the evening's discussion to Miriam's expected retirement. "Haven't heard what you want to do when you retire, Miriam? Any plans?"

As he asked, he also remembered that Miriam did not relish being put on the spot. He should have remembered that, and by the time he did he could not think of a way to ease her discomfort.

"You may not be ready," he said, attempting to find a way out. "I shouldn't have asked. Tell us in your own good time."

She responded quickly. "I'm not in shock, Gilbert. I'm happy to retire. Covid…I don't know, has helped me prepare. I'm ready to go. Where exactly, I don't know. Travel I suppose."

Gronsky left it there, except to touch Miriam's hand and smile. A Gronsky smile. Guaranteed to be real.

After dinner, they parted. Gronsky was still tinkering with the notion of travel. Not just travel but something more involving with Miriam. He poured an evening brandy and sat on his porch, his veranda, and smiled into the evening. He was concerned about the direction of *The Last Breath* but trusted that his creative juices would carry the day. Perhaps even two days. He sipped slowly, as was his custom, and absorbed the nights sounds. There were drunks on the street, car speeding much too fast, the usual sirens and sounds of urban excess, and he wondered if this was where he would end his days. On the street, quite close, he heard an unfamiliar sound. It almost sounded like "Gronsky."

And then it was gone. He gave it little more thought. It had been a long and tiring day, and the next two days would repeat the demands on him. There might be unexpected demands, things and events simmering today that he had barely noticed. He ever so briefly considered pulling what his generation and preceding generations called an all-nighter. There was nothing to be gained. Words, perhaps, but he had had his fill of words today. Words written, spoken, and most of all, unspoken. Sleep called. And he obeyed.

Morning, September 5th

Gronsky woke up Sunday morning with a sweet combination: thrill of adventure and doubt as well as a skinful of wine semi-remorse. As far as the three-day novel course horserace was concerned, he could barely see the finish line. He knew he had to double yesterday's total output and the thought exhausted him. "I am no Marcel Proust, no Victor Hugo," he barked. "I know my limits. "No one was listening, of course. Still, it was an honest expression of humility and truth, and he knew that somewhere in the ether, Proust and Hugo might appreciate the sentiment even if no one else did.

Sunday mornings offered a routine that even the three-day novel contest and the US Open could not replace. Eggs. Farm fresh eggs. If he could get them. Covid had flustered his usual buying habits, but he always had eggs even though sometimes they were not quite straight from the hen. There were people in the world who had never had anything to begin with, and the pandemic had added to their woes in ways he could not and did not imagine, so his little inconveniences were a trifle compared to real tragedy.

Though Gronsky's life was fairly dull, he hoped that he never let slip his grasp of world events during the week, and so every

Sunday was devoted to a game of catch-up just in case he had missed some pivotal event. This demanded a search of news of the world. He was surprised to note that anti-vaccine and anti-vaccine mandate protesters (apparently there was a difference) had taken to the streets here and afar. Some of those streets were even next to hospitals. Not the best place, he thought, to vocalize and spit out anti-public health, political and philosophical thoughts.

It was all so sad. So much was sad,

After watching a sufficient amount of news, he carried his scrambled eggs and coffee out to the porch to eat, to drink and to gather his thoughts before diving into the second day of the contest. All night he had woken up or dreamt he had woken up with notions of where he should take *The Last Breath* narrative. Mingled into those sleepless moments were thoughts of Miriam, of travel, of his stomach that seemed to react somewhat to the spicy sections of the previous evening's meal.

He knew from years of reading detective thrillers and watching film noir that there were a limited supply of plots. He supposed that many of these plots had seeped into his subconscious and might be driving his writing. This might not be a terrible thing, he thought. As much as readers liked to be surprised when they read a new story, they are also comforted by something strangely familiar. Gronsky wasn't all that sure of the validity of his suppositions, but he was glad that he was taking himself to task, measuring his literary steps, acknowledging his deficits, and turning them into strengths.

As he finished the last of his eggs, one of the neighbourhood homeless residents walked by, pulling his grocery cart, eyes darting to the left and right, ever a wary fellow. Gronsky was fairly sure it was the same one he had regularly noticed. There were a number of course. Some used a local park in mild weather. In inclement times, like last night, they would need a parking lot or a church vestibule, some sheltered area to secret away. It was always a depressing sight and Gronsky was vulnerable to moments of depression. He often thought that there might be something he could do for these dispossessed individuals, but they were transient thoughts, and he had a reasonable amount of faith in the political system that it would finally get a hold of a solution to homelessness. The current federal election would raise the issue countless times and in a few weeks, a new government would be in place and once and for all solve the matter.

As he thought that thought, the homeless traveller looked up at Gronsky sitting on his porch, his private veranda, finishing up his scrambled eggs, drinking his coffee, staring out at him, at the street, at the world. He smiled at Gronsky and pushed on.

Gronsky went inside, left the empty plate in the sink, grabbed some more coffee, and went to his den. He found the tennis channel, saw that an Argentinian and a Dutchman were playing, watched a few minutes and then turned on his word processor. Was murder afoot in *The Last Breath*? He would soon find out.

Chapter Four, The Last Breath

I walked around in circles for over ten minutes before I found a sign that stated "Gelbart Holdings; Ring for Service." I did as directed, and a voice came through the intercom: "Gelbart Holding: How may I help you?"

I was winging it again, having no idea what Gelbart Holdings did.

"Could I speak to Mr. Gelbart, please?"

My reasonable deduction that there was a Mr. Gelbart seemed to catch the disembodied voice off guard. She – it seemed like a she, but it might not have been actually human – said, "State your business, please!"

That of course caught me off guard, so I flew further along into the void of stupidity by the seat of my clichéd pants and said, "Special Delivery," to which he/she/they/it replied, "Just leave it at the entrance. Thank You."

It was time to retreat or rent a battering ram. Retreat seemed easier. I found my car, another ten-minute search through the business block maze, and sat in it for a few minutes. It was clear to me that I had little sense of how businesses are structured, layered one upon the other like some massive corporate orgy of greed and registration. Trying to penetrate Gelbart Holdings might be a waste of my valuable time. There were other things to do, but I opted to wait and see if the Two Gentlemen, or even one of them, might drive by in their mid-range corporate vehicle and lead me somewhere somewhat more hospitable. Time well wasted, perhaps? At any rate, I began my vigil.

Late Morning, September 5th

Gronsky felt the need to pace himself somewhat more lovingly than he had yesterday. The wear and tear on his body were noticeable. His breasts – yes, he had them – were feeling weighty. He supposed it was the position of his arms as they typed in the brilliance of his literary creation. He often leaned forward at a right angle to the word processor, so that his back was not fully supported. This led to a strain on his backbone that, while not excruciating, did ask for more tender care. He also realized that to manage this whole three-day affair at a measured pace, he would be best served by writing one thousand words an hour. That meant seventeen words a minutes. It might not seem like much, but it translated to one haiku every sixty seconds. That was a lot of poetry.

He also recognized that he would, hopefully, have spurts of creative flashes from time to time that would move things along at a greater speed. This would, however, be impaired by those wistful periods of reflection, fingers holstered, mind reaching for just the right word, selecting a less suitable applicant, and then whizzing along like a train rumbling down a mountain track, out of control, somewhat like the metaphor he had just concocted. And there was tennis.

He noticed that Svitolina and Halep had just begun their round of sixteen match. Halep was another favorite of Gronsky's. As with most of his 'favorite' people and things, there was no particular reason. In tennis players, it was mostly how they carried themselves, how they behaved on the court, and sometimes how they represented their countries. Halep is Romanian, and a star in her country. But as with many sports figures, she has paid a huge sacrifice for their passion. Often, they move away from home to train. Gronsky had read that Halep also had breast reduction in her mid teens in order to be able to play better, to swing more powerfully.

Svitolina, on the other hand, a Ukrainian, is married to the Frenchman Monfils, who lost on Saturday. Two different women, two incredibly different stories. Gronsky saw many metaphors in the wide world of professional tennis. He hoped others did.

He was about to turn his attention back to *The Last Breath* when Sam knocked at his door.

"Really hate to disturb you, Gil…"

"Not a problem. Lovely dinner last night. Spicy in places."

"Too much? I tried to restrain myself. Didn't want to cause you or Miriam any post supper grief."

"The little grief I suffered was worth it. Much appreciated. What's up?"

"You been out to your garage, lately?"

Gronsky only had a single car garage at the rear of the house. A back alley afforded entry. Miriam didn't have a car, and Sam, being a world traveller, often used taxis or Ubers and kept a small scooter in the garage for occasional use.

"Not for a few days. Why?"

"I don't know. I just get the sense that someone has been in there. Nothing taken that I can see. There's still your car, my scooter, Miriam's ten-speed, some wood, winter tires."

"I'll take a look later, Sam. Anything else?"

"Look, don't want to make a habit of this, but Miriam and I want to help you as best we can with this writing blitz of yours. She wants us to come to dinner night. If that would work for you?"

Gronsky loved the suggestion. It might mean that Miriam was indicating in her own oblique way that perhaps their relationship might be headed to, as the young folks said, another level. Or maybe it was just dinner.

"I'd love to," Gronsky said. "Same time?"

"A little earlier. Sixish...She might order in. Greek, she's thinking."

"I'll be there," Gronsky said. "See you at six.":

"Right. And good luck with the word count. You know I was just joshing you last night, right?"

"Course. See you later."

Sam closed the door and Gronsky tried to remember what Sam had been joshing him about. Of course. Fiction versus Thesis.

Barely noticed, thought Gronsky.

Greek, eh? Gronsky momentarily revised his notion of where he and Miriam might go, if indeed, they were to go anywhere. Greece. She was sending him a signal. A note. A food love note. He had to admit he was enjoying this romance in the bud, or was it a budding romance? Or just an old man's fancy turning to fall? Whatever it was, he was open to a change of some sort. Just not a huge change.

Gronsky was last in his garage on Wednesday, the day he went out to Costco to stock up on supplies. It was a once-a-month trip, and the summer had seen a depletion in his pantry's wares. He had worn his mask even though he had received his second vaccine dose back in May. It was such a small gesture, the wearing of a mask. He, Sam, and Miriam were a bubble of sorts and he eschewed wearing the mask in the house. He then remembered that he had popped out to the corner store one block over to get a bag of salted peanuts Thursday night. A momentary craving.

He wanted to get back to *The Last Breath* but was curious about the garage and Sam's concern. He went to the kitchen, out the back door, and up the two steps to the garage. It has a garage door off the street but had become locked in rust years earlier, so the garage was open to the universe. As Sam had noted, there were his winter tires and their three modes of transportation. (Miriam and Sam always locked their vehicles up, and Gronsky never forgot to lock his car doors and windows.) Nothing was amiss.

In the left corner facing the house, there was some newspaper and a bit of cardboard. That seemed new. It was probably destined for the recycling center. Sam's or Miriam's, likely. It was nothing to be concerned about. Gronsky returned to the house, then to his den, and considered his mystery plot line. As he did, he wandered into deadly pun territory. It was a diversion, but he could not help himself. Perhaps he was writing neither a novel, novelette, nor a novella. Perhaps he was writing a novelcro. Whatever stuck. It was feeling like that.

Chapter Four cont., The Last Breath

Twenty minutes passed. A few cars came and went. None seemed like the one being driven by the Two Gentlemen. Thirty minutes passed. I decided to check in on Phil. He should have reached the Conway home by now and perhaps had laid eyeballs on the effervescent Claudette. Just as I was about to punch in the numbers, my cell rang.

"Jimmy..."

Phil's voice was weak.

"Phil?"

"Jimmy..."

His voice was getting weaker.

"Phil, what's going on?"

"Damn dames..."

And then he dropped off. Whatever was going on, it would take me a fair time to get there. I called 911, gave my name and the Conway address, said a friend was in his car, gave a description, said something was wrong, sounded really wrong. They responded with an affirmative, took my particulars, and I said I would be there as fast as the law allowed.

Later Morning, September 5th

Gronsky again was drawn to the tube. Match point for Svitolina, and out goes Simona Halep. Gronsky would survive. So would Halep. There are wins and there are losses. There is no equity.

As Gronsky worked on *The Last Breath*, he could not help but measure the mystery he was fabricating with the course of his life. With anyone's life. In some biblical or evolutionary way, whichever side of that classic coin you landed on, writers gave life to their characters in much the same way that their personal lives unfolded. The written word was more manageable, he supposed. Although, with a few exceptions – his precipitous and ultimately failed marriage a prime example – his own life was chartered by himself alone. He liked to think so at any rate. He might be fooling himself, ignoring the generations of Gronskys and others who made up his genealogical breadbasket.

Gronsky needed to focus on the worldview he was creating. Jimmy the Slider Watkins was driving the narrative, but there were distinctly dark forces at play at the moment. Sunday morning, Gronsky's real time, was moving inexorably ahead. He had no control over that. Soon, he would be nominally halfway in. That meant he was at the top of the slide about to descend to Monday at midnight.

"Lordy, Lordy," he moaned. "Do I have the stamina? What happens if I fail? What happens if there is no denouement, no resolution?"

Swamped with a sudden wave of self-doubt, Gronsky decided to brush his teeth. That would brighten him up, help him step out of this bog.

Once that ablution had been concluded, he returned to the den. The short but ferocious Argentinian, Diego Schwartzman, had managed to win the third set after losing the first two to Botic van de Zandschulp, a player from the Netherlands new to Gronsky.

With his teeth refreshed and a few new narrative swings waiting in the word processing wings, Gronsky returned to his computer.

Chapter Five, The Last Breath

I may have broken a few speed records as I stormed towards the Conway house. Without even knowing what had gone down, I was preparing myself for the worst. I'd even started kicking myself for jumping into what might be a high-level kidnapping case without notifying the authorities. How stupid could I be! Just watch me, I said. Christ, Trudeau never seemed to be far away. The old man, to clarify. The snarky one.

As I turned onto the street where the Conways lived, police lines were already up. I pulled over, got out, and walked over to the cop handling the public right to know.

"I'm Jimmy Watkins," I said to the constable. "I called this in… from afar."

He gestured for me to get under the tape and follow him. He gave it a bit more thought and decided to frisk me. "It's licenced and in the car," I said indicating I was nobody's fool but my own."

He hailed one of his own over, a husky female cop, and said, "This guy says he has a gun in his car." He asked me for my keys and gave them to the gopher, asking: "Where?" I said, "Glove compartment."

"Fine. Get it, Sal. I'll show him to the detectives."

I had to ask then, "I'm gonna get it back, right?"

"Not up to me, buddy. Let's go."

We walked at a quicker than I preferred pace, a sort of perp walk in training stride down the centre of the street to the Conway house. Phil's car was parked in front, the passenger door open. A swarm of forensics and others were gathered round. An ambulance was pulling out. I was impressed at the speed of things. Someone was on the ball.

"Hey Lieutenant, here's the caller."

She looked up at me from a crouched position. A fresh face. "Emily Bradshaw," she said. "And you are?"

"Jim Watkins."

"You called 911?"

"I did."

"Because?"

"My guy, Phil Gains, reported in by phone. Sounded sort of off, barely able to talk. And then silence."

I almost said dead silence but held my tongue. I didn't want to go there.

"Your guy?"

"Private dick. On a case. Seconded Phil to do some surveillance."

"Of what?

"Confidential."

"Not anymore. Describe your guy, Gains."

"Fiftyish, ex-cop, a little hefty. Cool under pressure. Where is he?"

"Don't worry. He's still breathing. On his way to emerge."

"With what...?"

"Blade in the back. They think he'll make it. Now I need to know what the situation is?"

So do I, I thought. So do I.

Early Afternoon, September 5th

Gronsky was surprised by how draining *The Last Breath* was becoming. Just in the writing of it, the energy of thought he needed to bring to the plate. This particular scene was dramatic. He knew he was setting a bar that he needed to maintain. No matter how this whole exercise unfolded, it had to be exciting. Boring just wouldn't cut it.

It had been a while since breakfast. Lunch time was approaching. He looked out the window and saw a glimmer of sun poking through the clouds. The long-awaited rainfall had come and gone, and the earth around his community was still dry as ground bone. It would have caused grief to the homeless who had enjoyed – if that were the right word, and he thought not – the lengthy hot spell. The heat had been too much on occasion. Sweltering for a time. Hundreds of older people and disabled had died earlier on, trapped in their torture chamber apartment ovens. Gronsky's house had fine old windows that opened, were screened, allowed air in, even the blisteringly stifling air they had endured.

He accepted that this heat dome was a harbinger of things to come. He then remembered that Sam had complained about it and spent time in the basement sleeping on a spare cot. All three of them had slightly suffered.

As for tennis, the Argentinean had captured the fourth set and taken the battle with the Netherlander to a fifth and deciding encounter. The commentators were beside themselves counting up the number of fifth round matches the men were dueling.

Gronsky found the roar of the crowds encouraging, pretending that they were encouraging him on as he volleyed words back and forth, capturing, smashing, drop-shoting, serving away.

He grabbed some two-day old pasta, gobbled it down, took out kitchen garbage that was beginning to leave a foul impression, and returned to the den.

Chapter Five cont., The Last Breath

Lieutenant Emily Bradshaw had every right to expect full cooperation from me. Phil's stabbing changed the client confidentiality equation. Bogie knew that. Rather, Sam Spade did. Or Dashiell Hammett. All three of them knew that you had to do something if one of your people took it in the neck, or in Phil Gain's case, in the back.

I knew she would already know whose house it was we were clustered outside of. I wanted to give what information I thought necessary, but I preferred that she get to where she needed to be by deduction. Rapid deduction. I also wanted to get to Phil's bedside quickly. Phil's wife would want to be there as well. Alice Gains, separated but close. As I stood there waiting for brilliance from Bradshaw, I pulled up Alice's number and called. "Alice, Jimmy Watkins. Sorry, bad news. Phil's been injured. No, I don't know how seriously…." She had been with Phil when he was a cop. She always expected a call like this but not after he left the force. I gave her Phil's location and said I would be there as soon as the police allowed.

"Thanks," Bradshaw said. "Saves us the legwork."

"He was once one of yours."

"I heard," she said.

"Twenty years on the force, not so much as a hangnail."

"Rethinking what you can share?"

"Mind telling me what you know?"

"We aren't negotiating."

"I know. It's just …it helps me keep whatever confidences I can. I want someone to pay for this."

"Fine," she said. "I can handle that. This house," she said, pointing to what I knew was the Conway house, "belongs to Gerald and Claudette Conway. Neither are at home. We've entered to ensure that no one was injured or dangerous. The house is a mess. Everything turned upside down. The house appears to have a security camera. One of my people is checking it. Thinks it was turned off. We of course would prefer the help of either of the Conways. We are claiming exigent

circumstances for violating their privacy. Do you know where either of them is?"

Bradshaw was all business. I said, "No, I don't know where either of them are."

This was technically true. Claudette could be anywhere, and all I had was her statement that her husband had gone missing.

"Have you met either of them?"

"I've met Claudette Conway," I said, adding, "Someone who claimed to be her, at any rate."

She smirked. "Do you have any reason to think she wasn't who she said she was?"

Got me, I thought. Since she e-transferred money into my account I had no doubt, or practically no doubt, that Claudette Conway was exactly who she said she was.

"Absolutely no doubt," I stated.

"And what caused you to have absolutely no doubt about her identity?"

She had played me well. I would have to fess up. "She transferred money from her account to mine."

"How much?

"That is my business."

"Of course, it is. But she's your client?"

"That would follow."

"Good. What did she want you to do?"

I felt like I had been painted into the corner of a room with no exit. Maybe I didn't need one. I was getting jabbed left, right, and centre by a proficient swordswoman.

"Her husband had gone missing. His partner, Harry Stokely, may be being held for ransom. Conway and Stokely own CS Imports. Sounds like they borrowed money from bad people. Conway, according to Claudette, was trying to raise the ransom. He disappeared two days ago, if Claudette can be believed."

I threw in the bit about the two gentlemen yoyo's I encountered at Stokely's house and their link to Gelbart Industries. She didn't ask how I knew the link.

I was grateful for that.

"Good. You can go to the hospital. See your friend. And you can have your shooting iron back. Constable," she said indicating Sal, "escort Mr. Watkins to his steed and return his pistola."

It was a dark business, but she was trying to lighten it up a tad.

I tried to take that with me as I got in my car and drove to the hospital

Late Afternoon, September 5th

Gronsky was feeling quite satisfied with the progress of *The Last Breath*. The stabbing and the involvement of the police broadened the thematic possibilities. He wasn't quite sure how they were broadened, but he felt it always helped to involve the police. They were there to protect – in this case, protect a writer who may have boxed himself into a narrative corner. He was also happy to shift the tone to a more people-centred place away from shady high crimes and narrative misdemeanors.

A quick glance at tennis showed him that the young Canadian, Fernandez, was jousting with old pro Angie Kerber. Fernandez was almost up 5-2 in the first set before she began to falter and lose 4-6. Or perhaps Kerber was just ramping up. It was quite exciting, and Gronsky opted to spend a few minutes of quality time watching the second and possible final set. Kerber kept raising the ante.

Midway into the second set, Sam knocked lightly on the door and whispered, "Gil…Gil."

He turned the TV down and answered. "Come in. What's up?"

Sam came through to the den. "I was looking out at the alley, and I thought I saw someone sneak in the garage. Think we should call the cops?"

Having just left a bevy of imaginary policemen and women, Gronsky was loath to involve the real McCoy's.

"I'll take a look," he said to Sam.

"Then I'll come with you."

"That would be appreciated."

They went through Gronsky's kitchen, out the back door, and crossed the small patio to the steps leading up to the ancient shed that passed for a garage.

"Hello," Gronsky said, in as kindly and non-threatening a fashion as he could muster. "Is somebody there? Do you need help?"

There was silence. Sam whispered, "Should we go in?"

Gronsky shook his head, put his fingers to his lips, a gesture he remembered his mother often doing when he was too rambunctious. Which hadn't been that often.

"Let's just wait it out a bit," he said. He appreciated that this intruder undertaking was cutting into his writing time, but what could a poor time-challenged home-owning writer do but take a break and protect his property. Perhaps, he pondered, he should have called the police. The downside was that it would steal away more precious minutes and hours from writing. Once the police were there, you were captive to their time. Burglars, or whoever might be in the garage, theoretically should take less time to…to what? to process? Possibly.

He could hear the nearby Sunday traffic. A block away, there was an afternoon church service. Few would be attending, he hoped. Covid was still a force to be reckoned with. That and public health regs. For a second, he was struck by the reality that this moment, unlike the many moments he had stepped away from in *The Last Breath*, was not a moment he could just click and save. This moment needed to play out. Many of life's moments needed to be played out. This was not a fictional pause. It was a frictional pause. Something could ignite here. Something he might not be able to control or edit.

A few more moments passed. Finally, he said, "If you are hungry, would you like some food. I have a brand-new melon."

Sam gave him a querulous look, mouthed Melon.

He smiled back, mouthed, yes.

Sam shook his head but held his position.

Finally, the melon burst, or the moment, and a voice inside the garage, youngish – male or female, it was hard to say – said, "I like melons. I'm not a thief. Honest."

"Not much to steal anyways. Do you want to come out? I'm Gil and my friend here is Sam. We're pretty harmless…"

"Okay." And in a second a waif stepped out. Long brown jacket, skirt down to her ankles, boots, a cap. Female, Gronsky supposed.

"Let's go in the house and have that melon," Gronsky suggested.

"You sure you want to do that, Gil?" Sam asked.

"I think so. Let's go."

Gronsky led the way, Sam followed, and the young woman followed him. They entered the small foyer, and then went into the kitchen. "Let me get the melon. It's in the fridge." He retrieved the tempting fruit, said, "I will use a knife," which slightly startled both Sam and the young woman. He grabbed a knife from the block and quickly cut the melon into manageable slices. He then grabbed three bowls and divided the fruit.

"Let's go sit at the table, okay?" Both the young woman and Sam nodded.

They traipsed into the dining room adjacent to the kitchen. Sam turned on the overhead light, a chandelier that seemed too garish for melon eating.

"Sit where you want," he said to the visitor. She selected the chair nearest the door. Sam and Gronsky sat opposite.

"Dig in," he said, and they all did.

Two slices in, Gronsky decided to repeat introductions. "Like I said, I'm Gil, Gil Gronsky, and this is Sam. Sam Simmons. He lives upstairs. I live here. We have one other person, Miriam. Saw her a while ago. Haven't seen her in a bit. Might have gone out. Maybe not."

Gronsky expected reciprocity. A name. Something.

"Do you have a name?"

The young woman looked at him, seemed to be listening, perhaps poised to share…

"Anthea…"

"Anthea. Lovely name…Anthea what?"

She sighed, and asked, "Does it matter?"

"Names matter, I think. It's part of who you are. Yeah."

"Clapson…"

"Good, Anthea Clapson. Still hungry?"

Anthea nodded.

"What would appeal to you?" he asked.

"Peanut butter?"

"I have that. On bread?"

She almost laughed and said, "Yes."

"Jam? Honey?"

"Both?"

"Good, let's troop back to the kitchen."

As they got up, Sam said, "I think I'll go upstairs. Don't forget six, Gil."

Gronsky nodded, Sam left, and he and Anthea stepped into the kitchen. Gronsky bravely gave her the knife to slice bread and hauled out peanut butter, jam, and honey.

"Have at it."

Anthea dove in, and Gronsky tried to plan how he could be a good host and get back to the three-day novel enterprise and tennis and dinner at six. He wondered if Miriam might be up for a fourth for dinner. He also wondered if Anthea needed something else, like a shower and clean clothes, and whether a woman's touch might be advisable.

Suddenly, Miriam was there. "Sam mentioned you have a visitor, Gil." Miriam's appearance seemed to slightly startle Anthea, but she remained focussed on food.

"Anthea, Miriam. Miriam, Anthea."

Gronsky thought that went well. He decided to push the landlord /writer/selfish guy/social worker envelope. "Anthea, you're welcome to stay. Miriam and I haven't talked about this but, well, do you need or want anything else? Clothes? A shower? Supper?" The last thing he wanted to suggest to Anthea was that she needed a shower. She likely did, but that was beside the point. He was also trusting that Miriam would offer both clothes and her shower stall. Her front desk librarian role involved a lot of interaction with a challenged and challenging public. Also, he was desperate to get back to *The Last Breath* and the Kerber/ Fernandez match, which he assumed might be over but hoped not.

Miriam was quick to act. "If you'd like a shower and needed a fresh change of clothes, I could probably fix you up, Anthea."

He hoped they weren't overwhelming the girl, the young woman, with too much sudden largesse. Their home was a safe place, and he hoped Anthea sensed that.

She finished her bread and fixings and then burped.

They smiled, and she laughed and apologized.

She then nodded her head and said, "Yes, I'd like a shower, if that's not too much trouble."

Both Miriam and Gronsky indicated that it was no trouble at all. At that, Anthea and Miriam headed off to Miriam's suite.

With that Mary Poppins moment under control, Gronsky returned to his den, turned the sound back up, and caught the final minutes of the young Fernandez's third set dismantling of the great Angie Kerber.

It was all quite amazing.

Perhaps as amazing as his invitation to a young street person to come into his house, break bread, get refreshed, rejuvenated. This was not an activity he would have imagined he would ever do. And with so little thought. The moment simply presented itself. And the timing. He had never been so busy. Writing was busy work, important work and here he simply added Anthea and her needs to his checklist of activities.

Quite uncharacteristic.

And real.

But now he had time to re-enter his fictional sphere and do some sorting there.

Chapter Six, The Last Breath

I found a pay parking space, put on my mask, and entered the Emergency Ward of the local hospital. I asked at admissions if I could see Phil Gains or at least know where his wife might be. I had little doubt that Alice would have already made her way there. I also expected her to tear a strip off me. I wasn't sure I would deserve her anger except for the fact that the last thing I wanted was for something to happen to Phil. He wasn't muscle for me; he was a surveillance specialist. Granted, he was a retired cop, but he knew his limits, as did I. Watch and wait. That was his mission. He may well have been doing that. Something interfered with what should have been a sedentary surveillance assignment.

Admissions asked who I was, and I said that I was his employer. That seemed to help leap the hurdle, and I was sent to a waiting area. Phil was in surgery. His wife and son were waiting nearby.

I approached Alice gently. She may have been angry, but she accepted my elbow bump. She introduced me to Phil Junior. He nodded and then proceeded to ignore me.

"Any word yet?" I asked Alice.

"He just went in, Jimmy. It could be a while."

I nodded and took a seat. I hadn't been in a hospital since the onset of Covid. It was spooky, and not in the least comforting.

We all sat in silence, masking and distancing, for a while. Phil Junior asked his mother if she wanted coffee or food. She said she was fine. Alice asked me if I wanted something. I opted to test Phil Junior's generosity quotient and said a coffee and a chocolate bar would do me fine. Phil Junior went away to get the goods. Shortly he returned with an O Henry and a cup of coffee.

The bar was great. The coffee needed something. Different coffee.

We waited for almost an hour, and then the surgeon appeared and talked to Alice. The relief on her face, her entire body was palpable.

"He'll make it Jimmy. But he'll be out of the game for a time."

"I don't know what went wrong, Al. I'll check in with the lieutenant in charge. She seems like a crackerjack."

"A woman?"

"My assessment."

"Not a time to be funny, Jimmy."

"Sorry. Anyways, she impressed me. Name's Emily Bradshaw. Know of he?."

She shook her head. "Phil might. He still meets up with his old gang."

I let it go at that. I was ecstatic that Phil was going to be okay. With the gendarmes in the mix, I wasn't sure what else I needed to do. At a minimum, I felt a fiduciary duty to Claudette Conway. Overarching that duty of care was the need to complete my task, to feel that I had done my level best for my client. The police might find her, but I needed to try and make contact. I did have a chunk of her change and hoped to keep as much of that as possible.

Early Evening, September 5th,

Canadian Félix Auger-Aliassime was playing American Frances Tiafoe in a night match. They were equivalent players, Gronsky thought. It would be an excellent match. It could last for four hours. Gronsky would miss most of their exchange once he went to Miriam's for dinner. Greek dinner. Ordered in, maybe. Calamari, he hoped. A favourite.

What a weekend it had been for him. Flash novels, flash visitors, world class flashy tennis, grand Thai, and Greek food. Quite uncharacteristic.

He watched tennis for quite some time decompressing from the excitement of creativity and replacing it with spectator excitement, a slightly less stimulating buzz. He did wonder how Anthea was faring. He was, of course, curious about her story. What had life done to her to leave her on the street. She seemed about twenty, perhaps younger.

Gronsky decided to have a shower, long overdue, and dress for dinner. Once that was done, it was close to six and he was anxious to visit Miriam's, not only for the dinner and the companionship, but also to see if Anthea had hung around, taken a risk. It would be a different sort of risk to street life. He didn't know how to compare the competing perils. He had no genuine experience with a perilous existence. His own failed marriage was hardly close. It was more like the cancelling of a

TV series. Ultimately, meaningless. And usually without reruns. Even as he thought that, he apologized to his two children. They were never meant to be thought meaningless. And he would never have cancelled them.

At six, Gronsky knocked on Miriam's door. Sam did the door-opening honours and bade him enter. It was a cozy suite, made more so by a showered and re-dressed Anthea. Slacks, a beautiful age-appropriate white blouse, and quite a relaxed smile all added to the transformation. He assumed that all three adults were considering what the next steps might be.

A doorbell rang and Sam did the honours again, returning with a giant package of delivered food. Miriam plated and served. "I kept the calamari and salmon separate. Lots to eat. And by the way, I may be turning pescetarian."

"I've never eaten Greek food," Anthea announced, ignoring or not understanding the food preference conversion Miriam had just mentioned. "Even known that it existed. It looks, smells… grand."

Gronsky watched the meal unfold and relished every moment. There wasn't a ton of conversation but eventually some.

Miriam kicked it off.

"Gentlemen," she began, "Anthea and I had a couple of hours to…get to know each other. There are a few things she would like to say. I'll leave it to her."

Gronsky assumed that a lot of pressure was now on the young woman. He wondered if asking specific questions might ease the sharing of her life story. So he asked. "Would it be better if we asked questions and you could decide whether you wanted to answer?"

Anthea looked to give that some thought and nodded yes.

"Good. May I ask the first question?"

She assented.

"How old are you?"

She was quick with the answer. "Seventeen."

"So," Sam followed up, being a man of fact and clarification, "you were born in 2004?"

"Yes. I was."

That put a different spin on it for Gronsky. She was a child. She needed protection. What sort was another matter.

He offered a follow-up query. "Where were you born. And raised?"

"Nelson, I think. That's what I was told. Raised outside of town."

"Could you talk about your family. Would that be okay?"

Gronsky was getting curious. He wondered how much she would reveal, how much she knew.

"I don't know much. My mother and father died in a car crash a year after I was born."

"2005?"

"Yes. That's what gran told me."

"So, your grandmother raised you?"

"Until this spring."

"And then?" Gronsky asked.

"Well, she and I lived with the others."

"Who were they?"

"Our larger family. They cared for us. Me. Grandmother."

"A commune?" Gronsky pushed it.

"Our family. It always was there. My mother, my father, uncle, my grandmother. Always."

"In Nelson?"

"Away from the people. Close. But far."

"What was it like, this family?" Gronsky asked.

"It was fun. You should know."

"I should?" Gronsky asked.

"We played your game."

Gronsky laughed, said. "I have no game."

"Sure. It's got your name. Grandmother brought it with her. We all played it."

"What was this game called?," Gronsky asked.

"Beware The Gronsky. It was a great game. Beware The Gronsky. He'll steal you away."

The table was silent. The eyes of Miriam, Sam, and Gronsky were all levelled at Anthea.

They were all familiar with Gronsky's marital woes, the children who had been carted away, his children, never to be found. Was this the circle rounding?

Gronsky had so many more questions but sensed that later, perhaps in the morning, some time yet to come, would be the time to excavate the past. One thing he knew for sure: he didn't want to lose Anthea. She might hold the key to a chunk of his past that he thought would never be answered.

And he still had to complete the three-day novel challenge. Tomorrow would be as full a day as he had ever experienced. As the evening wound down, he could only echo, silently, the terrible children's game Anthea had been forced to play: Beware The Gronsky.

Morning, September 6th

It was the final day of the contest. Gronsky was buoyed, exhausted, excited, and frightened. He suspected, with absolutely no measurable evidence, that his granddaughter had found him, a granddaughter he had never even imagined existed. He wondered if that was another characteristic that he lacked, the ability to wonder about what might be. It was too late to self flagellate now. Nothing to be gained. Still, it was curious. This weekend he had begun to speculate about what might be possible between he and Miriam. Maybe the old dog was getting a new bag of tricks?

And, almost anticlimactically, he was two-thirds of the way to a complete, albeit choppy novella. Complete, perhaps, but likely far too short. Distractions, his own nurtured ones and a couple of surprise ones, had inserted themselves into his seventy-two-hour expedition.

He had not slept well. The conversation at dinner had delved into so much. Stella Fishbine had been named Dorothy. Dorothy what, he couldn't remember. If she was Anthea's grandmother, she had lost her daughter, Dawn, who had Anthea somewhat late in life – if Anthea was to be believed.

He believed.

As for his son, Robert, there was no clarity. He was thankful that Sam had raised the issue of Anthea and vaccine. Yes, she had said, a street health nurse had arranged both a first and second shot. They had totally not paid any attention to that concern when they had enticed her from the garage.

So many thoughts had snaked their slithery ways into Gronsky's mind at night, last night. He had tried to capture how Anthea's life had been, living some rustic, rural existence, some fanatic's life perhaps. It was unclear. While he had been living his life here, in this house, working at the paper mill for thirty-five years – a simple life, a working man's life, a lonely but not unfulfilled life – other worlds had been spinning away. His children…what had been the joys and sorrows of their lives?

His mind had seemed as tangled as his sheets became. He had to get up a few times to stretch his aching limbs. He would then crawl back into bed, try to get the sheets back to some semblance of smooth order. He would drift off, only to partially wake, plot Jimmy Watkins' next steps, get that confused with the unravelling mystery in his life, sense the two threads – fact and fiction – coming together in some satisfactory, mostly complete way.

The novella preyed on his thoughts. How important was it compared to this miracle of reunion? If it was a miracle. If it was a true reunion.

He needed coffee and food. Porridge. Something grounded, grainy, and wholesome. Was there anything more wholesome than porridge? He doubted it.

He got up and assembled the porridge, with honey, raisins, a bit of fruit, a peach moments away from being spoiled, saved just in time. He put the coffee on and lingered over the porridge mixture and the coffee machine. In eight minutes, they were both done. The time had simply slipped away. He scooped some porridge into a bowl, poured a cup of coffee, added milk to both, and went outside to his porch.

As he sat there, sensing what seemed to be a slightly warmer day arriving, he hoped that Anthea had slept well. It would be a strange new place for her, more comfortable than a cardboard and paper bed in a dank shed. She would have slept on Miriam's day bed. That couldn't last. He had a spare bedroom, a brilliantly bit of foreshadowing when the house had been renovated to accommodate his accommodation and two suites. The second bedroom was on the second floor, the floor Miriam mostly had.

Excellent forethought, indeed.

He finished the porridge directly and sipped some coffee. He knew he had to get back to *The Last Breath*. Would he keep that title? Whose last breath would it be? The story would take him there. It had to. He needed a guide. With flash fiction, there was usually a prompt, a touchstone. With this three-day novel, novella, novelcro, whatever it prove to be, he had to be the guide and provide the prompt himself. Not fair.

Anyways, back to it. He went in the house, placed the empty porridge bowl in the sink to soak, topped up his coffee, and went to the den. He wondered if he could manage his escalating responsibilities and the deadline, this final push, by having tennis playing in the background. He had managed to include its lessons, its highs and lows up to now. Why should Monday be any different? He turned the tube on and sat down at his computer. He fired it up.

He said, welcome back, Jimmy Watkins. Show me your stuff.

Chapter Six cont., The Last Breath

As I hadn't kept anything back from the police, Lieutenant Emily Bradford in particular, I decided to give her a call and bring her up to speed on Phil Gains' condition. I knew that she would already have reached out to keep up to date, so it was merely a courtesy call on my part to show I cared. Which I did. By now I suspected the cops would have found security cam footage, if there was any, that caught the events, the stabbing of my friend.

"So soon?" Bradford said in answer to my call.

"Thought I'd let you know that Phil Gains is doing okay. Lots of pain but they say he'll pull through."

"Good," she said, "Anything else?"

"Ah, I'd like to be not in the dark about how Phil got taken down. Can you enlighten me?"

There was silence. She was weighing the matter. She didn't have to give me dick. She knew it. I knew it. She knew I knew she knew. Neither of us were new to this.

"Across the street. The Morley's cam caught it all. Claudette Conway, we assume it was her, was leaving her house with two men, one older, one younger, and Gains attempted to engage them. Maybe he thought she was being taken by force. Anyways, there was a bit of a scuffle. The two guys didn't seem all that interested in fighting Gains who was handling himself quite well from the angle we had, doing good for a donut eating ex-copper. The lady stuck him. Pretty clear"

"Claudette?"

"Claudette. I'll send you a snap of the woman to confirm we are talking about the same walking redhaired felon."

The picture Bradshaw sent arrived in second.

"It's her."

"Your client, if I can be so bold, is now wanted for attempted murder. You don't owe her a thing."

We rang off. Actually, she ended the call. But she was wrong. I still owed Claudette Conway something. My fiduciary duty. Not to her anymore. To Phil Gains and to myself.

Later Morning, September 6th

Gronsky was pleased with how he'd begun Monday's take on the world of Jimmy Watkins. While it would be nowhere near the length he had hoped to get to, the story would be substantially longer than a piece of flash fiction. That fact mattered to him if to no one else. Whatever the length *The Last Breath* turned out to be, he would submit it.

He wiled away with a few minutes of tennis. The Swiss Olympic double medal champion, Belinda Bencic was playing the young Polish phenom, Iga Swiatek. Again, besides a couple of years between them, they were equals. Today, one would be more equal than the other, on another day, the result might well be reversed. Sports had that balance. He saw life as being less balanced, less equitable.

There were no footsteps in the house, so he assumed everyone was sleeping in. After some discussion last night, it was decided that Anthea would bunk in with Miriam for a few days and then, if she wanted, she could have his spare bedroom. It needed to be cleaned, and maybe painted, in any event. He loved Miriam for her gesture. She had made this emerging situation so much more comfortable. Sam too. He was immensely helpful.

As much as Gronsky needed to hone in on his writing project, hone it, own it, he couldn't help thinking beyond his Monday midnight entry deadline. There were a range of possibilities. Life, his life was no longer a straight line to the grave. He hadn't given much thought about the grave. He had an old will somewhere filed away, out of date, meaningless, as his lineage had ended, or so he had accepted. True, he thought he might still have a son and daughter, but the fraudulent Stella Fishbine had essentially erased them from the earth or at least accessibility.

Until now.

His mind was wandering in all sorts of untravelled spaces.

Chapter Seven, The Last Breath.

Like a newbie, I had forgotten to ask Bradshaw if she had any leads on Claudette's whereabouts. The revelation that Claudette Conway had stuck a shiv in Phil Gain's back meant that the police would not be sharing intel. Certainly not with me. I had a double dose of conflict of interest. I did wonder why Claudette had been carrying a knife. It didn't seem to be a usual weapon for a woman. Maybe I was behind the times. Not the sharpest…knife in the drawer.

Not Much Later in the Morning, September 6th

Gronsky pulled up short. The pun: not the sharpest…knife in the drawer. It was terrible. Totally unoriginal. On the other hand, Jimmy the Slider Watkins, needed to fall back on levity. He was under stress. Something Gronsky was starting to understand. Maybe he would make a teensy joke?

He'd leave it in.

Chapter Seven cont., The Last Breath

Though I didn't really know what made Claudette Conway tick, there were some clues. If she had really wanted me to find her husband, she would have likely not stabbed Phil Gains. Or anyone. That meant that she hadn't wanted me to really find her hubby, only to make it look that way. That made me an inadvertent shill. So, if that was her raison d'etre, then it was possible that she either knew where Gerry was, or he simply wasn't anymore. If he was alive or dead, he was either being kept secreted away by others, Claudette included, or he was part of whatever caper they had going. The partner, Harry Stokely, was also either part of the shenanigans or also toast. Or about to be.

The key seemed to be Claudette. She was my only connection to whatever was going on. Maybe Lucy Chenille could help me? A person's drivers license was also a record of where they had lived, other names they had used, and the like. I called Lucy and asked her to take a deeper dive. I indicated that the police were involved now, and I didn't want her to take any unnecessary risks. She was important to me, personally and professionally.

"'I'll take care, Jimmy. Call you shortly."

Shortly turned out to be ten minutes. Lucy was a whiz.

"Jimmy, it looks like she changed her name to Conway less than a year ago. Before that, it was Claudette Gelbart. I went all the way back to her teens when she got her first license. Gelbart is her maiden name, I'd make book."

"Any old addresses?"

"A couple."

Lucy gave three addresses to me. "Thanks, Luce. Much appreciated. Now protect yourself."

"Done."

"Good."

I had a lead. Three leads. I would start with the most recent. It was a small town, a popular beachside resort an hour down the freeway. Claudette Gelbart had kept that address for six years before becoming Claudette Conway. Was she the head of Gelbart Industries? I wondered.

"Maybe that's where I would find her. Maybe she would tell me. Maybe she would show me her knife. I could hardly restrain myself.

Late Morning, September 6th

It was time to take a break. Bencic had won the first set in an epic twenty-two-minute tiebreaker. Gronsky had been too engaged in Jimmy's deductions about Claudette to even look at the television, but the crowd and the announcers kept him informed. Competing excitements kept his writer's heart pumping. He was aware that *The Last Breath* was reaching some measure of completion. He wasn't quite sure what that would look like, but the odds were that Claudette Gelbart and Jimmy Watkins would have a thrilling and deserved denouement. Even as he anticipated that conclusion, Bencic seemed poised to have a round of sixteen conquest. As an Olympic Gold Medal champion, she would expect nothing less of herself.

There were sounds in the house. Pipes pumping water. Feet walking. He needed more coffee, so he went to the kitchen. He poured a final cup from the pot. He could hear steps approaching. It was Miriam and Anthea.

"Good morning, Gil. I thought…we thought… you two should have breakfast, talk, get more acquainted. I'll leave you to it."

Miriam left Gronsky and Anthea standing there. "Coffee?" he asked.

"I don't really …"

"Drink coffee?" he completed her thought.

She smiled and asked, "Do you have tea?"

He had some old teabags in the cupboard. Incredibly old teabags. He put the kettle on and dragged out an antique brown betty that had been his mother's.

When all that was done, he asked about breakfast.

"Peanut butter, jam, and bread, if that's okay?" she asked.

"Easy to do," he said. And added, "Very okay."

Once that was assembled, he asked if she wanted to sit outside on his porch. She agreed, and they carried the food and drink out into the Labour Day Monday sun.

They were quiet for a while. Anthea ate her breakfast, drank what he hoped was adequate tea, and together they enjoyed the quiet holiday morning.

Finally, she said, "This is nice. Here, I mean. Your house…and the porch."

"Much better than a garage, I would think."

"Yes."

He then asked how long she had been in the city, what had drawn her here, to him.

"In May…yeah, May. There aren't many Gronsky's, are there?"

He laughed. "Probably quite a few. I would think that after playing the Beware the Gronsky game, you would not want to actually find one?"

"Before Gran died this past spring, she told me…told me that she had once been married to a Gronsky. That he was the father of my mother, of my uncle Charlie, and that some day I might need to, you know, find him…you."

"I looked," Gronsky said, "as best I could. She made it impossible. My children were named Robert and Dawn. Not Charlie…what was your mothers new name? I suppose that had been changed?"

"She was Claudette."

"Hah. Claudette. Yeah. Why not."

Anthea looked a little confused. Gronsky could not believe that fake Stella Fishbine had changed his daughter Dawn's name to the same name he had grabbed out of the air to give to his femme fatale. He wondered if he should change Claudette Conway's name or just leave it alone and enjoy whatever it was, a weird coincidence, or irony, or both. Perhaps something just plain magical.

As he wasn't big on rewrites, he'd probably leave it as is.

"Sorry for laughing. Something just struck my funny bone. About your grandmother, my experience with her was that she really wasn't who she said she was. And until now, I was almost completely in the dark."

"She didn't talk about any of that. She was always who she was to me. She just told me so little. Enough, I suppose. As much as she cared to. But…it was so little."

Gronsky and Anthea dipped into a silent time. They had both known so little. and there might not be much more that they would ever discover. As he remembered Anthea's slowly evolving tale of her life from the previous evening, he wondered about Robert. Dawn had died in a car crash. There had been no real mention of Robert.

"Your uncle, my son, Robert, Charlie. What about him?"

"He left the Valley when my mother died. So, I don't know much more."

Gronsky understood that there were still mysteries to solve, factual ones and fictional ones. He needed to get back to his writing but didn't want to lose sight of Anthea at all.

"I mentioned," he began, "that I am writing this novel…in three days."

"I didn't quite understand what that meant," she said.

"It's a contest. I don't expect to win. Like to, of course, but don't expect to. So it's more a challenge I have made with myself. I have until midnight tonight to finish it. It's been fits and starts up to now."

She nodded, probably to be courteous. There was undoubtedly no real sense to be made of a crazy author spending a compression of time writing…what…whatever it became.

"But I want to be with you. Just get to know who you are. Would you want to watch me write? I have a television and I have been watching bits and pieces of tennis. Do you know much about tennis? It could be quite boring for you."

She nodded her head. "I could sit with you. I don't mind."

They agreed. He would need food in an hour or so. That would give her impromptu volunteer writer spectator role a break in case it turned out to be as monotonous as he imagined.

They dropped off the toast plate in the kitchen and then went to the den. She set up on the couch to the side of his computer, poured some more tea and started watching tennis. Zverev and Sinner were in the midst of a massive third set tiebreaker. In seconds, Zverev took the match.

He explained what had happened and then turned his attention to *The Last Breath.*

Chapter Eight, The Last Breath

I like road trips. It had been quite some time since the last one. Runaway kid then. Didn't actually go that far. The kid, or me. She was hooking up with an old boyfriend whom the family had concerns about. Turned out she was pregnant and was making a pitch to the baby daddy.

He turned out to be a disappointment.

An old story, I guess.

She whimpered the entire trip back.

I had little to offer her as compensation.

She would have to learn to be more selective.

If that was possible.

Most of my cases didn't require much travel. Short starts, quick stops, fair to middling endings.

Very few happy ones.

Life, eh?

And I intended to keep mine. It was a huge advantage to know that Claudette Conway was adept at back-stabbing. I was sure, given the chance, she would engage in front-stabbing as well.

There wasn't much I intended to do other then spot her and call in the calvary. To prepare for that, I gave Ellen Bradshaw a dingle as I approached the outskirts of my destination. As it was the last long weekend of summer, I expected a crowd. The crowd did not disappoint.

"Bradshaw," she answered.

I told her where I was and what I hoped to discover.

"Seriously. Holding out?"

I clarified that it was the result of years of experience digging into muck and that mostly it was a hunch. Yes, I had connected the Gelbart dots.

"Where do you get your intel, Watkins?" she asked and then said, "Forget it. I don't need to know. It would just give me grief."

"Last thing I want to do, Bradshaw. Anyways. If I do spot her, there may need to be some quick action."

"On a hunch?"

"Yeah. My hunch."

"I'll swing down. You get one busted hunch with me."

"Make it two."

She laughed and said, "Okay. Two."

I drove into the main drag and parked. There really wasn't much more than the one drag. It would take Bradshaw an hour to get here. I had that hour to play peekaboo. Claudette's house from before was on the beach side just at the far edge of the town.

Before I went to take a closer look, I acclimatised to beachville. Every shape and size was there, in shorts, muumuus, every conceivable type of summer wear. My slacks, shirt, and tie were somewhat out of place. I hoped no one noticed.

I gave my downtown surveillance half an hour. There was no sign of Claudette. I stepped inside a small but busy café, found a local telephone book, looked up Gelbart. There was an F. Gelbart. Same address as on Claudette's old driver's license.

The family domicile perhaps.

It was time to get a closer gander.

Afternoon, September 6th

Gronsky took a quick break to point out some facts about the two women tennis players Anthea was watching. Shelby Rogers, an American, was playing her best ever tennis. Eighteen-year-old Brit, Emma Raducana was a youngster born in Canada who moved with her family to England when she was two and was just beginning her career. He supposed he wanted to show Anthea that life held options, that the past didn't dictate the future. He neglected to point out that that was precisely what he had not done. He had allowed the past to direct him.

Gronsky's failings aside, Raducana was putting on a show, one he hoped Anthea appreciated.

When it was time for lunch. Anthea wasn't hungry. Just then, Raducana ended Rogers run. Anthea was smiling. The lesson had impact.

He grabbed a quick cheese sandwich, said the kitchen was hers and to help herself whenever she needed. He then returned to assist Jimmy Watkins wrap things up. Assuming that was possible.

Chapter Eight cont., The Last Breath

The Gelbart beach house was anything but a shack. It was a huge walled property oozing money and privilege. It would be nigh impossible to get a peek from the outside. That posed a problem. I couldn't visualize sneaking about the walled fortress looking for a viable entry. It was obviously a lot tighter that the Mexican-USA border, especially after that guy who used to be in the White House tampered with it.

The streets and beaches were festooned with a wallop of potential witnesses: sun worshipers, kite flyers, surfers, weight watchers, dreamers, and the odd crook. I wasn't worried about being reported to the police. In fact, I had already reported myself to them. I wanted them here. Bradshaw was my cop of choice, but any old cop would do in a pinch, especially if my fanny was going to be packed in a sling.

I suppose I could have just waited at the gate or nearby and keep track of the comings and goings. These days, tinted windshields made it almost impossible to see who was in a vehicle. I doubted Bradshaw would effect entry if there was no evidence of anything. She might, however come looking for me if I was inside and in peril.

That was a risk worth taking, assuming they would let me in. I called Bradshaw again.

"Impatient?"

"Yeah, where are you?"

"Ten, fifteen minutes out. Got your evidence?"

I'm outside the house now. Huge walled edifice. Can't see a thing, though."

"So, what?"

"I'm gonna knock on the door and visit. I expect they might try to hurt me."

"Then don't go. We don't have any bodies at the moment and I..."

"That we know of. The more I think about this, there might well be one or two...and if there are, she knows where..."

"Enough. Just wait."

"Tell you what, I'm putting junior on record, stuffing him next to my family jewels, and leaving it on. So, in a way, you'll be there with me."

"You're an idiot. Don't do it."

"Done. See you soon...or in the next life."

I left the car, recording the walk over, pressing the bell, waiting for the next act, wondering just what kind of fool I was. Maybe Claudette would tell me.

Later Afternoon, September 6th

Gronsky could feel the end approaching. The end of the mini novel contest. He was on a roll and didn't want to step away from the flow, but all weekend long he had taken breaks, treated himself to necessary and unnecessary diversions, small indulgences of drink and food, engagement with his big screen and his tenant/friends, the odd walk in the rain and now the sun, porch moments – every ancillary pleasure at his disposal.

It was the only way he could do it, live the experience. Self imposed, contractually required union breaks.

Anthea had returned from the kitchen and was now resting on the couch. Sleeping. She looked a bit like Raducana – slim, dark-haired, a slightly upturned nose. There was some resemblance to the fake Stella Fishbine he had once wed. Anthea looked softer. Considering her losses, the rough living she must have endured these past four months, she had bounced back quite nicely. Better and smoother than he would have done at her age. He'd always had his mother. His father had barely been there, dying on the docks when Gronsky was ten. They'd both had terrible losses, but hers would have been the more traumatic, the more enduring. And he suspected there was other unpleasantness that she might have undergone in the extended "family" that Stella had landed herself and her children in. His children in. Those might get disclosed in time. He would be there for her if she would let him. They could have a few good years together. Miriam would be a good companion to them both. That is, if she wanted.

As if preordained, there was a light knock on the den door. He said come in, and Miriam entered. She looked at Anthea.

"Asleep? Nothing much is open, but I thought she might like to go out for coffee and woman talk."

"Tea…not a coffee drinker."

"Oh."

Anthea awoke at the sound of their voices. Gronsky had muted the television a while ago. Miriam repeated her outing idea. Anthea looked to Gronsky for approval. "Go," he said. "Have a fun time. Incidentally, I haven't planned dinner."

Miriam said she would take care of that, this being an extra special long weekend and all. "Don't know what. Maybe Anthea has an idea. We'll talk about it."

With that they were gone, and Gronsky sidled up to Jimmy the Slider Watkins as he was about to enter the snake room of Claudette Gelbart-Conway.

Chapter Nine, The Last Breath

I had to ring the bell a couple of times. I resisted raising my voice, shouting, "Anybody home?" It was implied, anyways. Finally, I could hear movement. A voice, male, on the other side said, "We don't want any."

I replied, "I don't have any." And then added, "Tell Claudette I'd like a moment of her time."

I intuited that voice person on the other side of the wall was about to respond with "There isn't any Claudette here." I might have imagined it, but there was a gasp of air. Something was formulating when I heard Claudette say, "Let him in. For Christ sakes, just get him off the street."

It sounded less welcoming than I had hoped, but I trusted my cell had picked it up. Just in case they tried to have me arrested for illegal entry. Obviously, I had been invited in. The proof would be in the recording, which I hoped Bradshaw was recording as well. Just in case they found my phone and trashed it.

The gate opened and, lo and behold, it was my friends from earlier in the day. Younger Gent and Older Gent. And the lovely duplicitous knife-wielding Claudette Conway.

Each had a gun. Entry was highly encouraged, and I entered like a good guest.

Older Gent thrust me against the wall and frisked me. "Just a phone. No gun."

They left the phone in my pocket. It seemed a tad sloppy.

The house was done in a lovely Spanish motif. Tan walls, comfy larger-than-you've-ever-seen furniture, a grand view of the ocean until they drew the curtains. That seemed a trifle worrisome.

"Sit," Claudette directed me to a straight back chair.

I sat.

"What are you doing here, Mr. Watkins? My husband isn't here. You should be looking for him."

I smiled. She seemed not pleased with that.

"There's nothing to smile at here," she said.

I replied, "In fact, I wasn't smiling because I see nothing funny here. All I see are a couple of goons and a lady who stabs people in the back. Nothing funny about red-headed backstabbers."

The colour went out of her face. The hair stayed the same, but it looked a little more frazzled than I assume she preferred.

Older Gentleman opined with, "Jesus, Claude, they know."

"Shut up, Frank."

So, Older Gent was Frank. I was making progress.

"Claude, if he knows that you stabbed that guy, then the cops know."

"A good reason to shut up, Frank. Search him again."

"Younger Gent and Older Gent lifted me up from my sitting position, ran their hands semi-professionally up and down my body, took my car keys, wallet, and phone and pushed me back down to a sitting position.

Younger Gent looked at the phone, pointed to it, indicating that it seemed to be doing something they wished it weren't.

Claudette shook her head just as Bradshaw and her team rushed in and saved my bacon. No guns were fired in the completion of this arrest.

All three were taken away. The house was searched but there was no one else lingering about.

"Thanks, Emily," I said to Bradshaw. "Who knows what would have happened?"

"Oh, I think we know," she said with a somewhat provocative grin. "We got a search warrant for CS Imports. Harry Stokely, we think, has been there for days. Dead, of course. Conway, we don't know about. I expect he's dead, but he might be on the run."

"What was it all for?" I asked.

She shook her head. "Insurance, likely. The company was in the tank. Don't know why. Rescue equipment for traumatic events has to be booming. These jokers seem to have run it into the ground. Maybe Claudette and her brother and nephew just wanted to get out with some pride…and money."

"Brother and nephew?"

"Yup. A demented family affair. God knows what was going on with that menacing ménage à trois."

I have to say I was impressed with Emily Bradshaw's bedroom turn of phrase. It augured well. We said our goodbyes, though, for the moment, and then I went to visit Phil Gains. Told him what he had missed.

"Time to hang up my spurs, Jimmy."

"Give it some time. Divorce is still worth a few bucks to smart guys."

"Maybe, but not for me."

I said goodnight and started for home. Halfway there, the phone rang. It was Bradshaw.

"Fancy buying me a drink?"

"I am a fancy man," I said. We agreed on where and when.

I breathed in and smiled. It might be the last breath I would take as a lonely dick.

I'd leave that up to Emily Bradshaw. I fancied knowing her opinion.

Afternoon, September 6th

Gronsky put his pen down. Metaphorically. He had written *finis* to *The Last Breath*. Again, metaphorically. He was free now to watch the US Open without interruption. He and Anthea could share those moments. Perhaps she would learn to play the game.

He realized that *The Last Breath* was not of sufficient length, but time was about to run out. There were still eight hours, but his brain was fried. Nothing more was coming out. He was content with the product. Perhaps not a novel, nor a novella nor a novelcro. Whatever it was, it was done. And even though the fate of his femme fatality, Claudette Conway might leave an unresolved thematic wound in some readers, he felt that both he and Jimmy Watkins escaped relatively unscathed from her alluring tentacles. It was a crucial point to note: even writers had to be wary of their toxic creations.

What was not done however was the new adventure that had emerged in his life.

So unexpected.

So welcome.

The Girl in The Garage. Or The Woman Who Lives on The Second Floor.

He could call the next story one of those.

Something along those lines anyways.

Or maybe he could just live his new life and not write at all.

Seven weeks later, November 1st

Chapter One, Scratch an Old Wound

Danny Hawkins knew that he had to get as far away as possible from the ravages he'd seen in Europe. The horror that was Belsen-Belsen wouldn't leave him alone. The human mind, to say nothing of the heart, has a maximum number of corpses it can cope with at any one time. He didn't know what the precise number was, or even if there really was a number, except…yes, he believed that there was always a number.

And it always came up.

He had been demobilized in Nova Scotia at Camp Aldershot near Halifax, where he'd completed his basic training before being shipped overseas. The Maritimes were moderately interesting, but after a few days, Montreal was sharply in his sights, and he arrived there in February 1946. It was a new city to him having never ever been east of Winnipeg before except for the train trip from Edmonton to Aldershot after he had signed up.

He loved the size of Montreal. It was the antithesis of concentration camps. And of war. And the farm where he grew up. Or so he hoped. So, he decided to stay a while, soak it all in, get the flavour.

The flavour's name turned out to be Monique. Monique Lavoie. She was a little older than Danny and that was fine with him. Monique was settled in, sure of herself, strong and soft. Together. She managed a small restaurant, Maxie B's, which had okay food but was better known by some on the darker side of the street as a front for one of Harry Ship's smaller casinos.

Danny knew about its rougher edges from the get-go. While he had no significant yearnings to gamble, he had no qualms about suckers losing their milk money. "That's what the fucking war was about," he told Monique one night when he was heavily into gin and tonic, and she was in a mood to tolerate it. "The right to be a damn fool anytime you want."

Monique held her tongue, though that was not her usual practice and certainly not because she agreed with Danny. Wisely, she saw no percentage in arguing with his inebriated self. However, he demanded some response and so her discretion went out the window of their second-floor rooms.

"Well, don't they?" He had become unpleasantly insistent, fueled by alcohol and whatever else made good men mad.

"Of course, Danny. It's the right of any fool to be parted from their money. Even…" she hesitated, "even if their children go without food. I agree with you."

He caught the sarcasm in her comment and let loose. "Jesus Mary, Monique. You think I'm that fucked up. I don't want kids to be starving. Fuck, it doesn't matter what I want. It's what people do, what's in their nature."

Monique went over to Danny, who was standing at the window looking down on the street below. She took the bottle from his hand, put it down on the windowsill, and rested her head on his shoulder. "It's late. Let's go to bed. I need you."

Defeated in so many ways, he nodded yes, and she assisted him to their bed. She helped him with his clothes, and once they were lying down together, she cradled him as he struggled to get to sleep.

In the night, she felt him get out of bed twice. The second time, she thought she could hear crying. Sometimes she regretted begging Harry to hire Danny. He wasn't cut out to be a bookie. Harry had decided to call him his muscle-bookie. Danny had regular shifts at one of Harry's string of White Houses. He seemed to enjoy the work. Occasionally he had to do collections; some people just never seemed to want to pay up. Danny had a quiet anger, a bit of a simmering fury, contained just enough to be effective. Harry had even told her that Danny might rise in the business. "I like his style, Monique. Like it a lot. You did good bringing him to me."

Monique wondered if she was feeling that she did good. She understood that while Harry was riding high now, there were others – police officers, prosecutors, competitors – who wanted to bring him down. Harry, and anyone in his wake.

Tonight, game five of the Stanley Cup, would make Harry's enterprises exceptionally busy. And that would include the casino behind Maxie B's.

They slept late and arose about ten. It was Tuesday, April 9th.

She put on a pot of coffee and sliced up an aging cantaloupe.

"Tonight's the night?" she asked.

"Yeah," he answered. "Game five."

"You don't mind me not going?"

"It was kind of up to Harry, wasn't it! He wants you there. It'll be a busy night. I'm surprised he let me have the night off."

"He's …we say… imprévisible. What is it in English?"

"Unpredictable."

"Yes. Unpredictable."

"Maybe. I think otherwise. Harry always knows what he's doing. He needs you more than he needs me. We're alike that way."

That made her smile.

"You understand?"

"Of course."

"Good."

Later in the morning, they went out for a light lunch. They lingered over coffee and croissants at a little café that Monique called Notre Endroit even though its actual moniker was Chez Paul. They then came home and spent the afternoon in bed. Monique had to be at work by six, and so later, refreshed, they travelled together, she to work and he to the game..

The fifth game of the 1946 Stanley Cup was a goal scorers bonanza. Montreal won 6-3 and took the cup. The first two games had been played in Montreal, but Harry hadn't wanted to cut him loose. "It's our bread and butter, you crosseur. All that matters is that les perdants do what they do best. Lose their souls."

Danny couldn't resist sticking it to his boss. He'd come to learn that Harry enjoyed, to an extent, the occasional snappy comeback, a bit of a lively challenge from underlings. Not a whole lot but some. "All it means to you is money, eh! Pardon my French, Harry, but, Christ, you're a bloody bullshitter." As soon as he said it, truth though it was, he immediately regretted the risk. Danny had been a smart soldier and knew to keep a healthy social distance from his superiors. In the world Harry lived in, respect was everything. Even with the sense that he could play with him, he had no doubt that Harry was a viper, and you just never knew about vipers.

"Danny, Danny, Danny, boy. Maybe I am. And maybe its okay for you to call me out. But tread carefully boyo. I like to play but I don't like to be hurt. Anyways, go to the fifth game. On me."

And so, he did. And now the Canadiens were on top of the heap. At least for 1946.

The book, the casino, would still be open, so he swung by to pick up Monique.

The book manager, an old hand named Jean, gave him the news. "Harry sent a car and had her driven out to the farm at Cote St. Luc. No problems, as far as I know, but he wanted her to oversee it tonight. Just precautionary."

Danny had never been to the farm. It catered to islanders, made it damn easy to bet and not travel far. Quality service, with a smile…as long as you paid up. Monique had been out there before and knew the ropes. Still, to divert her from her scheduled shift and location. It didn't bode well.

"Will she be staying over?" he'd asked.

"No. I don't think so."

"It'll be a long night for her, won't it?"

"No. The people of Cote St Luc go to bed early during the week. And even earlier on weekends. Don't worry. She may even make it home before you."

With that reassurance, Danny left, hailed a cab, and asked to be let off a couple of blocks from their apartment. There was a small tavern he had discovered. It was mostly empty. A working-class neighbourhood, most of the men would be home, thinking, how morning will swiftly be upon them. Many would have listened to the game, been thrilled by Les Canadiens, their victory. The victory would belong to all Montrealer's, all the people of Quebec, even most Canadians, except for the hard-core Leaf supporters of Toronto and those others who still saw Canada as one nation composed solely of Englishmen.

Danny sat at a corner table and sipped his beer. He tried not to think about Monique. Of course, she would be fine. She was tough. Tougher than he was. When they had first met, the attraction had been so powerful. She'd asked how old he was. "Why do you care?" he had said. "A rule," she had answered. "If I am twice your age, it's a no go."

He had laughed.

"Why are you laughing at me? I don't like it." She had started to leave. He touched her arm. "Don't leave. I apologize. I'm thirty…hell, thirty-one."

She broke out into laughter. "You don't even know your age?"

He explained that he would turn thirty-one in March. It was only February, but he'd already made the leap. "It's a family thing. No matter what your birthday actually is, once you've journeyed into a new year, up your age goes. Nuts, eh!"

"Un peu," she'd joke… "Just a little."

It built from there. Faster than he ever imagined.

Montreal was a beautiful, exciting playground. He particularly enjoyed Parc Belmont and its rollercoaster.

This city and her energy were intoxicating. Never much for dancing, certainly not much more than country square dances growing up, he quickly adapted to her passion for a grand Montreal pavilion, Chez Maurice's Danceland. Jam packed most every night, swing and jazz, the youth careened in a force of musical extravagance. Monique was in top form, even though many of the dancers were a generation younger.

It was getting late, and Danny did not want to not be at home in bed when Monique rolled in from the Cote St. Luc casino. He paid up and returned home. He stripped down, crawled into bed, and waited for the woman who was saving him from his petty wars.

Morning, November 1st

There was no doubt about it. Gil Gronsky was confused. And he had no one to blame but himself.. He hadn't intended to start a new novel, but then a few weeks ago he learned about the whole National Novel Writing Month scenario. Which people succinctly, if awkwardly, called NaNoWriMo. Instead of three days he'd have a month. A whole month. No more than a week ago, he had a brainstorm, had his story within a story finally plotted out, at least in broad strokes. It would be a complex tale of lost love and revenge. It simmered inside of him. It waited to be told. Then, suddenly, it fell flat. Pancake flat. Flat tire flat. He hated flat tires. The swerve to the side of the road, the ka-lunk, ka-lunk, ka-lunk.

But today would see a rejuvenation. A resuscitation. He could feel the surge of emotion rise up in him this first of November. Writing the full story of *Scratch an Old Wound* – what he hoped would be a complex and exhilarating post World War 2 tale that he had begun, only to discover that, for a while, the juggling of time and detail was beyond him – would now be his catharsis, his ascension to some higher personal plateau. The world today was in such need. Certainly, the COP 26 gathering in Glasgow for the next two weeks would tell everyone what the future of everyone on the earth might be.

It was looking bleak, though. No doubt about that.

Still, as depressing as the environmental degradation of the earth was, as simultaneously hopeful and full of trepidation about the survival of the species as everyone seemed to be, Gronsky was on a roll. The past two months had brought so many new experiences, mostly never imagined. The revelation that he had a granddaughter, that she, Anthea, had sought him out, albeit out of curiosity as to what sort of beast he was that could have engendered Stella Fishbine's awful yet ultimately revealing game, Beware the Gronsky…it all served the process of reunification.

Stella, or whoever she was besides being his first wife and, previously, an identity thief, was now history. Dead. What a strange woman she had been. He hadn't thought that when they had met. Then, she had been a wild flamboyant Oregonian hippie chick. And he had fallen. Fallen hard. Carelessly hard as it turned out.

She remained a mystery even once Anthea had appeared as a waif in his garage.

Now Anthea had become a resonant part of his life, sharing his home, giving him a future, a future he had never expected or even felt that he deserved to have.

He had to get a move on, he thought. It was just past eight thirty in the morning. He had made coffee and spent a few minutes on the porch before he realized that it was too cold to dawdle there and had moved into his den to begin processing his words. They came out in droves. In the background, as was his habit, he had the TV on. BBC. News about gas production. The Russians and the Chinese not at COP26. Talking heads to hurl random thoughts into his writer's brain. He injected his own thoughts for a second. How often had he heard decision-makers and just ordinary Joes say that they supported climate action because of their kids, their grandkids. They all claimed that they wanted to leave the world a better place, not for themselves, old dying farts that they were, but for their progeny. He appreciated those sentiments, but until Anthea had appeared, he had never thought he could express his hope for the world in quite the same way. You would need children and grandchildren to be taken seriously if you said that. Dawn and Robert, his daughter and son, had been stolen away and memory of them had faded. They were not his anymore. Not in the way he thought they should be. Flesh of my flesh, flesh that I have held, hold, held close in the storm of life. Until Anthea had appeared like the proverbial Athena, albeit a slightly street-worn, adolescent version, he had not held the flesh of his flesh for over fifty years. He would never hold dead and gone Dawn again. As for Robert, Anthea did not know what had become of her uncle, her mother's brother, Gronsky's son.

Until Anthea brought that familial generational spark into his life, any wishes that he had for the future of the earth, any wish of wellness he might offer the future world, any wish for its survival, would have to be for all the children and grandchildren of everyone to come. He might still do that. Surely that was the better gesture.

But now, he had a flesh and blood granddaughter to wish upon.

As he thought that, there was a tap on the door.

"It's unlocked," he said unnecessarily. It was always unlocked.

Anthea entered. "Morning Grampa Gronsky. Hug?"

It had become their ritual. For the first few weeks after Anthea's appearance, they had not embraced. It was not in Gronsky's repertoire of behaviours anyways and Anthea did not seem to favor that sort of intimacy. Then in late September, they had bumped into each other in the kitchen, she coming down from her new bedroom and he, draped in his old blue dressing gown, bound for a morning shower and she touched the garment, laughed and said, "It's pretty old, Gronsky" and he had replied, "Almost as old as me," and they both smiled and somehow she had come even closer, and he did not step back. She asked, "Can I have a hug?" and he had dissolved into her body and she, so much shorter, had wrapped her arms around his embarrassingly chunky midriff and they had held that position for minutes.

For hours?

Not hours, but the barriers of time and troubles had thawed. It was their moment, and each day since, the morning hug was achieved.

"Come here," he said, and she approached and enveloped his shoulders with her arms, and he held her arms tightly.

"Let me get up and do this properly," he said.

"What's on your agenda for today?" he asked after the hug.

"What else: school. And you're doing that writing thing?"

"Yes. That writing thing. NaNoWriMo. You should try and say it."

She shook her head and said, "When I hear it, it sounds like Nanaimo." Nanaimo was a fair-sized town on Vancouver Island.

"It does sound the same…or similar. I'm thinking I may set some of the scenes in my book there."

"That *Scratch an Itch* book?"

He grinned. "I'm calling it *Scratch an Old Wound.*"

"Right!" she answered. "That one."

"But you're not wrong. I am scratching a writer's itch. My itch!"

"You're funny, Gronsky"

"I have to work at it. Anyways, you should eat something before you leave."

"I might eat at school. Pancakes this morning."

Gronsky nodded. Anthea had been enrolled in a local alternative school a short hop down the hill from their house. PURPOSE had operated for decades in the city and served a wide array of students, especially those who required more of an intimate community to learn and grow in. Shortly after Anthea had appeared in his life back on the Labour Day weekend, Miriam, had immediately suggested it as a logical choice. Gronsky had never heard of the school, and Anthea was initially resistant to school of any kind. However, after a few visits to the program, all with the encouragement from Miriam, she had enrolled near the end of September and now, over a month later, seemed fully engaged.

"Schools that feed you. Pancakes no less. Certainly not in my day," he joked.

"Did they have Cave Schools back then, Gronsky?"

"Get out of here," he laughed. "I have to get back to my art."

She left and he turned back to the keyboard. He had left Danny Hawkins resting in bed in the Montreal of 1946, waiting for his love, Monique, to return from work.

Gronsky knew that Monique would not return. He now had to find a way to tell Danny Hawkins the news and see what would unfold from that discovery.

Chapter Two, Scratch an Old Wound

Danny Hawkins woke after ten the next morning. It was April 10th. Monique was not in the bed beside him, and he immediately knew that she had not come home. He would always wake when she came in after him. It was just that way. Ten was too early for the Notre Endroit to be open, but he called anyways. Jean answered.

"Jean, Monique didn't make it home. Was there a problem?"

Danny heard silence.

"Jean? You there?"

"Harry's gone out there, Danny. There was trouble."

"What kind?"

"I'll have Harry call you when he gets back. I don't know."

"Don't know, or don't want to say?"

"Leave me alone, Danny. Harry will get back to you. Stay near your phone."

Jean rang off and Danny was left holding the receiver. He wanted to call someone, anyone. He had an awful feeling that something unimaginable had occurred. He didn't want to think beyond that. The war had given him similar premonitions. Every day was destiny. Nothing was guaranteed. Like those deaths the previous week in Puerto Rico he had read about in the Gazette on the weekend. Nine or ten Yankee sailors, watching manoeuvres in an observation tower. And a bomb accidentally dropped on the tower and that was all she wrote.

She, whoever she was, was always writing finis.

He made a pot of coffee, drank more than he usually would, and waited. At noon, there had been no call. He called Jean again.

Jean picked up.

"Jean? Danny. I need to do something. No ones called. I'm gonna bust a blood vessel if I don't hear something soon."

"I don't know what to say, Danny. I'm waiting for news too."

"Maybe I should come down there…wait with you."

"Sure. If you like."

They hung up and Danny got ready to leave.

There was a knock on his door.

He opened it. Maxie Fingers, Harry Ship's driver, stood large. "Harry wants to see you. He's downstairs."

Danny put on his coat and boots and followed Maxie out and down to where he could see Harry, short, pudgy, mid-thirties, dapper as always, sitting in the back of his Buick. Harry waved him in.

"Tell me, Harry," Danny said, climbing next to him in the back seat.

"It ain't good, kiddo. Ain't good at all."

Danny could feel his world sink into a giant slough of sorrow.

Afternoon, November 1st

Gronsky stopped writing, consumed by the grief he was about to impart to Danny Hawkins. Was this the way writing was meant to be, so painful for the author? It was quite something to feel the grief of a character you had created. Did this mean that he was so sensitive that he couldn't separate himself from his imagination?

Gronsky was aware of Monique's fate. Though not yet written, it was in the script lodged in his mind. That was part of the creator's plan. He was the creator. Such a godlike phrase, he considered. Gronsky was definitely a product of the fifties and sixties. Unlike those who came before who perhaps had to imagine death and bloodshed on the radio, he benefitted – if you could call it that– from the death and bloodshed portrayed daily on television during those decades. How insensitive our society had become, was trained to be.

Gronsky had to let the rest of the day go by with no more emotion-laden words, no more imagined deaths, no more real sorrow. He had not expected that being a writer would generate so much pain. Perhaps, he thought, it had little to do with the craft and more to do with whatever was locked inside the writer.

Anthea came home at four and later made simple omelettes for the two of them. Whatever her life had been before, she had benefited from an expectation that she learn to cook at an early age.

They were both tired from their respective days, but Gronsky suggested they watch a film, a classic called *Panic in the Streets*.

"A disease movie?" Anthea asked after Gronsky explained why it was such a timely film, even if it was seventy years old.

"Bubonic plague. A pretty impressive disease."

She made it through the first forty minutes before she begged off and went to her room. Gronsky sat through it until the end.

He had watched it at least five times in the past two years.

He thought of it as research.

Morning, November 2nd

Gil Gronsky had somewhat of a tossing and turning night. He had successfully maneuvered through the first day of NaNoWriMo and achieved his word target, given serious thought to the process of writing, both the art and a smidgen of the science, and was now poised to begin day two.

He had woken at six a.m. and listened to the news of the world. It was a lifelong affliction, the wanting to know the big stories of the day and the occasionally smaller tales that snuck in to capture the attention of humanity. How easy it was, how simple to rest in one's warm bed, being thankful that one had one, and to stretch and squirm and shimmy his toes to check on the arthritis that he was convinced was creeping into his aging joints, and listen, tsk tsking at this or that bit of news. Today had some breakthroughs on the illegal drug front. A move to decriminalize hard drugs. The commentator mentioned the cowardly ways of government, the inability to take a strong stand until thousands had died and the reality of poisoned street drugs was so palpable that only a rock would oppose the need to ensure that people who needed drugs, who were trapped in that mire, had the ability to get a safe supply.

Gronsky wished he had the courage to be public about all of the world's ills that he had the answer for. It amused him to think of the crowd parting as he strode to the podium. "Make way for the Great Gronsky. Make way! He knows the way!"

You are delusional, Gilbert Gronsky, he thought as he poured his first cup of coffee for day two of writing. He had some obligations. On the weekend, he and Miriam had found the time to share her bed. "Am I going to see you in November at all, Gil?" she asked as they snuggled at dawn.

"I'm not going anywhere," he had replied, aware that she was referencing the NaNoWriMo affair that was bound to occupy him.

"Don't be an ass. You'll be immersed in that cluttered head of yours, writing up a storm and barely conscious of those around you."

To counter that, he had kissed her left nipple and said something like, "Oh, my dear, I am conscious of your every charm."

She had repeated, "You ass."

And then laughed.

Just before he had returned to his bed, she asked to look more closely at his face.

"I am a handsome devil, aren't I?" he quipped.

"What is that?" she asked gently pulling his face to her dressing table mirror.

"This splotch? Yeah, this old man has a splotch on his face."

"I don't know, Gil. Maybe you should get it checked out."

He promised that he would, and this morning had planned to go to a nearby clinic. However, when he got up and shaved an hour earlier, the splotch was gone. Or had moved. Now he was uncertain whether a trip to a clinic was necessary. Covid had interrupted his annual medical checkup habits, and it had been over two years since he had been to Doc Marzak, his long-time physician. The pandemic had played fast and loose with his long-standing routines. He loved routines. His routines, mostly, but he also was not so selfish that he couldn't appreciate how so much had been lost, had changed with the current plague. The routines, such as they were, of all humanity.

As he dug deeply into the somewhat shallow pool of his most complex thoughts, he realized he was procrastinating. He had to get on with the novel. He topped up his coffee and went to his den. He heard Anthea walking above him on the second floor. Soon, she came down for her morning hug, they bantered a bit, he asked her to look at his face and see if there was or was not a splotch that shouldn't be there, to which she commented, "No new splotches." She left him alone with his writerly assignment.

Ah, Danny Hawkins, I'm sorry for this, he mused and set to the task.

Chapter Three, Scratch an Old Wound

Danny didn't want the answer but knew that he had to hear it. He gave Harry a few moments to plan it out. Harry usually blurted out whatever was on his mind unless it was something so terrible that even he had to pause. He was pausing. It wouldn't last long.

"Christ, Kid, I wish it weren't me doin' this. I hate this shit."

Danny sunk into himself even deeper. Harry didn't mind doing the most reprehensible of things so this, this thing…there were no words…

"Tell me, Harry. Whatever it is."

Harry sucked in a deep breath and let loose. "I got called in the bloody wee hours. By the gendarmes, no friggin' less. All sorts of shit exploding out at the farm. Get out there, they ordered. So, I hustled Whitey out of his slumber, and we zoomed out to Cote St. Luc. By the time we made it out there, there were a dozen cop cars and locals milling about like sheep."

Danny was getting agitated and took a shot. "Monique, Harry. Monique."

"Let me do it my way. Christ, don't get my bloody dander up, Danny. She's dead. Bloody dead."

Danny felt the universe crash in on him like some evil outer space asteroid had smacked him, crushed him into the ground. He believed she was gone yet didn't. Couldn't. Had to! Did he? Two completely opposing concepts. In an instant he remembered her, naked and lounging in their old clawfoot tub, smiling, ready to laugh, a sweet drink –Drambuie, whatever was handy – resting on a chair by the tub. Playful and so intelligent, so full of life. He saw her wet skin, the way he preferred her, her breasts, smaller than many, soft and inviting, her skin that was no more.

How primal he was. Primitive. Were these lustful thoughts, self sorrowful thoughts? Did thinking of her in a carnal way somehow demean the memory of her?

He knew that he needed to stop thinking and start feeling. Perhaps he was and didn't know it. Christ, the pain was there, and he needed to give in to it.

"Did you see her, Harry? Her...?"

"No, Danny, I didn't. By the time I got there, me and Whitey, they had taken the bodies away."

"Bodies?"

"There were three. Monique and two customers. It was a heist, Danny, and one of the dead customers was packing, and that tipped things deadly. Or so the cops said. But who believes cops? Not me, but maybe this time..."

Harry's voice trailed off and Danny was wanting to scream but not knowing how.

"Where would they take her?"

"Downtown. The morgue. Never been there. Never plan to."

Danny knew he had to make his way down to the morgue, but he was fed up with Harry. No reason, just afraid he might get angry at him for sending Monique out to where she was killed. Harry would have to take the blame, some of it, but Danny doubted he would. Guys like Harry, they knew not to admit anything. And if he were being honest, he knew Monique would give Harry a pass. She wanted more responsibility, believed women were equal or better than men and was always looking for ways to prove it. Danny had admired that about her. She took no guff. Gave as good or better than she got.

That might have been what got her killed. That and the goober patron who thought he could stop some professional heist jockeys. He assumed the robber-killers were pros and that the surprise element upped the ante.

He had to get away from Harry and go to her.

Afternoon, November 2nd

Gronsky was exhausted. The death of Monique was wearing him out. He was now convinced that writing and life were inseparable, that while he was doing one – that is, writing or living – he could interchange them, engage in both, back and forth, share moments of joy and sorrow in both his worlds. He would have to remember that he was the link.

Not confusing other people, his nearest and dearest, and his creations was also important.

He checked his watch and remembered that he needed to zip out to a clinic and get the mole or whatever it was that was blemishing his ratty old mug checked out.

Gronsky washed his face, put on a jacket and boots, grabbed his umbrella, and stepped out into the day. The clinic he intended to go to was just down the hill, a ten-minute walk. There was a slight breeze, but the walk, being downhill, was easy. Before he entered the clinic, he put on his mask, found his health card and vaccine passport, a paper copy. He wasn't sure if they needed to see it, but Gronsky liked to anticipate problems.

There were three other people in the waiting room, all masked, all distancing. He went to reception, explained his concern, accepted a form he was given to fill out, and took a seat.

At one point, fifteen minutes into his wait, a fellow popped in the door from outside. He was maskless. The receptionist asked that if he didn't have one of his own that he put on a mask from the supply at the entranceway. "Fuck that noise. I want to see a doc. And I don't wear no stinking mask." Gronsky kept a close watch on the fellow, angry at such stupidity but admiring what he assumed was a derivative movie reference from the classic Bogart film."

The standoff lasted for five minutes, and then two masked policemen arrived and gently escorted the Bogart lover out the door. Gronsky was captivated with how smoothly the police response had been. He would have to squeeze that proficiency into his novel.

Shortly, he was paged, went in and revealed his mole to Doctor Rebecca Theo.

"Do we shake hands?" Gronsky asked, not wishing to miss some finely tuned Covid-in- slight-remission-we-hope social etiquette.

Dr. Theo laughed and extended her right hand. "Such a simple gesture. My pleasure, Mr. ..." she peered down at the form he had filled out, "Gronsky."

"Gil, please."

They both used sanitizer, and Gronsky took a seat.

Dr. Theo looked at the offending spot with a small magnifying glass.

"Hmmm," she said.

"Hmmm good or hmmm not so...?"

"It's a blemish, Gilbert," the doctor said. "A simple blemish. I very much doubt if it is cancerous."

"Can you guarantee it isn't?" asked Gronsky

"I'll take a sliver, and have it tested," replied the doctor, a youngish woman who sounded confident in her knowledge.

Her offer satisfied Gronsky and after the scraping, he left. It was certainly less painful than what he was going through with Danny and Monique.

Going up the hill was definitely more difficult that walking downhill. On the other hand, Gronsky felt healthier after the physician's comment, so it all balanced out in his mind. Halfway up, he ran into Anthea and together they huffed and puffed the last stretch to home.

It was still relatively early in the mid-afternoon, and so Gronsky adjourned to his den to consider next steps for Danny Hawkins and his grief. His plan for Danny's future had begun to gel in his mind. But how to get Danny from his tragic time in Montreal mid-1946 to a small, growing community on the east coast of Vancouver Island a few years later? And how many years exactly was not fully fleshed out. Plotting was a conundrum.

He set all that aside and once again got caught up on the news of the world. Glasgow and COP 26 were aflutter with the salvation of the environment, but nothing seemed to be sticking as far as Gronsky could see. It still had a week and a half to run, so perhaps the environment would be saved before mid-month.

When Miriam returned to her apartment around five o'clock, he asked her if she wanted to share a pizza with him and Anthea. That seemed fine, and with a tossed together salad, the three of them ate dinner in his kitchen at seven. He reassured Miriam that he had taken her health advice seriously and had seen the loveliest of doctors.

"A lovely doctor? How *lovely* for you," Miriam tweaked him.

The rest of the evening was quiet, but Miriam invited the two of them up to her apartment at eight the following evening to watch the latest episode of *Survivor.* Anthea confessed that she had first watched the show a few weeks earlier absolutely loved how odd the show was, and how treacherous people could be.

Morning, November 3rd

Gronsky woke up Wednesday morning with an overwhelming sense of loss. He had totally forgotten that the day before had been Día de los Muertos, the Day of the Dead. How fitting, he thought, that he had experienced the fictional passing of his dear Monique Lavoie, a character barely sketched in but so real to him and, of course, his main protagonist, Danny Hawkins.

To get his head out of smothering emotional clouds and to set himself on the path of a productive writing day, he made coffee, a favorite Columbian blend, and turned on the BBC to get a sense of the day's larger domain. There was always a risk that some horror would await him, but he fully expected that COP 26 would be the kickoff story, and he was adjusting to another delay in earth's salvation.

Unfortunately, the lead story was a report on human rights abuses in Ethiopia on both sides of a war he was not sure he had been aware of. The starvation in that country had flitted into his brain, he was sure of that, but the war...what war?

There were so many wars.

Who could keep track?

He stepped away from world news, but not before noting that the Republican, Glenn Youngkin had clobbered Terry McAuliffe, the old Governor and Clinton loyalist, in Virginia. The impression was that Trump and his associates might be on the rise again.

Gronsky felt like crying but instead put on his coat and waterproof slippers and stepped out onto the porch to enjoy his coffee and a slight rainstorm that was pitter pattering away in delightful relief from slaughter and evildoers.

A few moments later, he was asleep. Around seven thirty, Anthea gently shook him awake. "Must not be sleeping all that well," he said.

"Let me microwave your coffee, Gronsky," she offered, and he assented. In two minutes, she was back with two hot coffees, passed his over, and snuggled into the porch settee.

"I love the rain," she effused, "especially here, with you."

They sat there and took in the start of the morning. Traffic was heavy, lights glancing off the pooling water, every second a horn beeping, the moments passing, and both expecting some sort of car crash.

"It's exciting, in a way," she said. "So different from the mountains where I grew up."

He nodded, wondering if she was yet ready to talk about some of the unpleasant things she had alluded to about her communal upbringing. Miriam had suggested giving her lots of time to talk and he had agreed. Especially after his other tenant, Sam, who had majored in psychology at university, had suggested the same.

Thus far, everything with Anthea had fallen into place like a preordained, if unexpected, jigsaw puzzle. That could change, of course, but for now, it was all to the good.

After a half hour of cozy communion on the porch, Anthea got up to get ready for school. She bent down, kissed Gronsky on his cheek, and left.

He stayed for another ten minutes, then got up, went to the kitchen, poured more coffee, and went to his den to revisit Danny Hawkins. In the night, at some point between deep and not quite deep enough sleep, he saw the means by which he could transport Danny from Montreal to Canada's west coast. That would be the creative trick. He hoped Danny would go willingly. Gronsky only had to find the words.

Chapter Four, Scratch an Old Wound

Danny was as numb as he'd ever been as he walked the streets of Montreal heading towards the morgue. His obligation was to see Monique, identify her, he supposed, for the record but more to just know that she was gone. He'd seen lots of death in Italy and later in Bosch land, but he had never been to a morgue. He had, however, felt numbed by death. One death, her death, would never be equal to the millions killed in the war, the hundreds, or thousands of deaths he had witnessed. How many he had witnessed was unclear. It didn't really matter. The deaths mattered, of course, and the numbers, they would always matter. They would continue to die in his minds eye, visit him at the most inopportune of times, laugh, bleed, blow apart. Once you have been to war, seen the horror that mankind delivers unto itself, you can't unsee it and it never leaves you.

He knew he would always see her and prayed that however she appeared at the morgue, it would not become his memory of her.

He arrived and they took him to where she was. A sheet covered her. The attendant lifted the sheet from her face. It was as if she had fallen asleep, as if it were the morning before when she had lain beside him, warm, willing, and forever.

He didn't cry. But he could hear his heart stop. For a moment he was dead too, sharing this final moment with her. Then his heart started beating and he thanked the attendant, someone likely who'd performed this routine task, this classic morgue moment, countless times.

He left and headed home. Once there, he breathed in deeply, desperate for her scent. He touched her clothes, and then crawled into bed and slept until dark. When he awoke, he tried with all the might of memory to recall the dream he had been in. It may well have been a dream from his just ended sleep, but whatever it was, he revelled in it, in her memory. In the dream, if it was one, he was beside her, running his palm up and down her strong sweet spine.

Danny was starting to be hungry, so he went out to a small café nearby that served English food. He ordered mashed potatoes, liver with onions, and a slice of apple pie. Monique did not eat liver even though she enjoyed heart of cow. Their respective food tastes had amused them both.

Harry was waiting for him when he retuned home. He got into Harry's car.

"You saw her?" Harry asked.

Danny nodded.

"What a terrible thing. Anyways, the cops don't have anything, but we've heard that it was a trio from Toronto. Maybe contracted by someone inside the family. I hate to think that, but it'll get solved. We solve out own problems. Even with traitors. But I don't want you to worry none. Take a few days. Get your head together. We don't want any vigilante stuff. I know that's what your thinking…maybe not now but soon. You'll get them thoughts. Don't have 'em. Take a few days, I've already arranged for the funeral."

Danny knew he should have resented how Harry had taken things over, the funeral being the big one, but he knew it was beyond him.

He spent the next few days sleeping and crying and wondering what the rest of his life might be like.

The funeral was small, and none of Monique's family attended. That hadn't surprised Danny. He had thought to ask Harry about who had been invited but assumed that Harry wanted to keep the whole thing – the murders and the funeral – quiet. There was next to nothing in the papers. He would have expected a triple homicide to get more coverage.

Harry had quite a reach.

As for Monique's family, they lived in the far eastern reaches of the province and Monique had been estranged from them since before the war. "They are much too Catholic, Danny. Tiresome. Maybe some day, we'll visit. Not now."

Whether it was true or not, he didn't have their information, names, a phone number, anything. He probably could look through her papers and find something. They had a right to know but that would likely have to happen later, much later.

And maybe never. Monique had been very secretive about her family, and once when he asked her about it, she had said they had never approved of her choices and that was their loss.

He went back to work the Monday after the funeral. It was busy work. Collecting bets. Simple work that kept his mind occupied and his pockets flush.

Then, in late July, Harry Davis, the Edge Man, the go-between who paid off the police at the behest of Harry Ship and others, was gunned down. There was no way to keep this assassination out of the papers, and the backlash against Harry Ship and the Jewish Mafia was intense.

Danny could see that his time in Montreal was ending. Still, he needed some direction. Harry provided it. "You've done excellent work, Danny. Now is the time to pull back. You have any plans?"

Danny had none and said so.

"I have a cousin, second, third, North Winnipeg. You ever been to the Peg?"

"The Peg?"

"Something I heard…or maybe I made it up. A little nickname. Quite catchy, don't you think?" Harry said.

Danny had passed through Winnipeg on the way to war. "Never heard it called that. Might have some family there. Blacker sheep than me! Never been off the train, though."

"My cousin, Vinnie Brass, bit of a dick. Bad joke. A private dick, you know. He could use you. A little muscle and a lot of brain. I'll check with him. You like winter, right?"

No, Danny didn't like winter, but this was Canada and winter was part of the package. And Harry Ship was giving him a lifeline. And even if it was connected to Winnipeg, he might as well take it. As for being Sam Spade, well, The Maltese Falcon was a good movie and Danny knew that he was observant. And he had a lifetime of taking risks. After the war and Monique's death, anything else had to be a breeze.

Late Afternoon, November 3rd

Gronsky stopped typing. He was as drained as he had been yesterday. More so, probably. It was after four and he had achieved enough for the day. Danny was on the move. Gronsky's writing mission for the day was accomplished.

Anthea was running late. Then he remembered that she was going to stay after school for math tutoring. He made a small salad and hauled out the leftover slices of pizza from the night before. He heated up a frying pan, splashed in some oil and slowly, very slowly crisped up the slices one by one.

Gronsky had never been a great fan of the iconic television show *Survivor.* For him it seemed to foster deceit and treachery. He'd not felt the need to tell anyone his reservations about the values espoused by the show. He understood that those character flaws, deceit and treachery, had considerable entertainment value.

Miriam, however, was a super fan of the show and argued that it taught people to collaborate, to work together. Two weeks after they had found Anthea, or she found them, the new *Survivor* season began, and it had since become a mid-week means of bonding.

Gronsky had to admit that he had fallen under the spell of the disparate individuals thrust together in weekly combat and games of the mind. He also thought that in many ways, as real as this reality show was, it was anything but real.

Shortly before eight, he and Anthea knocked on Miriam's apartment door. They gathered around her big screen and immersed themselves in the life-changing experiences of the dozen or so remaining participants. It was all quite entertaining and ludicrous and, in this particular episode, a horse race with much conspiracy and fake television suspense. In the end, a woman named Sydney was voted off the Island. It was mildly surprising. Sydney, in the final soliloquy, expressed her immense pleasure at being allowed to return to her real life.

Gronsky appreciated her unsportsmanlike point but kept it to himself. He wanted both Miriam and Anthea to enjoy every moment in the show.

They chatted afterwards, and then Anthea went to bed. Gronsky stayed, and he and Miriam shared a pot of tea.

"She seems content," Miriam observed.

"I am, that's for sure. There's still so much we don't know about her life in the Kootenays."

"I hope you're not pressing her. Clearly you two are building trust. I would hate to see that ruined by your need to know…"

He smiled. "I don't need to know anything. Whatever she tells me is fine. Though, I'm no spring chicken. There's only so much time."

"Right. You go to the doctor and now you have a week to live."

"I'm hoping for a few more weeks than that. At least three or four so I can finish this damn NaNoWriMo…"

"Perhaps, Hemingway, you should run off to bed."

"Whose?"

It turned out to be Gronsky's own bed. Both he and Miriam had called it a night, a noticeably quiet night.

Morning, November 4th

The rain clattered the rooftops for most of the night. Gronsky spent much of those dark hours tossing and turning the moments plotting his novel. In between every creative rain-charged flash, he slept,

He got up at six, dressed in his rain gear, and went for a walk to the park. It had been a while since he had done a morning walkabout in the rain. He'd have to do this more often. The morning car commute had started, and here and there he caught beams of headlights off in the distance. He entered the park from its southern entrance and quietly made his way through the trees. Shortly he passed the hockey arena and, beyond it, the playground. Off to the left someone had pitched a small tent. Whoever it was would be gone by the time the day formally began. He knew from press reports that the homeless were everywhere, both in his city and every city. Their numbers were growing in painful leaps and bounds, and no one seemed to have a solution. Housing, affordable housing was simply not doable.

Government at various levels had tried all sorts of measures to house the dispossessed, but Covid had challenged the economy, and even with rent moratoriums, people became houseless, homeless. Encampments were everywhere. Gronsky was befuddled by how these unfortunate people managed. He doubted he would have the wherewithal to survive the elements for even one night let alone days, months, or years.

Even now, after walking in the rain for half an hour, he felt the need to return home and get warm.

Once there, he ate some yogurt, made coffee, and adjourned to his den. He turned on the seven o'clock news and listened to the latest overtures from COP 26. Coal was on the menu for the day. Forty countries were declaring they would lessen its use. Not the four biggest consumers, though: China, India, The USA, and Australia.

It didn't sound all that monumental a breakthrough to Gronsky. However, he was loath to criticize any attempt, even the feeblest of efforts.

All that aside, the ways of the world were not, could not be foremost on his mind. The novel and the trials of Danny Hawkins were of the utmost importance. He had never been to Winnipeg, though friends had. He needed to locate Danny in the Winnipeg of late 1946. There, Danny would apprentice as a private eye. Gronsky was almost as excited as Danny was not. Danny would still be mired in grief. However, the drive to survive that had served him well enough in war would have to come into play. At the same time, he expected that Harry Ship would keep his promise to either avenge Monique or advise Danny who to go after.

Gronsky was convinced that Danny didn't much care who reeked revenge. Only that it happen.

As he prepared to enter Danny's world, Anthea slipped in, gave him a quick hug, and then left Gronsky to his time travelling.

Chapter Five, Scratch an Old Wound

Danny Hawkins left for Winnipeg in early September. Prior to that he had spoken to Vinnie Brass a number of times just to make sure that they would both have a fruitful experience. Vinnie proved to be somewhat of a jokester, the complete antithesis of the somber Harry Ship. Vinnie also clarified that he and Harry were not actual cousins. "I was his babysitter back in the old neighbourhood. Harry hates me mentioning that. Anyways, my folks and Harry's parents were neighbours. I moved to Winnipeg in the late twenties. Just before the crash. I had read all those Black Masks stories of Op's and crime and knew that that might be my schtick. Montreal was full of hooligans and hucksters, but I figured I needed to start small. I stayed small. Big fish, little pond small. It's got its rewards, staying small. And with luck, you'll live longer."

Before he was ready to leave Montreal, he pestered Harry into keeping him posted on the search for the gunsels who'd killed Monique and the two out of towners.

"You got it, Danny. It may take a while, but something will pop. Meanwhile, you make a new life. Don't worry about me."

They both knew Harry was under the gun from reformers the likes of Pax Plante, a Montreal lawyer, who was vehemently opposed to the wide-open gambling for which Harry was in large part responsible. Or thought he was. Harry had made a fortune and would do whatever he could to forestall the tide of repressive morality that Plante represented. Danny presumed that Harry understood that reform usually won the day and believed he felt an odd loyalty to his employees to get them safely settled if possible. Or at least, perhaps felt some guilt for sending Monique out to the farm where she died. Harry couldn't have anticipated that outcome. Danny understood that.

As for gambling, it was not a passion of Danny's.

He didn't have much passion left. For anything but revenge.

To live long enough to pay back whoever was responsible for Monique's murder, Danny knew he had to find a life, something to sustain him, and simply survive.

As the train pulled into Winnipeg's Union Station, Danny was both impressed with the building and experiencing a vague sense of reluctant hopefulness.

Vinnie met him as he disembarked, and Danny took a liking to his new employer right away. Vinnie was taller than he had sounded on the phone, running five foot ten or so. For a man in his mid-fifties, he was fairly trim. Vinnie flashed a broad grin that showed some healthy-looking teeth. He was wearing a black felt fedora with a small red frill in the outer band. His grey overcoat, buckled in the middle, showed the sort of style that Danny imagined he might well copy. He'd seen enough films about detectives to know that if you looked the part you were more than halfway there.

"Good to meet you, Danny," Vinnie said, shooting out his right hand to shake. Danny reciprocated, smiled, and they started walking out of the Station.

"That alright, calling you Danny? It's Vinnie all the way with me. Anyways, lets get you settled. I found you a little boarding house in the North End that I think you'll like. Midge Felker's place. She and I …well, Midge is okay in my book and not a half bad cook. In our game, it's smart to have a safe place to hang your hat."

Vinnie was driving a fairly new pickup.

"What year?" Danny asked.

"'42. Gets me around. Out in the flatlands, I can even be taken for a farmer. Useful sometimes."

Danny let Vinnie know that he appreciated his thoughtfulness at picking him up and arranging housing. Midge's house was a two-story affair, and Midge herself was a bundle of delight. You could tell in an instant that she loved to laugh, and Danny assumed right away that Vinnie was a source of pleasure for her.

"Right this way, Mr. Hawkins," she said, leading Danny and Vinnie up the staircase to one of three rooms on the second floor. "It's my largest and has a bed, a sitting area and even a table if you need a private space to entertain, dine in, as it were. Facilities are right outside," she said pointing to a large bathroom with a clawfoot tub and a second smaller room with a flusher.

Vinnie then told Danny that the first month's rent was covered and that they would start work tomorrow.

"I'll pick you up at ten and show you the cubbyhole I call an office. I already have a case lined up…"

"I might need some training, don't you think?"

"Not with this one. You'll be fine. Anyways, settle in, get use to Midge, enjoy her cooking. What's on the menu, Midge?"

"Perogy and ham," Midge revealed.

"I'd invite myself if I didn't have obligations."

With that, Vinnie left, and Midge said, "The house is yours. Dinner at six."

Danny unpacked and then sat at the under the touching the window looking out on the quiet neighbourhood of his new home. He lit a smoke and sat quietly, giving thought to his new life, perogies and ham – and, somewhere on that list, evening the score. He thought he might even be a little happy and wondered if he deserved it. He'd need to give that more thought.

Afternoon, November 4ᵗʰ

Gronsky was pleased with his progress. It was just past noon, and the entire morning had been devoted to achieving not just his daily NaNoWriMo numbers, a factor of no smallish importance to him, but a sense that he was channeling a fuller, more engaging story. Aside from the thrill of telling that story, nothing else much mattered. Whatever his novel turned out to be, he believed that he was capturing some relevant truths. Universal truths. Even if he wasn't, even if his tales proved not so monumental, the level of satisfaction he was feeling was worth the time and the emotion.

The days were getting shorter. That was always the way it was with November. On the other hand, it balanced out; the nights were getting longer. Gronsky appreciated this symmetry of time, not that it made much difference to a writer, to him. Light or dark, day or night, he was happy to write when the urge struck. If he had concerns about NaNoWriMo, it was that he felt there was a too rigid expectation on the number of words required. It was a small quibble. He was thankful that he wasn't a regular haiku writer. Fifty thousand words of haiku would be an awful challenge to mount. Far beyond him.

The rest of the day disappeared. He thought it might have been the morning walk that tired him out, even though he was rarely out of breath. Still, he needed more balance. His preference for living an interior, less physically active life warranted examination.

That evening, he and Anthea grazed on leftovers and a fresh feta omelette.

Just before bed, he caught a bit of news. The province's Premier announced that he had been diagnosed with throat cancer. It was not his first bout with the disease. Gronsky wondered at the irony of a man who made his bones by his voice getting throat cancer. If life was unfair, death was totally detached.

Morning, November 5th

Friday was Gronsky's main laundry day. Usually a man of timetables, he lay in bed and thought about Stella Fishbine. It had been decades since he had thought much about her but with the appearance of Anthea, Stella too – in her youthful hippie garb, the way she had first appeared in his life – now made daily appearances. Memories were like that, he supposed. They kept their own schedule.

There were aspects of the memories of Stella that were not unpleasant in the least. That first year, the aroma of her, the illicit smoke and hint of incense and lust, the patchouli oil, all of it, that clung to her, her clothes, her hair, her. And that summer, the freedom of the young people next door who had brought such a vibrancy to the old house they occupied – including, he remembered, their sauna in that old stone garage. He had glimpsed Stella, the young woman he came to know as Stella, running naked from that house one early evening and afterwards he was lost in that vision.

To step outside memory, Gronsky turned on his bedside radio to get the measure of the world. Glasgow topped the list. The young protestors outside of COP 26 were demanding real change. "What else would one expect?" thought Gronsky.

He wondered about the new Canadian Minister of the Environment and Climate Change, Steven Guilbeault. Guilbeault had excellent environmental credentials, and Gronsky vaguely remembered an episode from two decades earlier when Guilbeault had climbed the CN Tower in support of climate action. And he remembered reading somewhere that Guilbeault came by climbing as a means of protest quite early in life: as a five-year-old, he refused to come out of a tree he had climbed in an attempt to block development in his neighbourhood. Sadly, that protest failed, but it obviously stuck with him. He had now, as a fifty-year-old, climbed into the seat of power.

As Guilbeault and world leaders deliberated inside COP 26, outside thousands of youth and other climate activists, including the phenomenal Greta Thunberg, called for real change, not just policies. Gronsky wondered if Guilbeault had the urge to step outside and join those who were now what he once was. Would he climb a Glaswegian tree, perhaps? Or would it be called a Glasgow tree? Language can be so befuddling, he decided.

He also wondered what Ms. Thunberg might be doing in thirty-two years when she would be as old as Guilbeault was now. Would she be the Prime Minister of Sweden? Or was it President? Gronsky would have to check that out. Then he remembered Olof Palme. He had been Sweden's Prime Minister in 1986 when he was assassinated. Prime Minister it was.

He wouldn't wish that end on anyone, let alone young Greta. Gronsky could barely remember how young he was back in 1986. Not quite forty. Life still held promise. Youth was beginning to flit away but was still there. To Gronsky, Sweden was a country Canada might aspire to if it cared to reach beyond its colonial aberrations. And then the assassination of Palme destroyed that illusion.

He could ill afford the loss of an illusion at that time in his life.

As he wallowed in ancient thoughts of assassination, the news reported the rather shocking note that Covid infections in youth represented 20% of the epidemic in Canada at this point. Gronsky turned the radio off, gathered his sheets and pillowcases, descended to the basement, and tossed the items in his washing machine.

He then went upstairs, knocked on Anthea's door and asked if she was awake.

"Huh!" he heard.

"Awake?"

In seconds she opened the door.

"Sheets?" he asked.

She stepped back to her bed, removed her sheets and pillowcases, and handed them to Gronsky.

She then hugged him.

"Love you," he said. "Sorry for waking you. I'll make breakfast. Hurry on down."

She nodded, and he headed back to the basement to start the laundry.

His chores, such as they were, well on their way, Gronsky made coffee and fried up four eggs. He also cut two slices of pumpernickel and threw them into the toaster. By the time they were ready, Anthea had stumbled into the kitchen.

They sat down together and ate in silence.

"Plans for the weekend?" he asked.

Anthea shook her head, then added, "Some of the kids at school are planning a walkout at noon. To show support for Greta, for the environment."

"Where are they going to protest?" he asked.

"City Hall, I think."

"Are you walking out?"

"I might. I don't know. I've never done it before. What do you think?"

"Hmmm. I've never walked out either. Maybe I'll join them."

"Really?"

"It's close. I'd just be stretching my legs. I've started my morning walks again. Used to do that. Maybe I'll see you there."

Anthea smiled, finished her breakfast, gave Gronsky a second hug of the day, and left to get ready to leave.

Gronsky cleaned up, grabbed more coffee, and went to his sacred writing chambre. He turned on the television just in time to see Greta Thunberg declare COP 26 a failure and state "The world is burning. Our emperors are naked."

On that less than optimistic note, he ventured back to his fictional and possibly safer 1946.

Chapter Six, Scratch an Old Wound

Danny Hawkins slept like a baby on his first night in the north end of Winnipeg. But he was awakened in the morning by the sounds of others on his floor. At dinner the previous evening, Midge had introduced him to the two other tenants, a railway brakeman named Jim Sawatsky and a recently retired teacher, Henry Lewenski.

It had been a fine first meal, and afterwards, even though he was full of nervous energy, he wasn't in the mood for conversation or listening to whatever was on the living room radio. He begged off first night socializing and headed straight for bed. He had a new book that he had started, a mountain climbing thriller called The White Tower, written by an American mountaineer, James Ullman. As good as it was, he fell asleep after a couple of pages.

The bedside alarm clock said it was eight fifteen, so Danny assumed the sounds were not from Sawatsky, who had indicated that he'd be at work by six a.m. Danny could smell pancakes, or something approximating a pancake smell. He gave it a couple more minutes, got up, straightened the bedsheets, put on his robe, gathered his shaving gear and toothbrush, and peered out the door. The lavatory door was open, but the privy door was shut. He walked into the washroom, closed the door, and turned on the hot water. He shaved and then ran the tub. Once it was filled, he plopped in and gave himself an efficient two-minute scrub.

Totally refreshed, he went back to his room, dressed, and went downstairs. Lewenski was already devouring a stack of hotcakes.

"Smells great," Danny said as Midge served him. "After today," she grinned, "You serve yourself."

He nodded, added butter – or more likely, margarine – and then poured the waiting syrup.

"We've been hearing that butter will be more available soon," Lewenski mentioned. "It'll be a comfort to get back to normal."

Danny nodded as did Midge. "You overseas?" Lewenski asked.

Danny ate and nodded.

"I was in the first one," Lewenski said.

Danny looked up at him and could see something in Lewinski's eyes that he saw every morning in the mirror. He hadn't a name for it, but it spelled pain. More than pain. Hell. The eyes of Lewenski had seen hell.

Danny bobbled his head, hoping that it offered some commiseration. The last thing he wanted to do, ever do, was swap war stories. With anyone.

Breakfast finished, Danny returned to his room to grab his coat, and went out on the stoop to wait for Vinnie and his first case.

Afternoon, November 5th

It was close to noon, and Gronsky remembered the school walkout that Anthea had mentioned. He decided to go; City Hall was a block away. As promised there was a gaggle of young people, a few signs, and a local reporter.

The protest went well, though it was a somewhat smaller affair than he had imagined.

One of the youth gave a spirited speech reminiscent of Greta Thunberg. She even used the blah blah blah exasperated point about political leadership. Gronsky thought it was close to dead on.

He waved to Anthea, she acknowledged him, and he returned home. He tried to get back into Danny's first case but was feeling somewhat pensive and decided to spend the rest of the day watching a swack of Paris Open tennis before preparing his traditional Friday night pasta.

Later on, just as Gronsky and Anthea were sitting down to their dinner, Sam, who'd been away in Ottawa for a week, arrived back home.

"Welcome back, Sam. Hungry?"

"Hungry for quiet. Plain and simple quiet. And no discussions of policy. And no, I ate on the plane. Lunch. Looks good though."

"Pull up a chair, Sam. Join us…some wine…we'll be quiet," Gronsky added

"Sounds good. For a bit.

Gronsky stood up and got a wine glass for Sam. After pouring, he and Anthea ate as quietly as they could, though their munching and pleasure in eating pasta was evident. Sam finished his first glass of wine and accepted a second.

"So," Sam eventually broke the quiet, "how have you all been? Did you start that novel thing…the month long one?"

"Five days of it so far. Gets in the way of living but it's…it's taking shape."

"And you, Anthea, how's your week been?"

Anthea shrugged, likely quite full and past talking.

"Walked out of school today. Environmental protest…COP 26 and all," said Gronsky.

"Ah," said Sam, "they're not even halfway into COP 26, and they disappoint. There are no easy answers, I'm afraid."

"Yes, there are," thrust in Anthea. "There has to be."

The conversation wore down about then. The generations, though amiable, were as divided as they could be. Shortly, Anthea went to her room to read and text.

"I hope I didn't upset her," Sam said.

"I don't think so," Gronsky replied. "Big issues. Slow progress. Nothing is ever easy. How was your trip?"

"Meetings, like I said. I had planned a work visit to Haiti in the spring, but the kidnappings are a barrier. Not sure what part of the world I'll next set my skills to. But while I was there in the capital, I did do a little amateur sleuthing on your behalf.

Spoke to one of the Nelson MP's staffers to see if there was any tangible information an the Clapson clan."

"You didn't have to. But okay. Thanks! Anything?"

"Well, there was a Dorothy Clapson who passed away early in the spring. Left a granddaughter, Anthea. That much was easy to get. There was mention of a daughter who died tragically some years before. That would fit with Anthea's story that Dawn died in 2005. All this was online. There was nothing about any specific commune in and around Nelson. My source lived there for a number of years and was clear that there were pockets of dropouts and fringe religious and spiritual groups dotted throughout the Slocan. In other words, communes galore."

"I can well imagine," said Gronsky. "I suppose we'll have to take a drive up there someday."

"I'd give that a second thought, Gil. There's likely no hurry."

"I'm in no hurry, Sam. Just enjoying each and every moment with her."

"Look, I'm beat. Gonna crawl into bed. Miriam home?"

"A social evening with a few of the library folk. Sort of a pre-retirement drink tank…I mean think tank."

Sam grinned at the weak humour. "When is she packing it in?"

"Maybe year end. Maybe not. Don't know if she knows. It's hard to leave a job you love, I guess. Wouldn't know, myself. The paper mill was okay, but as soon as I could get going, I went."

"G'night, Gil. See you in the morning. And good luck with the writing thing."

"'G 'Night, Sam. And thanks."

As Gronsky was getting ready for bed, he gave some more thought to what Sam had said. He'd been meaning to have a more in-depth talk with Anthea about her life before arriving on his doorstep. He felt that they had built not only trust but love in the almost two months she had been in the house, with Sam and Miriam adding to that enhanced sense of evolving family.

Soon, he mused. Soon, he'd give that a shot.

Morning, November 6th

For over an hour on Saturday morning, Gronsky tried a number of times to get out of bed and get the day rolling. As was his habit, he had listened to the six a.m. news, and as usual, the weight of the world's woes weighed him down and made getting up difficult.

There was another big march in Glasgow by the youth protestors, the second march in as many days. There was an explosion in Sierra Leone's capital Freetown that killed over a hundred people. There was a riot at a rap music festival somewhere in Texas, he wasn't sure exactly where, that killed a few people in some rush of panic. The young Brazilian singer Marilia Mendonca, known as the 'Queen of Suffering,' died in a plane crash while on her way to a concert. There would be no more suffering for her, Gronsky thought.

None at all.

And then there was the story that seemed to redeem all of the world's sorrow. A woman sitting on her porch in Quesnel, having a smoke in the evening, was approached by a bear who licked her hand once and then tried for a second time before the woman thought better of it, stood up, snapped a picture. The bruin went peacefully away.

Gronsky had long since given up smoking but porch sitting... that was one of his singular pleasures. He doubted that he would ever have to face off against a bear on his urban porch. Raccoons, maybe! They were a different matter.

Finally, he pulled back the covers, got up, dressed, put on the coffee, and remembered that the semi finals of the Paris Open were happening. Except for yesterday, he had mostly avoided tennis this week, and that was unforgivable. He turned on the television in time to catch the third set between the great Djokovic and the upstart Hurkacz from Poland. Always one to root for the underdog, and anyone who played Djokovic had to be considered that, he watched the set unfold. While Hurkacz was down 4 to1 early on, he rebounded to 4-4. Then Djokovic served well to make it 5-4.

As foolish a thought as it was, Gronsky began to feel that if the upstart Hurkacz could win, somehow the planet would be saved. Hurkacz evened the match at 5-5. The Serb then made it 6-5, leaving it up to the Polish player to either even the match and take it to a tiebreaker or lose the works 7-5. The tiebreaker effort took that game.

Alas, as exciting and as close as the tiebreaker was, to Gronsky's disappointment, Hurkacz lost. Still, there was more of COP 26 to play out. Hope always sprung eternal.

Gronsky then remembered the seasonal time adage, "spring forward, fall behind." It was Autumn now, falling away into winter. Time was darkening the day.

He needed to pour his first cup of coffee.

Anthea was sleeping in.

Gronsky went to his writing station and what would prove to be Danny Hawkins' first day as a bona fide trainee private detective. Hope sprung for him too.

Chapter Seven, Scratch an Old Wound

Danny checked the time on his pocket watch as Vinnie drove up. It was ten on the nose. He got in and said good morning.

"It will be once we get going. I have a simple case...well I hope it proves to be...for you to get your feet wet." Vinnie then handed Danny a photo of a soldier.

The man in the photograph looked to be in his mid-twenties. Handsome, dark, unsmiling, a serious looking young man.

"Name's Richard Lacombe. Corporal, 2nd Canadian Infantry. Long tour of duty," exclaimed Vinnie. "Lives...lived north of Dauphin..."

"Okay. Wherever that is."

"Middle of the province. Don't fret. You won't have to go there. And if you have to, it's only a couple of hundred miles as the old crow flies. Anyways, we've been hired to look for the corporal."

"What's the story?" Danny asked.

"Four, five years of war. Was a kid when he enlisted. Saw what you saw, I imagine. According to our client, his commanding officer, by the way, a Captain Frew, tries to keep track of his

men, make sure they're doing as good as they can. Lacombe's not doing well. Was a farmer, mixed blood I guess."

"Mixed blood?"

"Metis," Vinnie elaborated.

"Ah. Met a few myself."

"Anyways, the last contact Frew had with Lacombe was a month ago. Lacombe sounded angry and said something about going to Winnipeg to get lost in the crowd."

Maybe that's what I'm doing, thought Danny. A smaller crowd than in Montreal. Maybe just as lost, though.

"So, I go looking for him?"

"Yup. Wear out some shoe leather. See the city. Get your bearings. Look for Lacombe. See what you can do in a couple of days of simple tracking."

It sounded somewhat relaxing, and the potential for reconnoitring his new city was an exciting prospect. In fact, it hardly sounded like a real job at all.

"I'll drop you off at the city center. Portage and Main. Take a cab home to Midge's at the end of your day. You'll get expenses, so keep track. Don't drink too much, but that is possibly what you might have to do. Check out the taverns…you never know. I'll check in with you tomorrow evening unless you come across him sooner and impress the hell out of me."

That sounded to Danny like Vinnie had zero expectations that he would find his quarry.

As promised, Vinnie dropped him off at the centre of the Dominion of Canada. Such was the nickname given the corner of Portage and Main. It was a very busy street, urban, with plenty of tall buildings. He'd expected something less grand of the prairie city. In any case, iconic corner or not, he'd just have to start strolling, grid fashion, and become acclimatised to this new city. It was a warmish day, and he didn't feel too much pressure to succeed. The entire case made little sense. He was tempted to think Vinnie had a different agenda. It seemed unproductive to just wander around the city and hope to stumble on one depressed soldier. On the other hand, it might just bear fruit.

He took another gander at the photograph. He could almost understand how Lacombe was unable to reassemble his life upon his return. It was a struggle Danny still dealt with. He couldn't fully grasp how complex and different it might be for a native son of Manitoba soil – farmer before the war and now a veteran of a terrible and scarring conflict – to readjust to an old way of life that wasn't there anymore, couldn't be there, because the war had changed the world, worn out old illusions, reconfigured everything.

Monique had saved Danny, pulled him back from the darkness. He wondered if Lacombe had found such a rescuer. He hoped that was the quest that Lacombe was on.

Just then, a trolley went by. Danny decided that would be a fine way to spend a couple of hour touring the city. Who knows, Lacombe might get on at some point, he thought. The worse that could happen was that he would get a better sense of the city. That was probably Vinnie's intention anyways.

After three hours of trolley travel that included changing trains, getting lost, finding his way down to an area people on the street told him was their skid road, he found a small greasy spoon and indulged on a burger and fries and way too much coffee.

He saw a number of people who bore some resemblance to Lacombe, but the few he approached with "Dick Lacombe, Danny Hawkins. You remember me?" were not Richard Lacombe. And if one of them was, he refused to acknowledge it.

After a late second lunch, he caught a series of trolleys back to Midge's and arrived a tad past four pm. He had a bath, read more of The White Tower before joining Midge, Henry Lewenski and Jim Sawatsky for dinner.

As they sat down for a macaroni and cheese casserole and the last of the lettuce and tomatoes from Midge's garden, all three were curious how his first day had gone. He regaled them with his trolley tour and his impressions of Winnipeg. He had in fact noticed that in many parts of the city there were lots of shoppers, and his principal impression was that the economy was improving.

"We're getting back on our feet," Lewenski agreed. "We had quite a lot of military economy during the war, but there were always shortages. Par for the course of a war, I suppose."

"We had good leadership, at least when the war began," Sawatsky opined. "John Queen was a right one. And a leftie."

"An old joke of Jim's, Danny," voiced Lewenski."

"He didn't enjoy being incarcerated by the Nazis, I can tell you," smiled Midge. "Lost the election after that, anyway. Not leftish enough I suppose."

That comment struck Danny as peculiar. "Nazis? In Winnipeg?"

"Ah, that was a day," smiled Midge. "When exactly was it, Henry?"

"February 19th,1942. Simulated invasion. They called it the IF Day. A cast of thousand. Captured the whole city. If anyone hadn't taken Hitler seriously before, after that day there was no excuse."

"And the reason for doing it?" Danny asked.

"The war effort. To sell victory bonds. Wars ain't cheap," pronounced Jim Sawatsky.

They all had a laugh at that truth.

It was a good story, something Danny had not heard before, and the conversation about the invasion lasted for three hours.

Around nine, Vinnie called to ask how the day went and did he want a ride into town tomorrow. Danny explained his day and said he felt more than competent to make the trip into downtown on his own.

With that, he crawled into bed, read for a few minutes, and fell into a deep sleep.

Afternoon, November 6th

Gronsky stopped typing. It was four thirty and he was exhausted. Tired as he was, he was very pleased with the way he was describing 1940's Winnipeg. Of course he didn't know how Winnipeggers would feel about his depictions. In rereading the dining table discussions about the war, and its impact on

Winnipeg, he felt that he had captured a couple of interesting and very specific touchstones.

When Miriam arrived home at a little after five, he asked her if she wanted to go out to dinner. Even with the limitations in restaurant seating because of the pandemic, she was more than agreeable and so he made a reservation at one of the local Greek restaurants down by the river for seven o'clock.

They left the house after six and strolled their way down the hill. As they walked, he asked her how her night out with her co-workers had gone.

"We had a fine time," she replied. "Lots of fun. You can imagine how it is when Librarians cut loose."

Gronsky had to laugh at the notion of out-of-control Librarians.

Miriam explained that there were four of them, long time fellow workers and they met at the home of one. The host prepared the entire meal, and it was a fairly relaxing evening.

"Seriously, Gilbert, I was aware, sadly aware, the whole time that they are also my family. As much as you and Sam are. And now, Anthea. And when I leave, I will miss them. Terribly."

"But, people keep in touch," Gronsky said. "Even I see a few of my buddies from the mill every once in a while. Around town. At least, before Covid."

As he said that, he knew that there was a world of difference between the close camaraderie of Miriam and her workmates and his relationships at the Mill in which he had once labored. He supposed without really knowing that there might well be those sorts of Miriam-like intimacies at the mill. He was clear that closeness was not something he had experienced. Or wanted.

Though Covid restriction had been lifted a few days earlier, Gronsky and Miriam showed their vaccine passports and wore masks. Patrons were well spaced out and the meal was delicious. So much so that they ordered a moussaka to go just in case Anthea was hungry. As it was, upon their return, she'd left a note indicating she'd gone out to a small party and likely would eat there.

Whilst her social life, the social lives of youngster everywhere, cooped up for many months as they had been, their lives significantly disrupted, was somewhat worrying, she was very careful and often explained that she planned to safely distance for the rest of her life.

Later, Gronsky and Miriam shared Miriam's bed, and he regaled her with tales of Winnipeg's IF Day. He had expected her to ask to read some of the book in progress, but she didn't. she seemed interested in the news of the fake invasion as a morale booster and stated she might do her own research.

Morning, November 7th

Sunday morning, Gronsky was fully awake at seven, bursting with energy and fully rested. He kissed Miriam, who offered to make an omelette in a while. She then went back to sleep, and he pondered the moment. He was often amazed at the pleasure he found in intimacy. Even with Stella Fishbine (who wasn't really Stella Fishbine and may well have been one Dorothy Clapson) he wasn't fully convinced; their relationship had gone from quickly carnal to passively so, then mechanically so, which may not have even been the right phrase and then not so at all.

Perfunctory.

Stella, who wasn't Stella, used that term days before she absconded with his children and his life.

"I am not sure I can live this way, Gilbert. It has become, perfunctory. I am in a funk."

He had looked it up. He decided he agreed with her but did not say it.

After she left there had been a very few times over the years when he was intimate with a woman. Then, fifteen years ago, he had his first conversation with Miriam one day at the library. It was about a book he had read, a film he had seen, which she had also read and seen: *Lost Horizon*, by James Hilton. It was a cursory conversation but over the next couple of years they had built on it.

Both the book and especially the film had offered Gronsky an image of perfection, a Shangri-la where one lived in peace, stayed young longer, essentially aging over a longer time. The book and the film had strangely consoled him in his few darker, more lonely moments. Sharing that respect or comfortable notion of paradise brought them together.

Then one of Gronsky's two tenants at the time passed away. In hospital, thankfully. Gordon…what was his last name? He had almost forgotten. Gordon McGuire. Robert Gordon McGuire. A veteran of World War 2, a quiet man, who had struggled with the stairs but appreciated the apartment.

He had mentioned his landlordship to Miriam at one point in their librarian/reader interchange, and then of course when Gordon passed, she asked, if it were appropriate, could she look at the apartment as she was thinking of downsizing from her small home near the hospital. And so she looked at it and moved in. Ten years now she had lived here, and they had found their own level of relatively consistent, but not overpowering, intimacy.

He did worry about the power imbalance, landlord and tenant, and, perhaps, in his rather old-fashioned view of the world, man and woman as well. He had mentioned it once to Miriam, but she had laughed and said, "Seriously, Gilbert."

He took that then to mean that it didn't bother her in the least. Once they had become more intimate on a semi-regular basis, he mentioned it again and she laughed again and explained that if there was a power imbalance in their relationship, she sensed that it leaned in her favour.

He did not feel sufficiently able to counter that interpretation and let it rest.

His ruminations at an end for the moment, he leaned over and kissed her brow and went to his quarters to dress.

He then decided to get a bit of exercise and went for a half an hour walk. There was a light rain falling. He went in the opposite direction from the large park he usually walked in and, instead, headed to the west of the city, to a neighbourhood with older, smaller homes planted on the steep hillside, the brow of the promontory as it were. As he walked he noticed that, here and there, in empty lots which once housed the workers of the community, small homeless encampments had popped up. Not many but enough to seem worrisome to him and social scientists and politicians – and he imagined, the neighbours. He hadn't come this way in quite some time, and he was saddened by the change. Land was valuable and would surely be built upon. Housing was out of reach to more and more people, and whatever was built on these empty lots – lots that once housed a family or maybe an extended ensemble – would only house the rich, certainly those wealthier than the homeless camping there now.

Gronsky completed his circuit and by seven forty-five was back at home and changing into his sweats for comfort and whatever style they demonstrated. He went back up to Miriam's apartment for the promised omelette and was pleased that both Sam and Anthea had been invited. They all crammed in around her table and enjoyed the food and the Sunday morning chatter. Sam, Miriam, and Anthea had already decided to go out together and watch the latest version of *Dune,* which would start shortly after noon. "We would have included you, Gil," said Miriam, "but you do have your November writing torture to get back to."

He granted the truth of that comment and, after a suitable amount of time, left the movie goers to their entertainment planning, went downstairs, made coffee, and then went to his den to begin his writing day.

Once there, he couldn't quite focus on the complexity of telling Danny's Winnipeg sojourn. He genuinely wanted to move through it quickly, limit the detail, if only because his Winnipeg history research was somewhat wanting. As much as he wanted to move Danny quickly to his final west coast destination, he knew he had to create a perception that Danny was becoming more equipped to not only be a fully-fledged detective but also combine that skill set with a sense of needing justice to be achieved for Monique –coupled, of course, with a mollifying morsel of sweet revenge.

To prolong his creative machinations, Gronsky turned on the television just in time to see Djokovic crush Medvedev in the third set of the finals of the Paris Open.

He switched over to the BBC and saw that there had been an assassination attempt on the Prime Minister of Iraq. Gronsky realized that he had heard little about Iraq in the last while. With an assassination attempt, that would change.

As for COP 26, he would check on it later.

Winnipeg and the past were calling.

Chapter Eight, Scratch an Old Wound

Sometime not long before dawn, Danny had what he could only call an epiphany. He had spent his first full day on the case of Corporal Richard Lacombe riding the trollies of Winnipeg, familiarizing himself with the terrain, hoping against hope, as they sometime say, that Lacombe would just magically hop aboard, and Danny would solve his disappearance. He could continue the search in that way, vary it somewhat, taking different trollies at fluctuating times, or – and here was the epiphany – he could park himself in one place, a high-volume location and hopefully have the opportunity to observe a larger mass of Winnipeg humanity. The downside to the epiphany was that likely the busiest of places in Winnipeg would likely be the large department stores.

In any case, he asked Midge at breakfast where most people went to shop. In a flash she said, "The Big Store." He asked, "That's what it's called?" She replied, "Yes. Eaton's. That's where I'd go." She then added, "Though, the Hudson's Bay would be a close second. Hard to beat that beautiful red brick Eaton's. Forty years old, I think. One of those two. Eaton's. Hudson's Bay. That's where all the people eventually go. One or the other."

If, Danny thought, the missing corporal was a shopper. He doubted he was, but still Danny felt that both businesses deserved a certain amount of his time.

Just before he left the breakfast table, Lewenski offered another location. "There's the Union Bus Depot. It's down on Hargrave. Lots of comings and goings there," the retired teacher said.

"I should have thought of that," Danny noted. "The train station as well, I suppose."

"Now you're cooking…with gas." Lewenski said, smiling.

With that guidance, Danny had his day's agenda pretty much set.

Shortly he caught a bus and made his way to the downtown heart of Winnipeg. It was a Friday, September 20th, and not as warm as the previous day. He thought it fortunate that it was a Friday, as more people would be out shopping, at least later. As well, more people might be travelling, going away for the weekend. He assumed that Winnipeggers liked to get away on weekends, but where exactly they might want to go was knowledge he didn't have.

Loitering in any place presented risks. To be successful in his search, he knew he shouldn't draw attention to himself. Inconspicuousness seemed a given. At Eaton's, he spent an hour walking various floors, watching the movement of people, enjoying the ordinariness of shopping, pleased by the faces, especially the vibrancy of the younger staff – the weariness too, and the beauty. There was nothing he needed to buy, nothing he wanted. War had been a great teacher in that regards. Water. Food. Warmth. Nothing much else mattered. If you had them, you had everything. You had life. War had also taught him how fragile life was. He supposed that was the lesson – one of them anyways – that Richard Lacombe must have absorbed. Soldiers with any experience of battle, whether at sea, in the air, or most assuredly on land, would have seen life snapped away constantly. Every day could easily be your last. To survive, you had to accept that you might not.

As he strolled among the Eaton's shoppers and staff, convinced that he was more or less invisible, he saw, intermittently, someone in uniform. There were not as many as he would have expected. He realized he should have asked Vinnie if Lacombe was known to still wear his uniform. A year had passed since most soldiers had been demobbed, and it was likely Lacombe would be wearing civvies. On the other hand, shellshocked, lost, seeking some form of stability, the sort that the military could offer away from the battlefield, perhaps he was still uniformed up.

As he thought about the uniform question, he remembered that he had read recently that verdicts were about to come out at the end of the month from the Nuremburg Trials.

He doubted that anything other than death would atone for the evil that the Nazi high command had committed.

There was a lesson there. Be your own person. Draw the line, even if you were a soldier. This was easy to say, much harder to do, he thought. The military was unforgiving. Orders had to be followed.

That rule made him wonder about Lacombe. His life before the military, before war, would have been determined by the seasons. Farming was like that. His own life in southern Alberta had been guided by the seasons. Planting, nurturing, harvesting. War changed all that. War did not nurture. Death was all that could be harvested.. Whatever ethic guided the corporal, guided Danny, guided anyone who physically survived the war, was shot to hell in peacetime. New rules were at play.

After more than an hour at Eaton's, Danny went over to the Hudson's Bay store and repeated his observation strolls through the plentiful aisles, watching customers and staff, noting anyone who bore the least resemblance to the photo he had of Richard Lacombe. In both stores the overwhelming majority of shoppers were female. School was back in session, so the shoppers were by far of a certain age. He had to admit that while his reconnoitre was relatively pointless, he had enjoyed the people watching, the absolute normality of shopping in a huge department store as if there had been no war, the normality of how safe everyone was now.

He decided to eat lunch at the Union Bus Station. He took a vacant counter seat and grabbed the menu. Salisbury Steak seemed to be the speciality, but he hankered for a grilled cheese sandwich, something he usually ordered when the opportunity presented. It reminded him of the sweeter moments of his childhood, his mother's delicious homemade bread and the fresh farm cheese that melted in soft delight.

When it arrived, it was accompanied by a crunchy looking dill pickle and a scoop of potato salad.

The entire day was worth it because of the grilled cheese sandwich. Danny knew that in some respects he was easy to please. And the pickle proved to be as good as it looked. A whole pickle. Heaven and Winnipeg were so bountiful!

The potato salad, however, seemed to be drenched in a lesser salad dressing. The war was still impacting some of the finer things, he mused.

Fortified, he decided to ignore the train station for the rest of the day and focus instead on the bus terminal. There were far more men traveling by coach then women and several looked not dissimilar to Lacombe. As the afternoon waned, he noticed a fellow enter the cafeteria. Danny had been sitting on a bench in the large waiting room, trying to appear as if he was waiting for his bus to leave. He let the fellow get comfortable at the counter, order, and have the waitress bring his food. Once his quarry was eating, Danny decided to bench in beside him and asked for a cup of coffee.

Once the coffee arrived, he took a sip, reached into his shirt pocket to get the photograph Vinnie had given him and slipped it along the counter. The quarry, Richard Lacombe, looked down, smiled, said, "Vinnie had a sense you'd find me. Though you didn't see me at Eaton's. Got you there. We'd better call him. Phone booth's over there."

Danny smiled, said, "You're not going anywhere, right?"

Lacombe nodded that he was going to stay glued to his stool.

Danny believed him. Decent food has a settling quality. He went to the phone booth to call Vinnie.

Evening, November 7th

Gronsky leaned back and saw that it was almost six. He'd vaguely heard the sounds of Anthea, Sam, and Miriam an hour or so earlier. He went to the kitchen and saw that Anthea and Miriam, along with Sam, were making a pot of something.

"Team effort, Gilbert," Miriam said. "Fish chowder and biscuits. Be ready in half an hour."

They sat around the table waiting for the biscuits to bake and the chowder to simmer a bit more. The moviegoers all seemed to have enjoyed *Dune*, found it sumptuous and well made. Gronsky listened as assiduously as he could, but he was not much of a science fiction fan, and his attention was still on Danny and Winnipeg and the quest. He knew that he often got distracted and that writing, particularly his Labour Day novella and now this massive project, was all consuming to the point that he must seem selfish.

He apologized and said he needed to do a bit more writing. Gronsky returned to his den and stared at the screen for a while. Anthea knocked some minutes later and brought in a bowl of chowder and a small plate of butter saturated biscuits.

"Thanks," he said. "Lovely."

She kissed him and, as she was leaving, said, "Call if you want more."

"Of course I'll want more, but this will have to do. Writing a novel is turning me into a lump. More buttered biscuits and creamy chowder won't help."

As he dug in, he turned on *The National* and watched the news. At one point mention was made of Indigenous veterans and the special recognition that was coming their way. Gronsky felt that Richard Lacombe would have been happy to hear it.

Morning, November 8th

Gronsky had gone to bed quite early. He hadn't been especially tired but assumed that the weight of this week's creativity wordsmithing a daily quota – a minimum daily quota, mind you – of words that actually told a story was finally pressing in on his body, slowing him down. Whatever it was, he had taken to his bed without mentioning anything else to Anthea or Miriam. He did slightly question what life might be like if their lives were more traditional. Their household *was* different. He slept with his tenant; his granddaughter had appeared out of nowhere, or Nelson, two months earlier; and Sam was a friend and tenant who travelled a lot doing a job Gronsky didn't totally understand.

International Development! What the heck was that?

Gronsky had flipped on the radio at seven and paid close attention to the news. He was shocked to hear the report that 95% of the citizens of Afghanistan were not getting enough food. The number was truly astounding. Gronsky had never starved, never come close, though occasionally he might have taken a meal later then scheduled. He recognized his privileged position in the world, donated to the odd charity, wished the world well, did his bit. It did not seem enough, he thought, but like so many, he wasn't sure what to do about it.

Even as he listened to that news story, as well as the unfolding events in Ethiopia, the press seemed enraptured by the deaths at the music festival in Texas. Eight deaths. Young deaths. Surely a tragedy for their families. How did that measure against 21,000,000 people in Afghanistan on the verge of starvation?

Again, he had no answer.

He did note that today was Indigenous Veterans Day. He had no idea how this separate day had occurred. He'd never heard of it before. It was three days before Remembrance Day, and his first instinct was that they should seek unity in celebration. Obviously, he was out of the loop on this. His research on Indigenous veterans, skimpy though it was, has drawn to his attention how difficult it was for them when they returned from World War 2.

Gronsky finally cranked himself up and out of bed, dressed, went to the kitchen, made coffee and porridge for both he and Anthea, pulled up a chair at the table, and waited for her to pop in. At quarter to eight, she wandered in, sat down, scooped her portion of porridge, ate, barely smiled, said, "Monday," as if it and porridge were a curse, then actually smiled, gave him a hug, and left with a "See you later, Gronsky."

It was all so deliciously perfunctory. The way many families were, he supposed. He smiled at his use of Stella Fishbine's favourite word.

The smile then waned, and he cleaned up and repaired to Danny's world.

Chapter Nine, Scratch an Old Wound

Danny was not particularly upset by Richard Lacombe's comments. He was almost amused by them. It had been an interesting two days, and he now had a fairly good sense of Winnipeg's geography. Vinnie arrived at the Union Bus Station cafeteria twenty minutes after Danny called him. The three of them then adjourned to a booth, Danny on one bench and Lacombe and Vinnie on the other.

Vinnie kicked off the conversation. "You did an excellent job. Found your man. Proud of you."

"Seems like I found your man, Vinnie."

"You could say that. More like David Frew's man. Sorry, Richard. Richard's his own man, of course. Cap Frew is an old friend of mine and when I decided to take a chance on you…remember, Harry Ship was recommending you, and Harry, much as I care for him, he's dodgy in places."

Danny nodded in agreement. Harry was nothing if not dodgy.

"Anyway," Vinnie continued, "I thought up this routine just to see how you would handle yourself. You have the fixings to be a good private operator, or so I've been told, but I had no idea how that would play out. So, I decided to make a game of it. A test. Dave had mentioned his concern for Dick. You know how it must be a bit, readjusting to civilian life. Truth be told, I may

have gotten a bonus, not only a shill to see how you would do but another detective as well, with a speciality that might prove useful. And maybe lucrative."

Richard Lacombe remained silent, but Danny could see what he thought were a range of emotions on his face.

"Where did I miss you at Eaton's?" he asked Lacombe.

"Couple of places. Women's dresses for one."

"Hmmm! That's not good."

"Maybe I was too camouflaged. Trick I learned over there."

"Maybe," added Danny. "Okay, so I passed the test. Do you have real work for me?"

Vinnie offered a grin, something Danny was starting to think that his new boss liked to do a lot. He actually thought Vinnie must be a pretty smart operator. He cast his mind back to his saunter through Eaton's earlier in the day. It upset him that he might have missed spotting Lacombe, especially if he was lingering in the Ladies Dress section. Try as he might he could not picture him in a skirt. Maybe Lacombe was pulling his leg. He might never know.

"We should head over to my office...our office... and I'll have you read the file I'm assigning. Dick has another operation lined up."

"A young girl from Churchill...took off last week with a young Polish boy, maybe heading to Winnipeg. Has family here so I'll pay them a visit," Dick said, summarizing his case.

"I like my ops to know what each other is doing, Danny. There's always the need for backup."

"How many of us are there?" Danny asked.

"Now? Three. Four including me."

"Who's the fourth?"

"You'll meet her at the office. Doubles as my office manager/ receptionist. But Gracie is a fine sleuth in her own right."

Twenty minutes later, they arrived at Vinnie's headquarters, the second floor of an old red brick five story office building. They entered the office. It proved to be a waiting room (no one was waiting), but a woman was seated at an oak desk that featured a Remington typewriter and a telephone which rang as they entered. The woman, Gracie, he assumed, looked to be in her mid thirties, with pale skin and short brown hair. Wearing hornrims and dressed in a blue blouse, she answered with a very efficient sounding, "Brass Investigations. Yup, just came in. He'll pick up in a second." She then pointed Vinnie Brass to what was clearly his office door and smiled silently,. "Grab it Vinnie. It's the little woman!"

Vinnie made a dash for the door labelled Vincent Brass and closed it behind him. That left Gracie, again an assumption, and Danny, figuring out their next move.

Gracie took the initiative. "I'm Grace Lambert. You're Dan Hawkins?"

"Danny. Mostly Danny."

"Then welcome to the Brass Circus ring, Danny Hawkins. Cup of coffee?" Grace asked, pointing to a hotplate and coffee pot.

"Sure," he said.

"Good. Pour me one too, will ya, hon? Black."

Danny took the hint, poured two cups of coffee into a couple of clean white cups and handed one to Grace. He immediately understood where he was on the Brass Investigations pecking order. He was quite okay with that.

"The little woman?" he asked as he decided to take a seat opposite Grace.

"Claire. Mrs. Vincent Brass. Vinnie's a great boss but not in his own home. Don't get me wrong, I love both of them, but Claire runs a tight ship. Expects Vinnie when he says he'll be there. He does get distracted."

Danny decided he needed more information, slowly acquired, before he ventured further into the Brass family domestic debate. Grace helped immediately by getting up and handing him a slim file. He accepted it and noted that she was wearing blue slacks to match her blouse. Very Katherine Hepburn, he thought.

"This is your next case. Sorry, first, or is it second case?"

He flashed a weak smile back at Grace and said, "Second, I guess."

"Second! Good answer. Anyways, classic two-timing wife case, we think. We need proof. You own a camera?"

Danny shook his head. "Got out of the habit in Europe. Nothing there I wanted to remember."

"No problem." She went to one of two side by side four-drawer filing cabinets, opened the second drawer from the top, and pulled out a camera. "It's a Kodak Ektra 35mm rangefinder camera. Know how to operate one like this?"

Danny didn't and let Grace give him a crash course. After a five-minute orientation, he felt relatively comfortable with the gizmo.

"Good," she said. "The file is pretty sparse. Have a read and ask any questions that come to mind."

Danny settled into the read. He also noted that it was almost three. Friday was drawing to a close. Night was on the way.

The client was Sergeant Fred Skylar. A still active soldier from Fort William originally. He suspected that his wife, Lucy, was two-timing him and wanted someone not military to look into it.

Why not military, Danny wondered? Many soldiers would want to keep their personal business in house. Although he could appreciate that sometimes in house was just a tad too close for comfort.

Skylar was born in 1908, which made him close to forty. The possibly promiscuous Lucy Skylar, maiden surname, Andrichuk, was born in 1924. A baby thought Danny. A fair gap in ages but not hugely significant. He assumed the task at hand was to verify that the spouse, Lucy, either was or was not playing the field. The camera was the potential instrument of proof. Of something. Danny had trouble imagining how one got close enough to snap sin.

November 8th Evening

Gronsky was suddenly tired. The entire day had passed by like a dream, and he had barely moved from his computer. Writing, researching, waiting for the storm that Miriam had reminded him was coming when she dropped in at seven p.m. to bring him a sandwich – all of it had consumed him.

He was ready for sleep. He wanted to write more, carry Danny Hawkins further on in his first real case, but his eyes were drooping, his brain locked in shutdown mode.

He had a short brandy and then went to bed, remembering too late that he hadn't showered all day.

Tomorrow would be soon enough.

November 9th

The windstorm had woken Gronsky a number of times in the night. The power had stayed on which was no surprise. He rarely suffered from that issue.

While the windstorm had disrupted his sleep, plotting the next phase of Danny Hawkins' journey also intruded. It was, by most measures, a welcome intrusion. Gronsky was enjoying his immersion in fiction, sensing that he would be a better writer the more he gave in to this obsession.

Yesterday he had missed much of the limited time he and Anthea had together, so he got dressed, knocked on her door, heard a mumble, went in, and sat on her bed. "Anthea," he asked, "How 'bout I cook up some pancakes?"

She nodded in the affirmative and buried her head under her pillow.

"Twenty minutes…they'll be ready."

Gronsky repaired to the kitchen, got flour, baking powder, eggs, and milk and mixed the concoction together. He also made coffee and got the griddle going. By the time Anthea appeared, the cakes were just done.

He served her, and they ate in silence until he said, "I love these moments with you. Sorry, there aren't more."

She shot him a smile but said nothing. Mid chew, she got up, went up to him and gave him one of her bigger hugs. "Me too."

She then returned to her chair, finished eating, said "These are great. Thanks, Gronsky," sipped a splash of coffee, and said, "Got to go."

In a moment he was alone.

He finished eating, cleaned up and, though desperate to get back to writing, decided to slicker up and go for a truncated stroll to see if there had been any storm damage.

There was still drizzle, but that did not deter him. His fifteen-minute walkabout did not present any signs of damage, which was a relief. Other areas were likely not so lucky.

He returned home in short order and turned on the television to satisfy his urge for world news. The Poland/Belarus border issue unsettled him. Belarusian migrants were trapped in the outdoors, unable to cross into Poland, unable or unwilling to return to Belarus. Children, women, over four thousand souls, were being, as one journalist said, "weaponized."

It was too much for Gronsky. He needed fabrication. Fiction! He needed to escape to the safety of his imagination where one was always able, given the time, to write anyone he chose to out of a dilemma.

Chapter Ten, Scratch an Old Wound

Danny finished reading the skimpy report. The key factor at the moment was that their client had left town to visit his mother in his hometown of Fort William. She had fallen and required some of his time and care. This sudden departure had spurred him on to hire Vinnie.

Danny glanced up at Grace, who looked like she was ready to say something. Whatever it was was interrupted by Vinnie stepping out of his office.

"Wives!" he exclaimed, adding nothing much else. Nothing really was needed. He had expressed his thought quite clearly.

"Ah, Mr. Hawkins, I see Grace gave you the file."

Danny nodded.

"There is some urgency. Skylar is gone for a week. Tonight would be a good time to start. His family has money, so I was thinking you and Grace could see what was cooking for Lucy Skylar Friday night while hubby is suddenly gone. Grace, you're free tonight, right?"

It seemed to Danny that Grace had been taken unawares and did not appreciate it.

"Sure, Vinnie. Who needs a life when adventure calls!"

"Good. Danny, Grace drives the company car. We pay for it. It's a rare car. Bought it in '42. Flying high in those days. A 1939 Chrysler Royal Windsor Business Coupe. Comfy ride."

Danny smiled and nodded to Grace. "I guess we should get to it, then."

"Enjoy the music, Vinnie. Give Claire my best."

Grace put on her outer coat, and she and Danny left the office. "The company car is parked in back. Vinnie had a shelter built to keep it safe from the elements. Winter, mostly."

As they approached the car, Danny was delighted. It looked like a skookum vehicle, and he'd be pleased to drive it, although it looked like he'd be a passenger for now.

Grace proved to be a skillful driver, and in thirty minutes they were parked outside the Skylar family home. The file had contained a picture of Lucy Skylar. A healthy specimen of womanhood: blonde, almost white hair, small frame, gentle features. Looking a bit like Tarzan's, Jane, Maureen O'Sullivan. Dainty but tough..

She'd be easy to follow, assuming she had plans for the evening.

As their waited in the near darkness Danny asked Grace, "Did you have any plans for the evening? Being new to town, I certainly didn't."

She looked over at him and said, "Flexibility. I planned to practice my flexibility. It seems to be working well."

The message was clear. Private was private, especially for this female private eye.

Close to seven pm, Grace said, "We'll need to eat."

"Anything open nearby?" Danny asked.

"A few blocks over. Let's give it a bit of time."

As if on cue, house lights were turned off, a porch light came on, and a woman, who under the outer light appeared to be Lucy, came out, went to the garage, and got into an older Ford.

The driver pulled out, and in a few seconds, Grace turned on the Chrysler and the chase was on. Night driving in a new city would be a challenge he thought, as he watched Grace keep close enough to the Ford without being too close. She was skilled, and he recognized that surveillance in a vehicle was one more talent he would need to nurture.

A short while later, the Ford pulled over and parked.

"Where are we?" Danny asked, seeking some orientation.

"Sherbrook Street. Hmmm, I think I know where she might be heading. You got on your dancing shoes, Mr. Hawkins?"

Danny scanned the street and saw Lucy enter a building. Others were going in as well.

"Dance hall?" he asked, almost knowing the answer.

"A Winnipeg delight! The Normandy. Even tripped a few lights fantastic there myself. One of the owners, Sid Boughton, is buddies with Vinnie. It can be a wild place, particularly back during the war. Military personnel accounted for a lot of their business. I imagine that has tapered off some, but it will still likely have a fair number of soldiers, past and present, dancing

up a storm…drinking up a storm, I should say. If little miss Lucy is meeting some fella here, she had better be careful."

"Are we going in?"

"We are on the clock and yes, we are."

Danny and Grace paid the admission, entered, and saw a remarkable site: hundreds of dancers whirling and twirling to a great fiddle-led band.

"Andy deJarlis and his Red River Settlers," said Grace. "If we were here tomorrow night we'd be on the radio. A Winnipeg tradition."

"But then, we wouldn't hear ourselves. Good to know though. It might be easy to lose her in here, though. Pretty crowded."

"Let's split up. Back here in say twenty minutes, okay?"

They separated and looked for Lucy. No more than five minutes later, Danny saw her dancing with a younger man – jacket, slacks, hair just a bit longer than military regs likely required. They made a handsome couple. He had no idea if there was more intimacy than just being dancing partners, but he had no trouble imagining them coupled in an embrace. The band was playing a two-step, wound that up, and immediately jumped into an unfamiliar polka. Lucy and her partner made the transition effortlessly.

He watched the young couple twirl about, saw that the wooden dance floor almost appeared to bounce. Hundreds of vibrating feet would do that. Monique would have cherished the hall, the liveliness of it, even the country music, which he remembered her mentioning as a fond memory from when she was growing up. Her family played music. Then he wondered why he couldn't recall her ever playing an instrument for him.

There had been no instruments in her effects when he had cleared her stuff out.

The sadness of a musician who had stopped performing played on his heart. Was it possible that fiddle music resurrected terrible memories for her? They rarely listened to music on the radio, even though he loved listening to dance band broadcasts.

As he summoned up these memories of Monique, Danny kept his eyes on Lucy and Mister X. Suddenly, he lost sight of them and scoured the crowd. He looked around for Grace, and she was invisible as well. He decided to go back to the hall entrance to see if Grace was parked there. She wasn't. There were steps leading upstairs. Grace had mentioned that the owners had a banquet hall on the second floor, and so he took a chance that Lucy had also planned to go to a banquet, although that seemed somewhat out of step with the ostentatious young wife/dancer and her husband's suspicions of marital duplicity. Regardless, Danny went upstairs to check it out, but there was no sign of Lucy or the young man in the celebratory banquet crowd.

He went back downstairs and took another look inside the dance hall, but he had lost momentum. Grace suddenly came up beside him and asked. "Lose them?"

"Guess I did," he replied. "Did you as well?"

"Just for a moment. There is another tradition I thought I would check out though. – trysting on an outside fire escape on the Telephone Exchange next door. Happens more on Thursdays when hungry young country wenches are looking for pleasure,

but Friday seems to share that hunger. Follow me and get the camera."

Danny trailed after Grace outside, ran to the car to get the camera, and returned to her side. She led him around the corner of the building and pointed up. There seemed to be a few shadows of people on the fire escape.

"Snap a few," she directed.

He tried but it turned out that the five-minute demo wasn't quite enough after all.

"Never mind, I'll do it."

Grace quickly took some shots, the flash glowing each time she clicked. If the bulb's brightness concerned any of the fire escape romantics, it was unnoticeable. They were all absorbed in their lovingly licentious activity. It was not an especially cold evening, and that probably added to the warmth and satisfaction of the moment.

"Hopefully, some of these photos will turn out," said Grace.

"Are we done?" Danny asked, beginning to feel hungry.

"A far cry from it, Master Detective. We'll put the camera in the car and go back in. I think we should dance. A slow one at any rate. I would like to see where, besides the Skylar home, the evening ends for the two lovebirds."

Danny nodded, took the camera back to the car, and rejoined Grace inside.

Once inside, he asked if there was anywhere to get food. He mentioned the banquet upstairs.

"I suppose you can go and beg for scraps. Otherwise, we'll have to find an open late-night restaurant afterwards. There aren't that many these days. Never were, actually."

Half and hour later they spotted Lucy and her companion. They were back on the dance floor and boogieing up a storm. Danny and Grace gave the jitterbug a shot and tried to angle closer to the couple. They managed to get quite close, but there was no talking to be overheard. Both Lucy and her partner were full of sweat and smiles as if they were the only lovers in the hall, as if no one else belonged in the same space.

Danny wondered if one or more of Lucy's husband's compatriots might be here and notice her, and if he, or they, did, might make a note to spill the beans. She was awfully careless with her indiscretions, he thought, and wondered if that was the point.

At eleven, Lucy and her partner grabbed their coats and left. Grace and Danny followed. Lucy's partner got in the driver's seat of Lucy's car.

"Nice to see a man driving," Danny commented.

"Isn't it," countered Grace. "Your turn will come."

The couple headed straight for Lucy's marital bed. They parked in the garage, but Lucy went in alone. The porch light went off, and Grace and Danny saw the shadow of Lucy's companion stealthily leave the garage and slip down the side of the house, likely to the rear door.

"Any chance of getting another photo?" Danny asked.

"The cat would be out of the bag for sure," Grace answered. "I think we have enough to make a preliminary report. One more

day should do it. I'll leave that to you to see what else you can produce."

They opted not to look for an open café, so Grace drove him back to Midge's.

Midge had waited up for him. "Sorry," he said, "I should have called. Late surveillance job."

"Not to worry," she said and then asked him if he had eaten.

He shook his head. "It won't kill me to miss a meal," he answered.

"Balls," Midge cursed delightfully. "How about a cold sausage sandwich…with a pickle? And a slab of cheese."

Danny wasn't dead but he felt that, just for that culinary moment, he'd met an angel and gone to heaven.

Mid-Afternoon, November 9th

Gronsky stopped writing at 3:00 p.m. feeling that he had leapt a major narrative hurdle. The mystery was moving at a breakneck speed – for Gronsky, at any rate – and Danny was getting more fully fleshed out. Perhaps a character flaw wrinkle needed to be considered.

As for major narrative hurdles, Gronsky was only one-third of the way along this November of Writing journey, and he needed to pace himself. However ahead of himself he might be, he didn't want to get there too early.

He decided to make soup for dinner. He scrounged around in his fridge, found a cauliflower and some carrots, and decided they were it, as well as an onion, garlic, and a finger of ginger. They'd become some sort of creamy curried soup. An hour later it was simmering, and he and Anthea sat down to the hot spicy broth.

"I love curry," Anthea said. "Granny cooked it a few times, all sorts of curried foods."

"So, good memories?" Gronsky asked.

"Our family ate a lot of Indian food, lots of curries. Fond memories of the food," she said.

"And some of the other ones, the other memories?"

"I can't talk about that now. Is that okay?"

"Anthea, we only talk about the things you want to talk about when you want to talk about them. Gronsky's rule," he said.

"I like that. Gronsky's rule."

"It's a small domain that falls under my kingyness, I confess," he laughed.

Later, they watched Stephen Colbert together. It was the comedian's Sexiest Man Alive episode. Often it was helpful to end the evening with a laugh.

It was almost an imperative.

Morning, November 10th

In the middle of the night, quite uncharacteristically, Miriam came to Gronsky's bed and crawled in beside him. Exercising wisdom, he did not question her conduct and allowed events to unfold as she likely had planned.

In the morning he expected that they might cuddle in bed and perhaps discuss her atypical behaviour, but she smiled after a quick peck on the cheek and departed for her own quarters. He admitted to himself that he found her mercurial mission somewhat disturbing but on the whole not unpleasant in the least. It seemed to him a subject worth discussing later in the day, thought he recognized that he sometimes overthought things.

With an additional quantity of Wednesday morning energy, he quickly dressed and went for a thirty-minute walk to the park and back. There were a couple of tents pitched in the park's woods, and on his way back, while taking a favourite back alley, he noticed a couple – a man and woman, he thought – sleeping in an open garage mid-way down the lane. He tried not to disturb them for more than one reason.

At home, he ate granola and made coffee. Anthea was up and about by then. She fended for herself, and they shared a laugh about the Sexiest Man Alive nonsense. Gronsky pointed out that he had no idea who Paul Rudd, the winner of the idiotic title, was and Anthea concurred.

With all of that grandfather-granddaughter folderol out of the way, he filled his mug and went to his writing den. He snapped on the television to catch a few moments of a young gun's tennis tournament from Milan. Alcaraz, the new phenom from

Spain, was two sets up in the tournament's truncated format. Gronsky put his feet up and watched the third set.

As much as he was enjoying the match, he was consumed by the narrative dilemma he was considering for Danny Watkins. There was no getting away from it. He would have to write the next scene that was pulsating for life and then judge how true it appeared. He remembered that today was the day, now almost over in Glasgow, where they would be issuing the first draft of many agreements that all the participating countries had to sign onto about how they, the soldiers of COP 26, will collectively fight climate change.

The entire process, whilst completely democratic, was ludicrous. Each country had a veto.

The final agreement was obviously going to be green-washed into nothingness. He would have to pay attention to what the People's Summit for Climate Action had to say.

He turned the sound off the TV and got down to Danny's Saturday.

Chapter Eleven, Scratch an Old Wound

All Danny wanted for breakfast was toast and coffee, as he was still rather full of Midge's late night sausage sandwich. He thanked her again for her kindness and apologized profusely for not calling and causing her to stay up later than she usually would.

"I might be late tonight as well," he told her, and she said, "Then here's a key. You can make your own sandwich when you get home. Unless," and she smiled, "I happen to be up."

He took the bus downtown and arrived just before nine. He waited in the hallway that led to the office until about nine thirty when Grace arrived.

"You're an early bird. It is Saturday, you know?"

"I should have asked about the hours. Things I need to pay attention to, I suppose..."

She unlocked the door, and they went in. "Vinnie probably should have given you a key to the office. Every once in a while, we sleep over."

"Really?" asked Danny. "Where?"

She took him into Vinnie's office and showed him.

"That's what they call…?" he started.

"A Murphy Bed. Vinnie had it installed a few years ago. Flusher times…around the time he bought the Chrysler. Old Murph doesn't get much use, and a couch, one of those pullout sofas, would have done the job just as well. But Vinnie wanted something unique."

Vinnie joined them as they were coming out of his office. "Such eager beavers I employ," he quipped.

"Showing him your staff sleeping accommodations, Vinnie."

"How did the surveillance go?" Vinnie asked, not wanting to kibbitz.

"I dropped off some pictures for Sammy to develop.. The Skylar women is clearly involved with someone. We didn't get any details about him, but he went home with her. It was dark for the most part. Hard to say if we'll get anything confirmable from the pictures. Smooching outside the Normandy. Classic."

"So you'll keep at it?" asked Vinnie.

"Danny will. I'm booked for the evening," said Grace.

"You're giving him your stamp of approval?"

"He'll be fine. You could always shadow him yourself, give him the benefit of your vast knowledge."

Vinnie smiled. "Danny, take the Chrysler. Follow the girl if she goes out again tonight."

"And if she stays in?"

"Take the camera. Do your best to get whatever proof would satisfy a cuckolded husband."

Danny had his marching orders. He got the camera and the keys to the Chrysler, an advance for gas, an admonishment to not drive all over "hell's half acre" which was Vinnie's description of anywhere someone didn't have to be with the company car.

Danny went back to his boarding house, rested up, read more of The White Tower, had supper, and by six thirty he was outside the Skylar home, set to follow the attractive Lucy Skylar wherever she went this Saturday night.

Late Afternoon, November 10th

Gronsky put down his metaphorical pen, lifted his fingers from the keyboard. He was prepared to keep going with Danny's Saturday night investigation but wanted to delay the gratification. He pretty much knew the direction he intended to go, but there would be some pleasure in withholding fire, being patient, exercising second thought.

He spent the next few moments remembering Miriam's unexpected visit to his bed. It had been mysteriously delightful. It also concerned him. He didn't know what it meant. Did it have a special significance other than showing affection in a surprising way?

Gronsky was a simple man who enjoyed the simplicity of his world, a world that was poised, perhaps, to become more complex. He had two women in his life. One continued to shake up his understanding about love and commitment in his later years. The other, new to him but also a delight, had resurrected long buried memories, all the old hurts and an odd faint measure of relief. Once he had been deserted, his life had returned to a simpler way of being. Incongruously, it was a condition he came to value. Now, he thought, he found himself more expansive, wanting to share more with Anthea than she had done thus far. He could sense his own contradictions. That was a price of life no longer simplified.

Tonight was Wednesday night. *Survivor* night. His den was still in disarray, a mess of papers and dust and yes, dusty papers. It had been agreed that he and Anthea would, as they had done last week, go to Miriam's suite just before eight and watch the show. They would bring the popcorn. Miriam would supply the worms…Or was it salted pecans?

They'd find out.

It was salted pecans…but in a silly turn of thought, Gronsky pretended they were worms…something he thought he remembered an earlier version of the show provided the contestants.

The theme for this night's episode turned out to be sacrifice, grilled cheese sandwiches and locally sourced papayas.

And the perennial theme; treachery.

After the show, Anthea went to bed, but Miriam asked Gronsky to stay. Unsure of the direction that might take, he willingly complied.

"Sit down, Gilbert," she said.

"I am," he replied.

"Figure of speech," she smiled. "I wanted to apologize for surprising you in your bed…"

"No need to. Absolutely no need."

"Gilbert," she continued, looking like a profoundly serious librarian reprimanding a child for returning a damaged book, "I woke up before I came to you last night. I woke up with, I don't know, doubts about us, about retiring. I wanted to talk, and we didn't…"

"I remember," he said. "There was very little talking."

"I know. Can we have a serious conversation about what we are doing and where are we going? I know you want to get to bed now and get up early to get on with your novel…How is it going, by the way?"

"Lots of good stuff, I think. I guess it could stall at any moment but so far, touch wood."

"You won't stall. I just know it. So, Saturday…maybe at, say, three? I don't work this Saturday. I don't want to take a lot of time, just enough."

He agreed, though he couldn't imagine it being a short conversation. He kissed her and went back downstairs to his bedroom. Tomorrow was Remembrance Day. Normally he would attend the ceremony. The city cancelled the in person one last year and had done the same for tomorrow. It would be virtual, starting at ten thirty a.m. He could do that, manage a short conversation about the future.

Morning, November 11ᵗʰ

Gronsky slept well. There were no surprise visitors. He almost regretted that. It had been pleasant, though he supposed it could prove too disruptive if it happened on a more regular basis. He jumped out of bed, a Gronsky slow-moving slightly arthritic jump, had a quick shower, dressed, made coffee, supplemented it with toast and blackberry jam, and repaired to his writing den. For a few minutes he watched a number of Remembrance Day ceremonies, especially the one from Ottawa.

As it was a holiday, Anthea was sleeping in. She hadn't any plans for the day.

After his toast and jam were scoffed, he plunged right back to the life of Danny Hawkins circa Saturday Night, September 21ˢᵗ, 1946.

Chapter Twelve, Scratch an Old Wound

Lucy Skylar left her house at seven fifteen p.m. She was alone. She pulled out in her Ford and Danny followed. The porch light had illuminated her in the moments she had headed for the car. Though she was wearing a longer evening outercoat, he caught what he thought was a glimpse of a red evening dress flash in the faint bulb light.

He immediately assumed that she was off for another evening of dancing.

He followed at a distance. She surprised him by weaving her way into unfamiliar Winnipeg territory, although he told himself that he knew so little about the city anyways that he had best just follow and not berate himself for his geographical innocence.

She pulled up in front of a three-story apartment building and honked twice. Someone had been standing in the inside foyer. He came out, walked to the car, got in. It was the same dance companion she had cut a rug with the night before, the same fellow she had taken home. Foolishly, he did not have the wherewithal to take a picture. Belatedly, he aimed the camera at her car and the man just getting in. He snapped two quick shots. With luck and an agreeable shutter speed, something might come of it.

Danny continued his surveillance and was not surprised when they arrived again at the Normandy Dance hall. He parked a few car lengths behind Lucy and watched as she and her companion held hands and walked toward the entrance. He got out without the camera and followed them in.

As it had been the previous evening, Andy deJarlis and his Red River Settlers were jigging up a country storm. He watched his quarry couple find a table, take off their coats, and immediately head to the dance floor. Danny decided that finding a table close to them might allow for some productive eavesdropping. He now had the lothario's address, so there was a fairly mundane way to get his name.

Mid-morning, November 11th

Gronsky stepped away from the Normandy dance hall to watch the YouTube virtual Remembrance Day ceremony from the steps outside City Hall, the very steps he had seen the young protestors standing on two days earlier.

It was a moving affair, as remembrance should be. A congregation of children read excerpts of "In Flanders Field." Local artists, a resident poet, a military band, and a host of others all gave those virtually attending a fairly close to authentic experience.

After a moment of silence, though Gronsky revelled in many moments of silence throughout many of his days, he returned to Danny Hawkins and his assignment.

Chapter Twelve cont., Scratch an Old Wound

Danny sat at his table against the wall, in the shadows. Candle-strength lights illuminated the darkness somewhat, and two tables down from where Lucy and her swing partner had left their coats, he noticed quite a lot of brown bags pouring liquid into cups. He wasn't all that thirsty, but he wondered if the local cops worried about this infraction of liquor laws. He had to admit he wasn't up to speed on Manitoba justice, and neither Vinnie nor Grace had raised the matter. Even as he observed some of the liquor in a brown bag action, a large fellow – the bouncer/floorman, he assumed – wandered over to a couple of yahoos across from him. "Hand it over," he insisted. One of the miscreants stood up and got into the bouncer's airspace. "Yeah, whatyagonnado Stevie?"

The response was instantaneous. Steve, the bouncer, twirled the yahoo around, raised the back of his coat, placed his giant mitt on the fellow's pant line, lifted him in the air like a sack of flour, shuffled him off the floor and, presumably, deposited him out into the street.

Lucy and her dancing partner returned shortly after the eviction, and Danny heard the dancing fellow opine, "Polish is on point tonight, Luce." She smiled and said, "I'll keep my mickey in my bag, Paul." The lothario, now revealed as Paul, said, "Shush, Luce. The walls have ears."

Paul looked around as if to make his point and saw that Danny was paying close attention. "More than the walls, Luce. You interested in our business, fella?" Paul asked in Danny's direction. Danny immediately played the newcomer card.

"Second night in town. Sorry, didn't mean to snoop. Just starving for company, I guess."

With that exchange, the band revved up with a new number. Danny was concerned that he may have failed in his assignment, exposed his flank. They now knew what he looked like, and any further surveillance, at least up close, would be compromised. Maybe, he thought, he should just pack it in, go back to Midges, and lick his novice investigator wounds.

As he debated the best course, he heard Lucy say to her aggressive companion, "Go on, Pauly, don't be like that. Invite him over."

Having another male at his table was apparently not to Pauly's liking. Danny could well appreciate that perspective. Still, if he played it right, he might just wangle an invitation. He got up and went a bit closer to Lucy and Paul. "Kind of you. Maybe two's company and three's one too many. I've heard that's the case pretty much everywhere."

Paul growled, but Lucy said, "That's sweet. Pauly, make room for our new friend…:

"Danny, he said, "Hawkins. Fresh off the train from Montreal by way of war and Edmonton and small-town points south."

"A prairie boy, eh?" said Paul.

"In the beginning. Yup."

"Sorry for my temper, just trying to protect…"

"Your interests?" Danny suggested.

Paul smiled and agreed, "Yeah, my interests. Pull up a seat."

Danny moved over to their table, which had two extra chairs.

"I'm Lucy," the girl introduced herself, "and this is my…my friend, Paul. Pauly to those who like to tease him."

"Paul to you, friend," he advised. "You said you were from Montreal. Why come to our fair town?"

Danny scratched his head and gave a compressed spiel. It was close to truth. "I'm still getting over the war," he answered.

Likely it was something both Paul and Lucy would have heard from others. Almost anyone, he thought, could tell the same tale, and it would always have the absolute ring of truth. If there was a lie in it, the lie was that you never got over war. Not just soldiers but all the civilians in Europe, on either side, and in the east, the Japanese – that damn bomb that had put an end to the conflict once and for bloody all. From where Danny stood, the world would not recover from the atomic bombs that blasted those two Japanese cities. It made him sick to think about it, to think he was on the side that did that.

If there was a saving grace to being on the side that unleashed that nuclear evil, it was that the other side would have done the exact same thing given the chance, so it was always good to be riding the winner's coattails.

"Aren't we all," said Lucy.

Paul remained silent.

Lucy didn't. "Paul couldn't go. Tried, but he was 4F. Isn't that what they called you, Pauly? 4F?"

"The yanks call it that. I have bad lungs. Pneumonia as a kid. Couldn't get pass the damn physical. Tried…"

Danny nodded, unsure what comment would work best.

"But you were in the war, Danny? Where? if you don't mind my asking?"

Lucy had asked gently, and he needed to respond in kind.

"Europe," he answered, "and no, I don't mind you asking. If that's as far as it goes. I just want to forget it. And talking about it doesn't help with that. That's why I looked for a happy place. Heard there was a lot of happy people here in Winnipeg…and here at the Normandy. Was here last night too. Just to check it out. You two come here often?"

"Whenever we can," said Lucy.

With that, and the music, Paul grabbed Lucy's arm and pulled her up. They were a fine-looking couple and looked first-class together on the crowded dance floor. It was easy to see their mutual attraction.

But Danny was hoping for a point of division. He sensed that there was some animosity withing the pair. At one point, Lucy and Paul returned to the table and Paul sat down while Lucy reached for Danny and said, "Let's see how Alberta Boy moves his feet." They had two dances together. The second one was a slower polka that required holding her close, which she seemed to encourage. He could feel the sexual energy in her. Married or not, he knew she could be a handful. Perhaps more than one man could handle. Or even two.

"You and Paul are a good-looking couple," he finally said, almost whispering in her ear. "Been together long?"

Lucy looked up and said, "We're related…"

"Related?"

"Third or fourth cousins. Ukrainians, the both of us. I am little Lucy Andrichuk. He's Pauly Starchuk, so related. But not enough to be…not together. We've known each other all of our lives."

He nodded. "So close, for such a long time. Are you gonna get hitched?" he asked as innocently as he could. He had no idea if third or fourth cousins could get married. He didn't really care anyways, as he already knew she was married. He wondered if she would tell him. There didn't seem to him any reason why she would.

She quickly switched the subject to him. The dance was almost over; there wasn't much time to plant a new seed. "And what about you? What are you now? What do you do?"

Her question suggested to Danny that she was hoping he might have a skill she could use. It was a longshot, but some embellishing wouldn't hurt even if it went nowhere. He took his time forming an answer, and she picked up the thread of silence. "Montreal, you said. Lots of crime there, I hear. Lots of big bad criminals." She made it sound childlike, as if she were a coy young creature repeating a tale told in the dark.

He nodded. "Yeah, there are some."

"Did you know any?"

He smiled, thinking that might be a better answer than anything he could say.

"Are you someone like that?" Lucy had difficulty with silence.

"Now, we're getting too personal," he whispered. "You probably don't really want to know."

The dance finished and they returned to Paul and the table.

Danny wondered if the next few moments might be pivotal to the case.

Evening, November 11th

Gronsky eyeballed his computer clock and saw that it was after six. He felt that, again, he had found a new direction. A little addition to an untested plot twist. He couldn't tell if it rang true, but he likely would follow it to the end of one thing and the beginning of something else. That was the way he liked to write. There was no real ending, no direction he had to follow. Of course with Danny Hawkins, he did have a destination. A small town on the coast of Vancouver Island. He'd picked it out when he had first conceived of Danny. Anthea had given it voice when she played with how NaNoWriMo sounded. It was good to have a final destination. How one got there, how he shaped the tale for Danny to get there, was a whole other creative journey.

He poked his head into the living room and saw that Anthea and Miriam were working on a giant jigsaw puzzle that totally covered much of the floor. A fire was burning in the fireplace. He looked at the jigsaw box. "Perfect Dawn," he said. "How long will it take?"

"Christmas," Miriam answered. "It could take to Christmas. Or New Years Eve. Maybe forever at the speed we're going. You don't use this room much do you, Gilbert? You seem to be spending all your time in your den."

He smiled back and said, "The perfect room for a Perfect Dawn. Can I help?"

"Pull up a rug, Gronsky," said Anthea, and he did. They worked on the puzzle for an hour until they got hungry, ate some leftover soup and crackers, and then went to bed. Before he did hit the sack, Gronsky watched *The National*, in his mind Canada's key news source, though he allowed that others might disagree..

Two stories made his heart sink: one, De Klerk's dying statement that he apologized for Apartheid, something he said he never believed in. It was a heartrending final soliloquy.

The other story was even more wrenching: the Canadian Government urging Canadians to get out of Haiti which, they were clear to point out, was on the verge of collapse. There was a huge shortage of everything including gasoline to run the generators needed for businesses and hospitals. Seventeen kidnap victims were being held for upwards of a month so far and, as far as Gronsky could remember, there had been no word of their fate. One was a toddler. He couldn't remember how old.

It was a horrible story, but then, he thought, the world has millions of horrible stories, stories that end just as others begin.

Or overlap. Horror lapping horror.

A smaller irritation was the story of anti-vaxxers interrupting a Remembrance Day ceremony upcountry. The self-righteous were legion, Gronsky supposed. How sad a species are we?

Sleep would temporarily assuage all the horrors. For him, anyway.

Morning, November 12th

As Gronsky stirred just before seven, he remembered that today was the final day of COP 26. He had to look it up sometime ago to find out when COP 1 had occurred. 1995 In Berlin. In the spring. Twenty-six years earlier. There had been one Conference of the Parties every year since. Twenty-five previous failed attempts to the save the earth.

Maybe not failed but hardly successful.

However, he hadn't paid much attention back then or in the intervening years, really.

He was paying heed now, although he sensed that his participation, whatever that might amount to – one older citizen out of billions – was somewhat meaningless.

That was the big picture of the world on this late autumn morning.

Gronsky finally got out of bed, shaved, made coffee, nibbled on toast, ate a withering Mandarin orange, and walked towards his den. He heard Anthea getting up, talking to a friend on the phone, making her plans for school, for the weekend. He saw Sam approaching, said, "Morning, Sam. Haven't seen much of you this week?"

"And that's why I am catching you early, Gilbert. You've heard about Haiti? The warning to Canadian citizens to leave?"

"Last night on the news. How does that impact you? You're here."

Sam smiled, weakly Gronsky thought. "Here for the moment. I'm on my way there. With a small security force…to try and get a few stragglers out."

"Not exactly international development, is it?"

"No, not exactly. But I know the country all too well. Ottawa thought I could be of assistance. Maybe I will be. I could be gone upwards of two weeks. Less time, I hope but maybe not. No telling. But I also wanted to mention that in looking at the list of Canadians possibly still in Haiti, I came across the name of a Robert Clapson. That's…"

Gronsky nodded his head. "Could be my son. Too much of a coincidence. Haiti, hmm. Likely someone else."

"And whoever he is, perhaps he's not even there, anymore. The list I was given was culled from a number of sources. Reliability would be a concern."

Gronsky shook Sam's hand, wished him well and went back to his den.

He didn't know what to think about the name Robert Clapson. Whoever he was, he would be a stranger to him. No point in getting his hopes up. It had been decades since he had given much thought to his two children. That wasn't totally true. He remembered the babes they once were, holding them, thinking about their future. But he had few glimpses of that time anymore…until Anthea appeared, the almost magical appearance of a granddaughter, his granddaughter, along with her report that her mother, his daughter, had died in a car crash sixteen years earlier, and the news that she had been raised by his ex-wife, Stella Fishbine who wasn't Stella Fishbine, but who became again what she had once been, Dorothy Clapson, who was now deceased…it was all a bit much for poor Gronsky to digest.

He much preferred to plot Danny Hawkins with his next sleuthing steps.

Chapter Thirteen, Scratch an Old Wound

After Danny returned to the table with Lucy, Paul immediately hauled her back onto the dance floor: Good, thought Danny. They can discuss him, who he might be, might not be, what skills he has that might serve their purpose, if any. He had not been at all obvious for an exceptionally good reason: he had no idea what was going on aside from the tawdry reality that Lucy and Paul seemed to be immersed in. He had a brief history about Lucy, but the client had not mentioned Paul, or at least, if he had, it hadn't made it into the file.

Danny had another troubling thought. He was likely in over his head. He shouldn't have been permitted to go out on the case alone.

Just as he thought that thought, someone came up to him out of the shadows and said, "Could a lady ask the gentleman to dance?"

Danny blew out a ton of anxious breath, got up, took Grace's hand, and they went together to the dance floor. It was a fast-swing song, and they faked it. The next song was a slower waltz like affair, and they held each other close and talked.

"Thanks," he whispered.

"I'll dance with anyone, Danny. No need to thank me."

"For being here. I was sinking."

"Thinking?"

"No. Sinking. Like in quicksand. Not that I have ever seen any."

He hastily filled her in on some of his assumptions and some of Lucy's assumptions, what he thought she might be thinking.

"She thinks you're a gangster?"

Danny laughed and said, "Well, I worked for Vinnie's old friend, and he was into some iffy stuff…so, it is not too much of a stretch."

"But you think she is thinking that you…"

"Yeah, another Bugsy Siegel…"

"A contract killer?"

"Yeah, maybe. Yeah, I bet you that that is exactly what she might be thinking."

"To kill who?" Grace asked and then answered, "The sergeant. Her hubby."

"Unless there is someone else in her sights we don't know about."

"Why would she want to hire one. I mean, why not do it herself. Or get the boyfriend?"

"Paul. Paul Starchuk. Third or fourth cousin…something like that."

"Why not have him do it?"

Danny thought as he held Grace tightly, and she squirmed a bit, said, "Not so tight…"

"Sorry." He released her a mite and said, "About Paul, I get the feeling from my few minutes with them that Lucy thinks Paul might not have it in him. Me, I think everyone has it in them. Paul didn't serve…maybe health reasons, maybe a character flaw."

The music ended and Danny thought that Grace might want to fade into the crowd. He asked and she said, "That makes sense. I'll check back in a little bit. I want to find a phone booth and talk to Vinnie."

Grace slipped away and Danny returned to the table. Paul and Lucy watched him approach.

"Made a new friend?" Lucy asked.

"She like my looks. Might be back."

"You should invite her to join us."

We're an 'us'?" Danny asked. "That was quick. Don't even know her. Or you two."

"Lucy says you have an interesting pedigree, Danny."

Danny looked at Paul, said, "Don't we all." He sensed that Paul, maybe even more than Lucy, wanted to mine whatever nuggets of information they could extract from him. They were inching into dicey territory. He understood that. If he were who they assumed he was, he would be incredibly tight-lipped. Contract killers, he had no doubt, didn't go advertising their wares to any

Tom, Dick, or Harry. Not if they wanted an extensive career. For Lucy and Paul's part, blabbing that they wanted someone killed was also something best kept quiet. It was a wonder anyone ever got killed this way. The hiring process was murder.

Maybe, he thought, he should let Paul stew in his own cowardly juices. He asked Lucy for another dance. A slow one was just starting, and the thought of feeling the slim body of a potential murderess in has arms was an exciting prospect. The tune the band was playing was a novelty song, I Always Wanted to Waltz in Berlin. Danny had heard it a couple of time before, likely on the radio.

He took the opportunity, drawing Lucy in quite closely, to ask, rather provocatively, "Paul, Pauly, is he your one true love?"

He had taken her unawares. He wondered if she had ever asked herself that very question. She was curious why he had asked it. "Why? What makes you think he is…or isn't?"

Danny smiled, far more of a wise smile than he was feeling. "I just don't see it. I see you with someone…stronger. Tougher."

That seemed to unleash her emotions, her reality. "I am married," she whispered, "to a tough, strong man. But it was a mistake. I need it to be over. You're right, Pauly isn't the man I need. Now, I need a tough strong man…to free me from my husband. Are you that man, Danny? Or am I wasting my time?"

Danny did not know the next step. He needed Grace to pull him out of the muck.

Evening, November 12th

It had taken Gronsky most of the day and early into the evening to get Danny Hawkins positioned to have an impact on his first real case. He had to stop, though, needing more time to conjure up next steps. The narrative was taking over, and he needed respite

He went to the kitchen and saw a note left by Anthea announcing that she had made some mac and cheese. The note also said she had gone to the house of a school friend for a few hours and would be home by ten. The note additionally advised him not to work on the jigsaw puzzle, as she and Miriam saw it as *their* project that he could help out with only when they were working on it. He had no trouble respecting that directive.

He reheated the mac and cheese and took it to the den to watch *The National*. He was not surprised to see that COP 26 was morphing into another day of compromise. The earth was likely doomed, but he expected that the COP 26 delegates would manage to eke out at least a dozen more compromises for their community of countries.

COP 40 was bound to be a biggie. And all the intervening ones down through the years.

He opened a bottle of Pinot Noir, drank two glasses as he watched the news, and fell asleep in his chair. Later, around midnight, he struggled out of the chair and made his way to bed.

He fell quickly into a deep sleep.

Morning, November 13th

Gronsky was up and ambulatory by seven. He and Miriam had their heart-to-heart discussion scheduled for some time later in the day. He couldn't quite remember when, but the topic was clear enough: What direction were they going?

Serious domestic discussions.

He had never had any that he could recall.

Although his mother had offered marital advice before he had married Stella. He hadn't listened.

It was frightening...exciting in a way, but for a semi-romantic fellow who had underutilized those predispositions, frightening and exciting.

Even more frightening, he remembered, was the situation Sam was placing himself in. Haiti was on the brink. Sam would likely be arriving in Haiti, by whatever means he was travelling, today or tomorrow. Gronsky was worried for his friend and tenant but knew that any second-hand fretting from afar would serve no purpose. Whether Sam would be able to track down Robert Clapson, if he were still in Haiti, and whether that Robert Clapson was his long missing son were two such large questions that Gronsky, for both his sanity and his creative literary venture, needed to put it all to the side. He had more pressing fictional concerns.

Before he attended to the challenges of the day, he opted to go for a morning walk. It was light out and that made it somewhat safer. He decided to walk down the hill, along the downtown business district, and then hump his way up the big hill toward home.

Downhill was a breeze. It was too early for most businesses other than coffee shops to be open. The main street that ran parallel to the river had suffered greatly from Covid, fires, and a declining customer base. Conversely, the denizens of the street, the homeless, the lost, had overwhelmed his city – so many towns and cities – and it all seemed so hopeless. The school Anthea attended was in the middle of this urban decline, and he worried for her and her compatriots. But he was not fooled into thinking this situation had any comparison to what Sam would shortly find in Haiti. He was thankful that there was no comparison. Except, he mused, our ability to repair what was before our eyes. All of this, the difficulty in his home community, was challenging but miles away, in every sense of the phrase, from the challenges that existed in the third world.

The climb up the hill to home wore Gronsky out, but there was a short stretch that was flat at the end that refreshed him. Almost.

Once home he walked into the kitchen, made coffee, mixed some yogurt with granola, took his breakfast into the den, snapped on the TV, and caught the second half of the men's World Cup soccer qualifier between Canada and Costa Rica. Almost immediately, Canada scored a goal.

As much as he wanted to re-enter Danny's delayed dilemma, he settled in to watch the end of the game. Literature was one thing; patriotism and sport were quite another.

Canada won and was slowly making its men's soccer way onto the world stage.

Just as the game ended, he turned to the BBC to catch the last-minute shenanigans at COP 26. The assembled were debating the latest compromise statement. He admired the verve, the tenacity that the delegates, the ones who had not walked out, who were not demonstrating, exhibited. They had phenomenal staying power.

He vowed to follow COP 26's final steps throughout the day.

But first, the 1940's in Winnipeg were calling. Perhaps he'd find a mystery he could solve.

Chapter Fourteen, Scratch an Old Wound

Lucy was taking a substantial risk. Danny could tell that right away. How desperate she must be, he thought, to make such a blatant overture to a man she had just met.

How desperate and how foolish.

He knew he needed to stall in his response. Grace had wandered off to find a phone booth to call Vinnie; they were treading deep water and needed his leadership.

She had just asked him, while he was holding her young body next to his, whether she was wasting her time. What, he wondered, would a contractor, a hired hitman, say to that? Wasting time was in no one's best interest, he figured.

"I'm just passing through," Danny answered. "I've got a little time on my hands. No account time, I guess you could say. Maybe we need to be more private about what we are, and we aren't talking about."

She seemed to think that that was a smart idea. They returned to the table.

"Pauly," she said to her third or fourth cousin, "I think we ought to get together with Danny and have a frank discussion."

Paul looked angry. "What the hell are you talking about, Luce?"

"Don't speak so loudly. Trust me. Tonight, maybe!"

Danny interjected. He needed to play for time. Time and guidance. "I'm thinking tomorrow. Maybe late morning. After you get back from church?"

Paul and Lucy smiled together. "You got us all wrong," Paul said. We ain't churchers."

"Huh…my mistake."

"Okay," said Lucy. "Paul, your place? Should we meet there?"

While Paul gave that some thought, Danny wondered if a more public place, or a place more easily accessed by others, might be a better location. He hadn't thought it fully through, but he was desperately trying to think like the seasoned detective he knew he wasn't quite yet.

Finally, Paul went along with a meeting and suggested a location. "Not my place. What about the Marlborough? Rent a room on the fifth floor?"

Lucy looked at him with disgust. "That's morbid, Paul. Morbid."

Danny was in the dark both about what the Marlborough was and what was morbid about the suggestion.

"Famous Winnipeg murder happened there," Paul informed Danny. "at the Marlie, just a couple of years ago. Fine old hotel though. I'll rent something if you want, Luce. For tomorrow. Summer season's slowing down Should be able to get a small room for cheap."

Danny nodded. "A hotel's fine. On your dime. Your cheap dime. And not too early. After noon…okay?"

"Consider it done," Paul said. "Not sure I'm all in on this, whatever this is, but for Luce's peace of mind, I'll go along. Give me a phone number where I can call you in the morning."

"I'd rather call one of you," Danny interjected.

Lucy started to reel off her number, but Paul interjected. "Here's mine," and Danny took out the pen he had taken to carrying and wrote it down on his wrist."

"Good," said Lucy. "That's settled. Now, I feel like dancing."

"And I think we should head out," said Paul. "You and I have some talking to do."

Lucy resisted this notion initially but then relented. They grabbed their coats and departed.

Danny sat by his lonesome for a while until he spotted Grace re-entering the hall. Just in case Paul and Lucy had remained to see what he was up to, he welcomed Grace, and at the start of the next dance tune, they started to dance.

He scanned the crowd but saw no signs of Paul and Lucy.

"Let's check to see if they've left," Danny suggested. They went outside and determined that Lucy's car was gone. The two of them went to the company car. "Where are you parked?" Danny asked.

"You are driving what I would normally drive, Mr. Hawkins. I took a taxi."

"Then will I drive you home?"

"Oh, so gracious. Before that, fill me in."

They sat in the Chrysler and Danny filled her in on the latest details. Then he asked what Vinnie had to say.

"He was both impressed and shocked. He prefers his operatives not to get too close to their quarry. You've pretty well jumped into bed with both of them. She is a pretty little thing, isn't she!"

Danny let that comment slide. But Grace was right. Lucy Skylar was a pretty young woman. "We agreed to meet and talk further tomorrow. A hotel called the Marlborough."

"One of our finest, though I prefer the Fort Garry," Grace said.

"Now I have heard of that one," Danny answered. "Lucy mentioned that the suggestion of the Marlborough was 'morbid' and that the 5th floor…was the scene of a murder."

"Terrible story," Grace explained. "A murderer who served years in prison for an earlier murder got released, moved to Winnipeg, rented a room at the Marlie, met a child who worked there, sixteen-year-old girl. Edith…Edith Cook, I believe. She was a chamber maid, I think. Happened just a few years ago. Murdered her as well. He was hung. Fully deserving of that. Westgate was his name. Didn't help with the Marlborough's image, but people forget most terrible things."

With that bit of murderous history under their belt, Danny asked Grace to elaborate on Vinnie's thought.

"Well, he doesn't know about the Sunday rendezvous yet, so we need to speak to him pronto. We can try and reach our client, but we might need to involve the police. It's too risky

without notifying them. Drive me back to my place, we'll call Vinnie from there, work out a plan."

Only one problem with that plan," Danny said coolly. I don't know where you live."

Grace got out and motioned for Danny to do the same. She shifted behind the steering wheel and drove to her apartment. It was a four-story building with an elevator. She lived on the fourth floor. Once inside, Danny took a seat on her couch whilst she contacted Vinnie.

He heard Grace give Vinnie a very concise update. They went back and forth until she said to Danny, "he wants to talk to you."

Vinnie didn't mince words. "You went too far for my liking. You never should have made contact. Observe and report. That's all I wanted. Maybe I wasn't clear enough. BUT we're in it now and maybe it'll turn out okay. I'll contact the police. Georgie Smith, been chief forever. Close to retiring. We've shared secrets before. You think they'll rent a room at the Marlborough?"

"That's what Starchuk said he would do," Danny parroted back. "Maybe not in his own name, but he seemed willing to do it. You never know."

"I'll know. You don't plan to kill serving soldiers in this town, even if they are lousy husbands, and think you can get away with it."

"I don't know what kind of husband Skylar is, beyond not being wanted."

"But you think he's not a good one."

"His wife seems to have some issues with him," Danny added. "Other than that, of course I don't know."

"Well, we'll maybe find out. Doesn't matter what kind of husband he is, though. If they spell out what they want done to him at the Marlborough tomorrow and we get it on tape, if the Winnipeg Police Service gets it on tape, they're done, and we'll get brownie points. That's the important thing. Not him and his behaviour. He's not trying to kill her. There's not much else in this for us, but the points add up. Give me back to Grace."

Danny handed the receiver to Grace and she and Vinnie wrapped up their discussions.

She hung up and said, "You can head home to your bed. I'm beat. We'll know what's arranged in the morning."

Grace didn't seem interested in more talk or any other adult activities, so Danny tipped his hat and left.

He made it back to his bed just after midnight. He was excited with the challenges that this case was providing.

And he was learning a lot in a short while. He could see a future in the profession.

If he didn't get killed first.

Afternoon, November 13th

Gronsky checked the time. It was just after two. He needed a break and some food. He turned on the television, hopped channels, and found the second set of the Guadalajara WTA

Open between Sakkari and Badosa. A time waster, but his brain needed some escape from murderous behavior. He had read that the tournament was intended to draw exciting female players and encourage the young girls and women of Mexico to play tennis.

A noble goal.

The Greek player had lost the first set in a tiebreaker, and it looked like she had just been broken leaving Badosa the opportunity to serve for the match.

The tennis season was ending. This tenth game of the second set went back and forth, and Sakkari, giving and taking her opportunities to break, in the end, couldn't.

He remembered that he and Miriam were scheduled to have the TALK at three. It needed to happen, regardless of where it led. He believed that he loved Miriam, that she cared for him, and that they were very compatible. She had taken to Anthea wonderfully, and by any measure he could imagine, they were, along with Sam, a family of sorts. It was an important day.

For the world as well, this day was pivotal. COP 26 had ended with a concluding document, and as Gronsky watched the BBC, he saw what one compromise had become: coal power to be 'phased down' instead of 'phased out.'

He supposed one could phase coal down, but it didn't seem as monumentally pleasing to the earth as phasing out would have been.

What it meant was anybody's guess, though they likely had described it in their concluding document. Someone hopefully understood.

At three, Miriam knocked on Gronsky's den door. He let her in, and they sat down on opposite chairs. He turned the television off and offered her wine or brandy.

"Maybe…maybe a small glass of brandy," she acquiesced. Once the glasses were filled, Miriam asked, "This is okay to do this now?"

"A natural pause in my creative process, believe me," he reassured both himself and her.

"Good. I just wanted you to know what I 'm thinking about…my life, you, my profession, the library."

He nodded. He nodded often when he was very unsure what to say. He then ventured in to what likely would amount to conversational quicksand. "So, about work…you're not planning to retire soon?"

"Part of me wants to. Most of me, I think. But I love my job, Gil. I *love* it, and it rewards me with meaning. I'm finding it hard to think of letting go."

"Then don't," he advised, perhaps a little too quickly. "Don't leave until you are ready. I know Covid really messed up the transition. You were almost ready for a while even if you *were* working. People not coming in, the pleasures of your job, it changed."

"But *you* want to travel, Gil. We've talked about that. You and me, all those places we've never been…"

"Did you talk to Sam before he left yesterday?"

"Oh, yes, I did. Such a dangerous thing he is doing."

"There's that. There is also just flying and how bad it is for the environment. I'm not going to say this in public. I'd get swarmed by an armada of snowbirds yelling 'Whaddayamean, no flying?' But I am thinking it."

They both laughed.

"Come here," he said, and she came closer and sat gingerly on his lap. "I don't know what you should do, but I do know I need you. I'm not sure that I can do right by Anthea all by myself. You've been a godsend, and I have appreciated how you two have bonded. I need both of you. I don't want to lose that."

There might have been more to say, but Gronsky was talked out. It hadn't been as suffocating as he had imagined.

They spent a quiet evening at home, as per usual. All three had dinner and they worked on the jigsaw puzzle until almost ten. Gronsky was enjoying the challenge, but he found jigsaw puzzles infuriating.

Miriam and he spent the night in his bed. Nothing was finalized, though both had the sense that some progress had been made.

Morning, November 14th

Though Gronsky mostly slept the sleep of a noticeably quiet baby that night – a situation he had never been much privy to, he mused – likely because Miriam was by his side until she returned to her apartment around six, he had been very aware of the clatter of fat rain pummeling the earth overnight and into this very damp morning. He wished for anyone who lived on the street to be indoors. The wet, windy, chilly rain would not treat anyone left outside well.

It was day one after COP 26. In a few days, the post-mortem would be in full force. He could not devote much time thinking about that nor his previous evening's discussion with Miriam. They were connected, of course. He was rapidly becoming an earth savior, one who would never fly again. He understood that some people had to. Sam on his mission to Haiti and other places would have to. It was incumbent on the billions of people like Gronsky who didn't really need to travel by air to stay firmly earth bound.

Easy to say, he knew. Especially if no one was actually listening.

Most everything was.

He rose, decided to take a rare morning shower, made coffee, thought about pancakes which would include his traditional Sunday egg requirement, but instead poured cereal in a bowl, splashed some milk, reminded himself that he should do a bit of grocery shopping sometime later in the day, tomorrow at the latest, and, once fed and propelled from the first cup of java, poured another, and went to meet Danny Hawkins back in the day, a specific day, Sunday, September 22, 1946

Chapter Fifteen, Scratch an Old Wound

Sunday was evidently not a day of rest at Midge Felker's boarding house. By seven thirty, Danny was at the breakfast table with housemates Jim and Henry, and all three men were being served pancakes and syrup by Midge, who was a whirlwind of graciousness. "Lots more on the griddle," she announced as she plopped another plate of the fresh hotcakes on the table.

Midge eventually sat down and joined them. "So, Mr. Hawkins, what have you planned for this fine Sunday morning?"

"Some work, I'm afraid." he said.

"Oh, that's too bad. My impression of Vinnie is that he is usually not such a taskmaster. I'll have to have a talk with him."

Danny replied that, alas, the labour was of his own making.

"Then you need to practice restraint. And Jim and Henry, what have you got to do today?"

"I believe," said Jim, "that I will be cleaning the eves of your fine establishment Midge. And Henry is helping."

"I am blessed," said Midge. Danny was amused but then, after breakfast, asked to use the phone.

That proved no problem. He called Paul to get the details of the Hotel Marlborough reservation.

"Room 502," said Paul. "Lucy and I will meet you there at one. No tricks."

"I have none. I'll be there. And I expect the same…no trickery on your end. It wouldn't be a smart thing."

He hung up and called Vinnie and gave him the details, including his less than veiled threat to Paul. "Good," said Vinnie. "George is ready and willing to set up a recording device and capture the conversation. Hopefully, they'll be in the next apartment. Get them to repeat exactly what they want from you. Exactly."

Danny understood. He could sense his nerves jangling. "I understand. Will you and Grace be there?"

"Yes we will. Quite a bit earlier. So I'd better hang up and get the wheels in motion. With any luck we'll stop another Evelyn Dick from ending her marriage in a grisly fashion."

Danny bobbed his head and hung up. He hadn't been thinking of the ignominious Evelyn Dick, a woman shortly to go on trial for the gruesome murder back in Hamilton of her luckless husband, but he should have. He wondered if that murder case had influenced Lucy's planning in any way. He would have thought it would have given even the most vengeful of spouses cause for second thought.

He rejoined his boarding house companions in the dining room. "I could give you an hour of assistance," he announced.

"Excellent," they all chimed. "Good man."

For the next hour, Danny worked hard and felt that he had contributed to the small community of which he was now a part.

Around ten, he cleaned up, dressed in his best clothes, pretty much his only civies, and began his journey down to the heart of Winnipeg and his rendezvous on the fifth floor of the Marlborough Hotel.

Late Morning, November 14th.

Gronsky needed to catch his breath. He desperately wanted to complete this part of his narrative by noon, but he switched on the television, watched a few minutes of British women's soccer, then listened to the CBC. The message from post COP 26 was, as expected, wavering. The 'phase down' coal power language was disheartening to many. Not the least, Gronsky.

Then Doctor Tam, Canada's top public health officer, reported that aerosol transmission of Covid was increasing. Winter behavior, indoor gatherings, would escalate the virus' hold.

He heard Anthea knock on his door, and he bade her enter. "Morning," he smiled. "Sleep well?"

"Yup. Still at it, eh!"

"You mean the book? That I am."

"You wouldn't like to sneak out and catch a movie with Miriam and me? Spencer."

"A mystery?"

"No, Gronsky. About Lady DI."

"A new movie?"

"Where have you been?" Yes, a new movie."

"I've been here. You guys go. I'm…well, fully occupied."

"Change your mind, we won't leave until noon. Just down the hill. We're walking."

"Pretty darn wet."

"We have umbrellas. Particularly useful invention."

"So I've heard."

With that she hugged him and left him to his creative devices.

Gronsky got another cup of coffee. The machine had turned off, so he poured the liquid in a mug and put it into the microwave. Fortified, he stepped back into the novel.

Chapter Fifteen cont., Scratch an Old Wound

Danny arrived about twelve thirty. It was half an hour before the appointed time. He parked himself in a comfortable chair in the lobby and took in the sights, few though they were. The hotel clerk did give him the once over a couple of times but must have decided that he looked harmless. That was worrisome, as Danny needed to look somewhat menacing if he was going to pull off this assignment.

Close to one p.m., he went to the elevator and pushed the button. The elevator opened and the operator asked which floor.

"Four," he said.

"Four, it'll be," said the operator.

Danny got off on the fourth floor, found the stairwell, and walked up one more floor. It hadn't been necessary, but it helped him to get into the role.

He knocked on the door of room 502. Paul Starchuk opened it, stepped aside, and let Danny in.

"Take a seat. And let's make this quick," Starchuk ordered.

"You're driving this bus," Danny said. He looked at Lucy, who was standing at the window looking out on the world she was darkening. She turned around and asked, "What can you do for us, Danny Hawkins?"

Danny shook his head and replied, "Hey, it doesn't work that way. You tell me what you want done and I'll tell you if I can do it and what it will cost."

Lucy and Paul looked at each other as if to determine who should speak next and what should be said.

"We're on a budget," Paul finally chimed in."

"I do nothing cut-rate, fella. Nothing," Danny said.

Lucy then took the lead. "I told you last night that I need to be rid of my husband. Fred...well, he has been...physical with me. Thinks he owns me. Nobody owns me, and I can't stand him anymore."

"Then leave," Danny said. "Why not do that?"

"Fred's not rich, but he's not poor. The house is in both our names. It's free and clear. And he inherited money when his father died. His father was a piker. Saved every penny. Like Fred."

"So," said Danny, pausing, he hoped, for significant effect, "what do you want done and how much will you pay me to see that it gets done?"

Lucy and Paul each looked at the other, almost in panic, as if whatever they wanted done had never been spoken in front of a living soul before.

Paul started pacing. He went over to Lucy and put his hands on her shoulders. "Are we doing this?"

Paul was demanding that Lucy make the final decision. It was cowardly, but she was the married cohort who wanted to terminate the connubial partnership. After some hesitancy, Lucy nodded yes.

Paul turned and addressed Danny. "Best we can do is scrape together three hundred bucks. Maybe a little bit more. Best we can do."

"How much of a little bit more can you scrounge up?" Danny asked.

"Fifty. In a pinch, fifty. That's it."

"And," Danny pressed, "for three hundred and fifty dollars, what do you expect?"

"To kill my fucking husband," Lucy screamed. "Sergeant Fred fucking Skylar. I want him dead."

It had finally been spoken. What Lucy Skylar and her twisted third or fourth cousin, her Pauly paramour, had in mind. The job was done. That clinches it, Danny thought, just as a force of cops, followed by Vinnie and Grace, burst in the room and subdued Lucy and Paul.

Case closed.

Until the trial.

Evening, November 14th

Gronsky checked the time. It was dark outside, yet it was only just five p.m. A little while ago he'd heard Anthea and Miriam return from the Lady Di movie. He trusted they enjoyed it and would regale him with tales from the film, how it was made, and the like.

He hadn't been able to get to the supermarket today, so that would have to be on the Monday agenda.

He popped out of his office, saw them working on the jigsaw puzzle without him, and asked what they would like for supper. He was in an ordering mood and wondered if they could go for something new, East African and Indian fusion, perhaps. They were game, and so he ordered three dishes of cayenne spoke prawns with masala fries. An hour later the meal arrived, and they dug in. Gronsky was in an effusive mood, as he had passed a self-imposed hurdle and was close to concluding the Winnipeg portion of Danny Hawkins's journey. In actual literature time and space, Danny had a couple of years to remain in the story, but Gronsky was planning to compress that interval into a few paragraphs, no more than a full chapter at most. Writers could do that, play with time and space, but it required a level of believability. That was the test.

In any case, Danny was about to be on the move. His stay in Winnipeg had been fulfilling and educative. He felt 'healthier,' emotionally and physically. He would be marking time but as long as it lasted, it would only enhance him, his character, his soul.

Morning, November 15th

Gronsky turned on his bedside clock radio to listen to the six thirty news. He was immediately taken by the announcement that the newsreader thought it was seven thirty. The wonky clock radio he had been meaning to replace for quite some time had done it again. Moved back an hour of its own accord.

Machines might not be taking over the world, but they seemed to have established a beachhead in his bedroom.

Whatever the time was, the weather outside, as the old song went, was frightful. Tons of rain, of flooding, pooling water everywhere, cars and people trapped, mud oozing far and wide. Nature was really upset with the results of COP 26, Gronsky reflected.

He decided to make a pot of porridge to warm up the day. Anthea was not a great lover of porridge. She had confided that, for much of her life, porridge had started most days. It explained why, when he and Sam had first found her and brought her in to the kitchen, toast, peanut butter, and jam had been her first request.

So much and so little had happened since then.

She had blended in quite swiftly, and Gronsky could almost not remember a time when Anthea hadn't been there.

Shortly, he was up and dressed, had the porridge simmering and the coffee percolating. The rain was intense and provided a dramatic backdrop to the morning.

"Nasty night," Anthea said as she entered the kitchen. Looking at the pot on the stove, she made a face but then smiled at Gronsky.

The porridge only took ten minutes. They sat down to eat, each looking at the other, each enjoying the thunderous rain outside, the peaceful moment of togetherness inside.

"You really want to get writing, don't you?" Anthea asked.

He nodded. She said, "I'll clean up…and run down the hill to school. I'm already a bit late."

"Blame me if they ask," he said.

"I will," she smiled, and he left the mess for her and repaired to his den. Once there, he opted to get the word count moving and then, in a while, look at the news of the non-fictional world.

Chapter Sixteen, Scratch an Old Wound

Danny was relieved that this first real case of his was over. Vinnie didn't sit still for long, and business started booming. The local press covered the arrests of Lucy and Paul later when the police held a press conference. It was clearly an embarrassingly rich and deliciously lurid scandal.

Vinnie took the credit for the resolution of the case from the perspective of his agency which was fine with Danny. The last thing he wanted was notoriety. Vinnie had given him what he really wanted and needed: experience and a skill set that would allow him movement.

After the arrests, Danny, Grace, and Vinnie had returned to the office, where Vinnie poured a celebratory brandy, and they toasted their success.

"You both did great. And Danny, I'll let Harry know that he sent me a winner. A real pro."

That felt good; Danny was pleased with the acknowledgement. Later that Sunday, he sat down with Vinnie and stated his position. "I'm good for a while, Vinnie. I can learn a lot from you. But I am waiting to hear from Harry about who killed Monique? Ugly as it is, that is my main goal…"

"I'm okay with that," Vinnie said. "I know that's your primary objective. It would be mine too if I were in your shoes. We'll see how things roll out. Are you planning to stay at Midge's? She seems pleased with you."

"I'm stayin'," he said. "She's a good woman. And I am comfortable there."

They left it at that.

At the end of September, the Nuremburg trials of the highest Nazi leadership, some of the most venal and sinister men and women the world had ever produced, came to an end. A number of the accused were found guilty and sentenced to be hung. Martin Borman, who was sentenced to death in absentia (it was thought he might already be dead by suicide); Hans Frank, the Governor in charge of Poland; William Frick, the Minister of the Interior; Hermann Göring, once head of the Gestapo, and who committed suicide the night before his October 16th 1946 date with the hangman, Alfred Jodi; Ernst Kaltenbrunner, another Gestapo acolyte; Wilhelm Keitel, Defence Minister; Joachim von Ribbentrop, Minister of Foreign Affairs; Alfred Ernst Rosenberg, a Nazi theorist and ideologue; Fritz Sauckel, Plenipotentiary of the Nazi slave labor program; Arthur Seyss-Inquart, and Julius Streicher two other highly place Nazis. All, except Göring who, as Danny noted, took his own exit – were executed on October 16th.

From Danny's point of view, these names had to be mentioned but once more, a final newscast, perhaps, and then forgotten, never spoken of again. Of course their repulsive deeds needed to be remembered so their names would likely always linger, and that was perhaps a necessary price; evil needed to be remembered in the hopes that it would never be repeated.

Over the next year he received excellent tutelage under Vinnie and Grace's good guidance. None of the cases held a candle to the first. Danny had expected to testify in the Skylar case at some point, but once the initial furore settled, Fred, the client, the intended victim, was not anxious to go to court. The military brass was also unhappy that Fred's alleged abuse of Lucy would be the key defence strategy. It wouldn't leave the sergeant or the brass in a good light.

Eventually the case disappeared in a snowstorm of cowardice on everybody's part. Danny wished them well from afar.

In November of 1947, fourteen months into his time in Winnipeg, Vinnie passed along the message Danny had been waiting for. Harry Ship had kept his promise. There had been three in the gang responsible for the robbery that had ended in Monique's death. Two were identified. They were brothers, Rocco and Giovanni Genna out of Toronto. Harry's message was that they had been interviewed and given up what little they knew of the third gangster. He was new to them and younger, maybe late twenties or early thirties, and was the wheelman. They only knew him as 'Hubcap.' Hubcap didn't know who the Genna brothers were either; he was supposed to be just their imported driver. Though he might have other skills, they hadn't needed to know and hadn't asked any questions. They said, though, that he was also one of the shooters and that he seemed to relish it even more than the brothers.

As for where Hubcap' was now or where he was from, that was unknown. "Maybe out west, maybe that's where that bastard hangs his shingle," were almost the last words Rocca Genna apparently uttered. Giovanni had remained tight-lipped to the end.

In early December, Danny finally was able to get Harry Ship on the horn. "Good to hear from you Danny. How's life?"

"It's been good here, Harry. Time to hit the road, but which road? I don't know."

"Good thing you called when you did. It's looking pretty bleak for me. Damn reformers have me by the nuts. Squeezing tight. Anyways, I don't wanna be jabbering on the line about who hired those guys to go up against me. Just know they have been paid back in spades. We did learn that this Hubcap mug is from Vancouver Island. Little burg out there built in the shape of a hub. Nanaimo. Stupid name, but at least you've got a place to get to. Beyond that, I'm a dry well."

Danny thanked Harry for all his trouble and wished him well with the troubles that were coming his way.

"Price of doing the kinda business I do, kid. Watch your back… and your front."

The call ended, and Danny began to put his journey west into action.

It was deep winter, and he didn't fancy crossing the country when most of it was covered in slush and high drifts. Some months earlier, with Vinnie's connections, he had bought a '41 two-door Coupe for a decent price. His plan was to drive wherever he had to and maybe even drop into his hometown. Southern Alberta was to the west. He had always expected to be headed that way.

And now he was. In the spring. He was in a hurry to extract revenge, but weather played a part and weather said there was no rush. Springtime. 1948. That would do fine.

Midday, November 15th

Gronsky was happy with the plan. He was looking forwarded to Danny's journey from Winnipeg to Nanaimo. Getting through the winter was difficult no matter "where or when you lived." Or maybe that was an old man talking. Danny Hawkins would also be considering a side trip to renew acquaintance with his community of birth. If it hadn't been in the same direction he was heading, its possible that he would have skipped it.

Gronsky had reached the end of his creative juice squeezing for Monday. The extreme rainfall that had disturbed his sleep had reached into many towns and cities in the province. One town, Merritt, had to be fully evacuated because the rising water took out the town's water system. Seven thousand people had to leave their homes. Another town, Princeton, was also under water and hundred of families had to evacuate. Mudslides had trapped people overnight on Highway 7, the old highway that preceded the Trans Canada.

Gronsky walked up to a local supermarket and did some power shopping. Vegetables, fruit, cheese, veggie burgers for a change, cottage cheese and pasta for later in the week.

For supper, Gronsky cooked the veggie burgers, boiled some potatoes, and made a spinach salad. Anthea had no complaints, as she was easing into a vegetarian life and the burgers were even tasty.

He was in bed by nine.

Danny Hawkins' epic journey west was preying and weighing on his mind.

Morning November 16th

The night winds were mostly quiet, and Gronsky slept well. When he arose in the morning, the sky was clear, and the rain had stopped. He went for an hour's walk, twice his usual distance, all the way past the old prison, now a congested upscale neighbourhood, and further along, up into the old neighborhood by the hospital. He circled around above the hospital, wandered through the cemetery high above the river, cut across the highway, and ambled back via several back alleys, listening for sounds of the city awakening. Though he couldn't tell for sure, in several of the open garages, it seemed people were burrowed in towards the back, sleeping, huddling, having sought shelter as the rain dwindled in the night. If they were there, they would surely be on the move shortly, headed for a meal and the companionship found in the company of their brothers and sisters of the street.

Once home he had toast and jam, made coffee, and immersed himself in his den. He quickly scanned the news of the world on TV. His province was still assessing the impacts of the vicious rain event that had pummeled so many people. Concern was expressed that some folks might have been caught and buried in mudslides. There were also numerous examples of people helping others, providing safety, comfort, food, and conversation.

Gronsky liked the notion that people would care each other when the world ended. Anthea rushed in just as he was beginning to make note of Danny's planning regimen. She hugged him, said, 'I've gotta run,' and she did just that.

Chapter Seventeen, Scratch an Old Wound

Now that he knew he was going to be on the move, Danny was more conflicted than ever about whether to return to his hometown or not. It was nestled in the southern part of Alberta, and there were reasons he might not want to revisit the community. His old man had passed away while Danny was overseas. Early in the war. No way to make it back.

Danny still had an older brother, Eddie, and a sister, Fiona, living, but Eddie's twin, Teddy had died in infancy. Lucas, the eldest, had been struck by lightening when Danny was four, just after the first world war.

Three months after he entered the world, his mother had died. She had been twenty-six, given birth to a swack of children, wanted, he imagined, to prepare them for world she might not herself have been prepared for. She had only those brief ninety days with him. He hoped that she had suckled him, perhaps ill or dying as she did. He was her last and whether she knew she was dying or not, he would like to think that he had brought her pleasure even as she prepared to leave. He would never know. It would have been a struggle for her no doubt. All of it.

When Danny's mother died, a decision was made that Danny was a burden his father. He thought it might have been phrased like that, that he was a burden. It would have been a heavy responsibility for a widower to run a farm, look after four surviving kids including an infant.

There had been the four siblings, but two he barely knew. The other two were older and because he was parked with his mother's mother and father for a dozen years, he didn't know his remaining siblings all that well.

That had been the decision. Did his father initiate it? Did his mother's mother offer? They must have all been grieving, Danny thought. A wife, a daughter, gone in the prime of her life. Even if an early death, often from a complicated childbirth, was more common then, the grief would still sting, linger. No wonder he was aimless now, driven only by retribution for the loss of Monique. Was his need for revenge a replacement for the anger he sometimes felt for being kept from having a mother's love? Knowing a mother's love.

He lived with his maternal grandparents until his grandmother died. She had loved him, clung to him in her grief. But once she was gone, it was then decided that he was of an age where he could move back with his father and his two remaining siblings and work on the farm.

They were pretty much strangers to him, and he to them.

Danny Hawkins wasn't one for picking at emotional sores. He knew he had been shortchanged, but he also knew that most of the world had been as well.

The man he was as the Depression ended and the war was about to begin was not always a careful man. One summer night in Lethbridge, he had met a girl, a Catholic girl, – like Monique in some ways – and they had become intimate in his 1925 Ford. His old man's car if the truth be known.

Elise. Her name was Elise, and she had gotten pregnant.

He didn't love her, or thought he didn't, because he believed he was unlovable.

Why else would his mother have left him, have died?

Still, Danny married Elise, and she had her baby: Constance, little Connie. Then he had absconded. Shortly after abandoning his family, he enlisted. War might be good for redeeming this errant father he had become, he hoped.

Now he was thinking of visiting the town where it all happened, but he couldn't imagine it would go well. His remaining older brother, Eddie, had moved to the States and joined up there. He had also abandoned a wife.

Fiona had gotten married and was working as a cook on a ranch her husband worked on as a cowboy, a cowpuncher, a wrangler.

They were childless as far as he knew.

We all made a mess of it, he thought. And he couldn't see a way back.

He could, however, see sliding in through the back door of his hometown and catching a glimpse of his past, reassessing choices made, choices delayed, and, based on that, maybe undoing or at least patching up some of his mistakes.

He wasn't sure if that was worth it.

As he had done the previous year, Danny celebrated his second Winnipeg New Years Eve at Vinnie and Claire's. Grace was there with her roommate, Stella Samuels, as was Richard

Lacombe and wife Milly and a range of extended family and friends of Vinnie's and Claire's, including Midge.

At the end of 1946 Danny had been numb, so in a sense this was his first real New Years celebration back in country and it was by far the best ever in his life. If he'd stayed in Montreal after Monique's murder he likely would have spent that New Years winter hustling drinks for Harry at the club. Before the war, most New Years were piss-ups, and during the war, New Year's was just another day in a war that didn't know how to end. After hostilities were suspended, he'd remained behind to do some mop up work through the end of '45, and so that New Years was spent in Berlin. It was a lonely experience, and in January of '46, he had shipped back to Canada.

As 1947 slipped in to 1948 the Brass home was a gentle gathering of good people. Danny was enjoying the jazz on the RCA, the occasional dance, some light drinking, and then around ten, the phone rang in the kitchen. It was Harry Ship, and he wanted to talk to Danny.

"Wanted to give you a warm hello from Montreal, Danny. Surprised you're still there."

"Still on my mission, Harry. Heading out in a few weeks maybe. Helping Vinnie out till then."

"Then its swell I caught you. Look, it's not looking too good for me. Those fun-loving reformers are closing in. But I've got a description of Hubcap. Maybe six feet. Thirty, thirty-five…talks about fishing when he talks at all. So somewhere on the west coast is likely. Nanaimo, like I said before, or any little village up and down the east or west coast of Vancouver Island. It won't be a cakewalk."

"Thanks, Harry. I hope they go easy on you."

"They won't," Harry said. "Take it easy kid… I know I don't miss her as much as you, but I loved Monique. She was steady, and she was tough."

"Take care, Harry. You want to speak to Vinnie?" Harry did, so Danny passed the receiver.

Shortly before one a.m. when the party broke up, Danny and Grace found a quiet place, and she let Danny know how much she had enjoyed working with him.

"I owe you, Grace. You taught me well. It's a been a pleasure. I'm going to miss you."

"Who knows, you might see me sooner than you think. Stella and I have been giving some thought to moving out to Vancouver. Bigger view of the world. A little more tolerant, I hear."

"Then we should keep in touch," Danny said.

"We should."

Danny drove Midge home.

Later, resting in bed, he knew he was ready to leave Winnipeg.

Soon.

Evening, November 16th

Gronsky was tired. Writing about a New Year's Eve party was almost as exhausting as going to one.

He flipped on the television and caught the third set of the Guadalajara semi final between the fierce Estonian Anett Konteveit and the equally fierce Greek, Maria Sakkari. Sakkari was always popping up in his narrative. She was more than welcome.

He then flipped the channel to the Canada/Mexico world cup qualifying match in Edmonton. It was twenty below. Canada was up one nil when Cyle Larin scored to make it two zip.

That would be it for Gronsky. Sports would ring out the night.

Around seven thirty, Anthea brought him a sandwich and tea. She watched some of the tennis match and tolerated his channel hopping.

The tennis duel in the eighth game of the third set went on for thirteen minutes, a titanic duel won by the Estonian who went up 5-3. It looked like doom for the young Greek favored by Gronsky.

And it was. Tennis matches don't kill, but losing hurts, until the next game.

As for the Canada/Mexico duel, Canada won 2-1.

The cheese and lettuce sandwich was very tasty, and the tea more than welcome. Gronsky and Anthea hugged goodnight, she expressed her concern for Sam in Haiti, realized communications might be spotty, but Gronsky reassured her that he would be fine and that he might even e-call at some point. He didn't mention Robert, her long lost uncle, his even longer lost son. There seemed to be no point until there was some news.

He ended the night with the CBC and *The National*. The weather in BC had been so destructive, but heroes were everywhere. An ER nurse helped save some people pushed off the highway and down an embankment by a thunderous eruption of mud.

The hour-long news program ended with a clip of a fellow in a boat rescuing a herd of horses from rising water.

It was a grand story, and for a change, Gronsky went to bed with a smile.

Morning, November 17th

Gronsky woke up to the news that out in the valley, flooding was still happening, and in Abbotsford, the pumps were close to failing. He remembered hearing stories of the flood of 1948, the lives ruined, farmlands underwater.

He quickly dressed, ate breakfast, got coffee, and went online to find some of that history. It might or might not play in Danny Hawkins' story. For Danny, it was late winter in early 1948. The floods occurred later in the spring. A writer of fiction could only do so much. Facts were useful but could be inhibiting. Gronsky had a mission. Danny Hawkins had a journey to make, a place to be, a diversion to perhaps take, a resolution not only to his story but, for Gronsky, a means to finalize his tale.

He had so far negotiated NaNoWriMo on time and on budget, or a writer's equivalent of that. This was the final push. He still had thirteen days to finish the project, but the pressure was mounting. Still, he was fabricating the pressure, and it was not like the pressure out in Abbotsford, the rising water pushing against the system of dikes, built to withstand what they knew of their water systems but never factoring in the massive rainfall that was now walloping the land.

As he researched the spring of 1948, Gronsky came across a reference to a ten-day storm that impacted the prairies from late January to mid February 1948. He was elated. That storm would serve as a useful character, something to delay Danny's journey. This would allow Gronsky time to better plot out the narrative.

As part of his due diligence, Gronsky double-checked the story and discovered that all the other links to the storm placed in in January/February 1947. Gronsky was incredibly disappointed. Deflated though he was, he'd revise the story to include that it happened during Danny's first winter in Winnipeg. Gronsky would further take advantage of this to suggest that Danny was so traumatised by the storm of 1947 that he delayed his January /February 1948 departure until later in the spring.

Gronsky was impressed with his narrative flexibility. He wondered if others would be so enthralled.

Much of the balance of the morning was spent in research, revision, and narrative guidance. Gronsky wished he could be more certain that his narrative direction was believable.

Around noon, he took a break and checked out the flood situation in the Fraser Valley. He noted two new things. There was a massive fire in an RV storage park in Abbotsford that was challenging the community's emergency resources. Then the Premier, John Horgan, declared a state of emergency. His deputy Premier, Mike Farnsworth, described the difficulty of getting people safe and goods moving. The supply chain was at risk.

Gronsky was beginning to feel a bit of a fool for worrying about his imaginary dilemmas created by the fabrication of Danny Hawkins. On the other hand, he was too old to help out much in an emergency. In the long run, literature did have value, so it was up to him to write something meaningful. Staying at home writing lies was more useful than going out to Abbotsford to make sandbags and probably have a heart attack and then becoming a health emergency nuisance.

Gronsky was proud of his reasoning process. Writing was meaningful work in a state of emergency. He wondered how he would incorporate that philosophical concept in his novel.

It would be a challenge.

Chapter Eighteen, Scratch an Old Wound

Danny waited until January disappeared before giving serious thought to taking his leave of Winnipeg. He had planned to hit the road on Saturday, February 1st, 1948. One year earlier, the world's most notorious gangster, Al Capone, had gone kaput. Heart attack, it was said. The man had a heart. Danny wondered about that. Capone's death reminded those who might have forgotten that no one was immune from being taken down. Harry Ship would soon know that if he didn't already.

That same month the previous year, nature had gone not kaput but seemingly crazy. On Thursday, January 30th, 1947, a ten-day blizzard hit throughout the Canadian prairies. It was one of the worst Canadian storms on record. Towns and trains and highways from Winnipeg to Calgary were buried under an avalanche of snow. Later it was noted that some rural roads and railways in Saskatchewan would remain closed until the spring. For a week, Winnipeg came to a standstill. Little detecting occurred, so Danny found himself shovelling snow daily at Midge's. Jim was off work as well since no trains were running, so he, Henry, and Danny formed quite the shovel brigade.

But now, as Danny was about to leave he was worried that the extreme weather that had happened the previous year might reappear. Vinnie couldn't convince him otherwise but offered to keep him on until the time arrived when Danny felt comfortable to safely get on the road. Midge was more than happy to house him while he waited.

Danny knew that he was feeling trapped by his own reluctance –partly to leave and partly to arrive.

Finally, March came around. Danny waited until the fifteenth and then irreversibly began the seven-hundred-mile drive cross country, with a modest plan to stop over in the town of his birth. A few days earlier it was reported that one of the many Nuremburg trials had come to an end. This one was the eighth, the RuSha Trial. There were fourteen defendants, all officials of various SS organizations responsible for implementing the repulsive Nazi pure race programme.

He had tried to keep up with the score of various trials occurring but life interfered, and getting complete news was difficult. The papers had much of it right, he thought, and he was thankful for that,

The scale of the retribution the Allies had inflicted on the criminal Nazi government might hopefully deliver other nation states from similar power- and race- related overreach. Danny trusted that the trials would serve as an object lesson, even as he knew that the millions who died during the war would never be avenged.

His personal loss did not compare, but he knew something of the unnecessarily dead that villains always left in their wake, the unnecessarily dead and those left behind.

It would be good to be alone on the drive. Winnipeg had been a pleasant enough place to reenergize, but Danny had rarely been alone. Work was always bustling with people – his fellow detectives or clients and their associates – as was the boarding house, which had given him an oasis of home cooking and pleasant company for his entire stay.

Once on the highway, he somewhat overenthusiastically resolved to try and make Regina by day's end. It was about midway between Winnipeg and his hometown, three hundred and fifty miles as the veteran crow flew.

Saskatchewan was achieving amazing things the past few years starting with, and because of, the Socialist government of Tommy Douglas. Danny had to admit he favoured the CCF, though he had never voted in an election. That was another resolution he had made.

Given the opportunity, he would support a party that was there for the little guy. That was evident in almost everything Douglas and his party did. He'd heard that Douglas hated the Nazis and tried to enlist but there were health issues keeping him back.

Maybe it was for the good of Canada that he didn't go to war and die. He had done so much, including forming a progressive provincial government.

As Danny thought about his journey west, the reason for it, the remaining unknowns – so many unknowns, the needle in the stacks of hay unknowns – he realized that it might be better to pace himself. He wanted to reach Regina in the first couple of days but there really was no rush. It was still winter and gaining a flavour of the country he had gone to war to defend might serve him well. He decided that he would stop over in Brandon the first night out, a town he had little knowledge of except that Vinnie had mentioned that he and Claire had spent their honeymoon at the Prince Edward Hotel located next to the train station. "It might be a trifle fancy for a young man going

*from one place to another but treat yourself. Gloriously regal…
for Manitoba."*

*"Why not?" he said to his invisible companions. He had earned
a fair salary during the past year, and as he ventured into the
unknown, likely a dangerous, possibly deadly unknown, a little
luxury would not be out of the question.*

*Later that day, around four in the afternoon, he pulled into
Brandon, drove around looking at the sites, and then registered
at the Prince Eddie.*

*After checking in he sought out the billiard room located in the
basement The felt was plush, and he enjoyed shooting pool
with a couple of other residents. Later they went to the bar,
swapped drinks and stories, and then dined together. Both
were ex-paratroopers who had trained in Shilo in the early
forties. They proved quite knowledgeable about Manitoba, and
especially Winnipeg. They parted at ten, and Danny went to his
suite, stretched out in the bed, and faded into dreamland. At
some point he was sure that Monique had crawled into bed with
him and warmed his body. When she left, when the impression
that she had been there vaporized, he was sure that he heard
her warn against risking his life to avenge her. "Live for me,
Danny. Live a life that was taken from me. Marry. Have children.
Live and love. Do not hate."*

*She had been like that. Forgiving to the end. He was not made
for forgiveness. Still, he was delighted to sense her presence,
even if imagined.*

*In the morning, he had a full breakfast, gassed up, and headed
for Regina.*

Early Evening, November 17th

Gronsky noticed that it was close to six p.m. His mind was still on the highway just outside of Brandon, driving along with his character Danny Hawkins, pondering the journey, a possible family reunion, a child he had abandoned, a west coast town to move to. And possibly death at the hands of the hired killer.

As he had done so often, Gronsky turned on the television and was blessed to find a tennis match. It was a special match in that his favorite player, the six-foot tall, lanky svelte Spaniard Garbine Muguruza – a beautiful woman, to be sure, yet who in some ways reminded him of a soft featured Anthony Quinn – was playing for the Guadalajara Cup, or whatever it was called, playing against the Estonian, Anett Kontaveit, who'd cleaned the hair-sprayed clock of the young Greek player, Maria Sakkari, the previous evening. Gronsky couldn't help himself. He had to watch. Then he remembered that *Survivor* would be on at eight. He called Miriam and asked if they were good for the episode tonight. She said she would order pizza and reel in Anthea and, "Not to worry, just show up."

He vowed that he would.

He then settled into the match and tried to let other pressures drift away. It had been five days since Sam had gone to Haiti, and Gronsky was concerned. Months earlier, Sam had given him a number to call if he was ever worried about him. He'd never used it but was feeling that this situation, a surreptitious mission into the collapsing infrastructure of that tragic country, was of sufficient concern that he should reach out. Perhaps a call after the first set. After all, it was a great tennis match. At the moment, they were 3-3 in the first set. Too exciting not to give his full attention.

Just before six thirty, with the Estonian serving, Muguruza leading 40-30 and the game score 5-3 in her favour, she flung a lob over Kontaveit and won the set. With that mystery solved, Gronsky dialed the long-distance number that Sam had given him and let it ring. A message from an unfamiliar voice said, "Leave your name and number and the person's name you are calling in reference to." He did as he was directed and hung up.

The second set began in a few minutes, and again Gronsky settled in. He had no actual reason to be unduly concerned about Sam, who was a pro at third-world diplomacy. They had often talked, not about specifics, but about the need to respect and embrace the customs of any country in which you were a visitor and where you believed you had something to offer. Gronsky had countered that there were a few countries that might not be open to that level of respect and need. He was specifically referencing Haiti, a country that had never seemed to get a break. Sam had laughed it off and said, "Sometimes there is no coming together, no meeting of the minds. I am ready for that too, sadly."

As for the match, it was tied 3-3 until Kontaveit broke Muguruza and it became 4-3. It was looking like they would need a third set tiebreaker. Shortly it was 5-4 Kontaveit. Then Muguruza broke back, and it was 5-5. Gronsky was impressed that she had recovered from a brief bout of rampant overhitting. She then pulled ahead at 6-5. The tiebreaker was not necessary. Muguruza had come from 5-3 down to take the second set 7-5 and win the tournament.

The final scene of the contestants, Kontaveit and Muguruza flanked by Chrissie Evert and Billie Jean King, spoke volumes about the growth of women's tennis, not just in Mexico but around the world, as well as the resilient women who have marched it forward.

Gronsky almost said, "Whew," but didn't.

It was a few minutes to eight. He rushed upstairs and Miriam opened the door. The pizza was already there, and Anthea had not waited.

Red wine was poured, and the show began.

Almost immediately, there was a titanic *Survivor* challenge, and the result would be two players heading home.

Ah, torture and then release. All through the show, he thought of Sam and *his* challenge. He hoped he wasn't missing the call. He should have call forwarded it. It was thoughtless not to have considered that.

The show proceeded, with chicken and fish stew the prize for the winners. Nazeer, who had an idol, didn't play it, and was the first of two to get voted off the island. And then, the final reject: The PHD candidate, Evie. He would miss her.

It was predictable though. She offered a final message to the world: "If there are any queer kids out there, be yourself."

A fine message, Gronsky thought. He was definitely going to miss Evie.

The show ended. The pizza, Greek in theme, feta, olives, artichokes, and dried tomatoes was excellent. The wine was a suitable companion. Anthea even had a glass.

She seemed to enjoy the red.

Before they separated, they chatted about the episode. As with most television, a deep dive into theme was uncalled for.

"I just like it," Anthea emphasized.

"Me too," said Miriam.

"Me as well," added Gronsky, though he didn't quite mean it. He enjoyed the occasional character, the intrigues they fabricated, the awareness they must all have that the camera is on them and a number of their predecessors had made media careers out of being on this show. Social issues were occasionally touched on, only to be diluted by the entertainment aspect of the production.

Anthea and Gronsky then left, she to her bedroom and he to his den to check on calls. There was no message.

He stared to watch an old movie, *The Conspirators*, a hybrid *Casablanca* knockoff set in Portugal, and shortly after it started, the phone rang.

He turned the movie off.

"Hello," he said.

"Mr. Gronsky?"

"Yes."

"Unfortunately, we have temporarily lost track of our mutual friend."

"I see," Gronsky said, not wanting to really acknowledge the information.

"We will continue to try and make contact. And when we do, we'll contact you."

"Thank you," Gronsky said.

"Good night sir."

"Goodnight." And he hung up.

That was that, Gronsky thought.

Sam was missing.

Possibly with his son, Robert.

There was no one else to call. He would have to wait.

Morning, November 18th

Gronsky woke at seven. He felt a weariness that was unfamiliar. He'd been weary on occasion before, and certainly this lethargy was not much different, Still, he was beginning to believe that there is a type of exhaustion that can affect the artist, the writer, the painter, the potter. Gronsky had no doubt that he was suffering from writer's malaise. Ideas, once on the tips of his fingers, almost as if he could touch them, now reposed on the ground, washed away like leaves, stone, wet from torrent, streams of muddy water flowing into the gutters of the city. He winced at the mess of metaphors he had just concocted.

As for the fatigue, it was a sunless stupor and required intervention.

He got up and went for a twenty-minute stroll up his back alley, out on the next street over, and then up to the Public Library. He circled and returned home.

Once home, he woke Anthea and Miriam and offered them coffee and toast.

"Sit down," he said. "I have some news. Well, news that isn't news."

"Is Sam okay?" Miriam asked. "He's not..."

Gronsky shook his head. "They don't know where he is. I called the number Sam gave me. Court or Call of Last Resort like," he added, referencing a television program from his childhood. "They got back to me late last night and it seems he has gone off the grid. Their grid. They haven't a way to contact him at the moment. That could change in a heartbeat."

The three of them sat there and looked glum.

"Lets just get on with our day," he finally said, "and realize that Sam is perfectly capable of looking after himself. Have faith."

With that flaccid note of optimism, Gronsky poured more coffee, hugged and kissed the two women in his life and said, "The novel awaits."

Gronsky closed the door to his den and sat down in front of his computer. He knew he needed to get a move on, put his concern for Sam and maybe even for the existence of his son, Robert, to the side. He was tempted to again call the number Sam had given him. Surely they knew something they weren't saying. Where he last was. Where he planned to go. They couldn't be so lax as to have their emissaries, their operatives, dashing off with no plan. Surely the world, the government, his government was more organized than that.

To refocus on Danny, Gronsky reviewed his last entry. He'd left Danny gassing up and heading off to Regina. He'd zero in on that.

Then a tsunami of mental exhaustion flooded over him. It would not happen today. His brain needed a break, needed to refresh. He decided to go for a marathon walk into the big city to the west. It would take hours. He would stop from time to time, have a coffee and a croissant, imagine that he was in a foreign land, and relish the journey. Tomorrow he would resume his tale telling. There was no rush. He was still ahead of the game.

Morning, November 19th

Gronsky's almost fifty kilometer walk the previous day along the BC Parkway Urban Trail had given him a new perspective, not only on himself but on Danny Hawkins's quest. This new perspective seemed so vivid during the walk and focussed on the end, not only the end of the journey, the story, but the end of November as well.

They were, he supposed, one and the same. Whether there would be a reasonable resolution for Danny was not the issue any longer. Or in doubt. The novel demanded it. Monique deserved it. Gronsky was in control of that. That was the power of authorship.

He would not let his characters down. He certainly hoped not, anyways.

He had returned by seven p.m., chatted briefly with Anthea and Miriam and, exhausted, gone straight to bed, full of red blood cell excitement and a few too many croissants.

He had a most interesting dream that night. He was at a party, a small affair, a party not overly concerned about Covid transmission but still everyone was doubly vaccinated though that seemed to be not a guarantee any longer. There were approximately fourteen people at the party, equally balanced between men and women, the way many parties of a manageable size traditionally were. The gathering was held in a decent size country home, one that he seemed to be familiar with and comfortable in. It was on one level, and people alternately mingled in conversation standing and sitting.

A very pleasant affair, it seemed to Gronsky

All of the guests were older, his age or in the vicinity. He seemed to know some of them, though their names escaped him.

As was his habit at most parties he had ever attended – though he had to admit he rarely ever went to parties and, as a child, he had no memories of going – he would find a position that afforded him the opportunity to observe much of the interaction and not fully immerse himself in the event. Often that would be by standing near the kitchen fridge, hanging from it almost, watching the comings and goings, nodding, smiling, sipping from whatever drink he had at hand – a beer, usually, in his youth and later, a glass of dark red wine.

His position this time, in the dream, was deep into the living room, a chair, a comfortable chair, next to a large stone fireplace. Though it was winter, the only fire in the fireplace were the flames from of an array of candles. A lovely touch, thought Gronsky. The room was warm anyways, so a roaring fire would not have been needed.

Many of the guests, certainly most of the women, were dressed elaborately. Gronsky was not surprised to note that he was wearing shorts, a recent affectation he had adopted. He had always felt that his legs were his best feature, but he had never mentioned it to anyone, and so none were ever in a position to disagree. That was one of the advantages of silence.

As the party progressed, Gronsky seemed to be having brief verbal exchanges with this partygoer and that partygoer. They were mostly a well travelled group, convivial, sharing experiences, drinking, smiling.

The hostess, he presumed she was the hostess, was blonde, shapely, enthusiastic. She announced that there would be a party game, in part "of an ice breaker," she said, or he thought she said. She then went about the room attaching, with scotch tape, sheets of paper to the backs of the attendees.

Each sheet had the name of a famous person. The task of each dream partygoer was to ask a yes or no question to determine who we were, what name was on our back. Gronsky immediately sensed that he would be dragged into the real party, that he would no longer be the observer he cherished being, but some fop involved in a game. So be it, his dream self thought. What was the harm!.

One player, a statuesque woman in a long, gloriously blue, jewel encrusted robe asked," "Am I a woman?" to which another replied. "Yes." She then asked, "Am I alive?" and the disheartening answer was, "no."

The entire gathering got into the game. Even dreamlike Gronsky. After a number of questions, he had pared down his paper self to a deceased male who was not a politician but who once lived in California and who had changed his name.

As he watched the crowd, as they played the game, he began to notice that they were changing. From a gathering of older, well-dressed men and women he barely knew, each began to look like a famous male of female tennis player.

Gronsky, dream-Gronsky that is, sat down and enjoyed the rather psychedelic transformation. One of the women began to look like Garbine Muguruza. Another woman bore an exact resemblance to Martina Hingis. One fellow, Nadal. And on it went.

Then he woke up, none the wiser about his paper person.

It was, all in all, a modest dream, with good wine and hors d'oeuvre but not particularly memorable. It was the usual state of his recalled dreams, except for the tennis players.

Once out of bed, Gronsky put his dream life behind him.

He was in the mood for a Friday morning omelette and asked Anthea if that would suit her. She was in accord.

His favorite omelette by far was a cream cheese/anchovy mix, but Anthea had yet to see the pleasures of that concoction, so he rescued a few old mushrooms, some cheddar, and five eggs and mixed up the ingredients. It turned out quite well, combined with sourdough toast and coffee.

With the most important meal of the day out of the way, compulsive Friday laundry chugging away, and Anthea about to depart for school, he gave her a big hug and prepared to disappear into his fictional world. Before he did, he quickly checked the news and was impressed that Austria had reached a decision to make vaccination for Covid mandatory. By February 2022, that is. Gronsky wondered how far behind his country was now or would be by then. There were escalating pockets of resistance. Canadians were a spoiled people, entitled to so much freedom that their understanding of social responsibility, their individual responsibility, was not always in the forefront.

There was one more newsworthy note that pleased Gronsky. For just a few hours that morning, eastern time, Kamala Harris was President...while Sleepy Joe Biden was under an anesthetic for a colonoscopy. By noon, Eastern time again, Joe had resumed his seat of power.

What an interesting metaphor, he thought.

Chapter Nineteen, Scratch an Old Wound

As Danny drove out of sight of Brandon, he was smiling. It was as if Monique was still with him. She had visited last night. One of the side benefits of a bit of drink and a good night's sleep. He had found pleasure in the reunion, though it was much too short to fully satisfy.

He wondered if he really needed to stop over in Regina. There was an increasing urgency of sorts, a need to implement his plans, and he could sense that he was delaying the obvious. Holing up in Winnipeg for much longer than he probably should have had slowed the process of justifiable retribution. At the same time, he wanted to do it right, wanted to find the remaining killer, the enigmatic 'Hubcap.

Suddenly, only a few miles on the road, he saw a soldier hitchhiking up ahead. As much as he was enjoying the aloneness of the prairie morning, there was no way he could drive past a brother in arms. He pulled over. The soldier – maybe twenty-five years old, tired looking, uniform showing the wear and tear of a wet morning thumbing by the side of the road – removed his cap, opened the door, asked, "Kit in the back?" Danny said "Stow it there, brother, and hop in."

He did and Danny reached out his hand, said, "Corporal Danny Hawkins, formerly of the First Canadian Army."

The hitchhiker reached for Danny's hand and said, "Bobby Waldron, Air Force Mechanic Class B, 438 Squadron…Once upon a time."

Bobby Waldron got in and Danny pulled back onto the highway.

"Cold out there I bet. Why travelling by thumb? Trains still running last I heard."

In a low, barely audible voice, Bobby Waldron said, "I needed to be alone. Just got out of.. well, hospital. Been there for quite a while. You get tired of people. Fawning over you, you know. Feeding you. I certainly did."

"I'll keep my trap shut, brother. Glad you decided to get a ride, though."

"Hell, it was a stupid idea. They were paying my way back to Rosetown, but I figured I'd make it on my own…"

"Rosetown?"

"Little place. Southwest of Saskatoon. Where you headed?"

Where am I headed, Danny asked himself? He knew. "Tonight? Regina. Beyond that, a small town in Alberta. After that, if I go there, Vancouver Island."

Bobby nodded, said, "Lots of places. It sounds like you have it worked out."

That got Danny to smiling again. "If only. So, Rosetown where you from?"

"Something like that. About time I returned. Got a big family. One brother, Jack, died at Tobruk. I still have lots of these big *ugly pictures in my head. Belsen Belsen. All the bodies we had to bury…"*

Danny couldn't believe he'd picked up a vet who'd seem pretty much what he had.

"I was there too, Bobby. Can't shake them either."

Evening, November 19th

Gronsky set his pen substitute down. It was Friday night. The day had whisked by. He hadn't made all that much progress, but he was satisfied. He had cluttered Danny's life up with a new character. Bobby might stay for the ride to Regina, or he might stay longer. Gronsky had no idea. He wondered if the coincidence of two vets who'd been at the grotesque scene at Belsen Belsen would be a bit much. He thought Danny needed to flesh out this war experiences a mite. Having another person who had experienced the same horror, allowing them to talk about it should they decide too, might be cathartic.

Gronsky needed something cathartic.

A favourite old western was scheduled on TCM at eight forty-five. John Wayne, Dean Martin, Angie Dickenson, Walter Brennan and even Ricky Nelson. Howard Hawks' *Rio Bravo*. That would put a great comfy cap on the night.

Neither Miriam nor Anthea seemed enamoured of the Duke.

He rummaged in the fridge, saw two slices of pizza, heated them up, threw on some canned anchovies, got a big glass of wine, and had a grand time at the movies. There was a moment in *Rio Bravo* when all four male heroes were hunkered down in the jail waiting for events to unfold. Three of them were singing and playing two songs: "My Rifle, my Pony and Me," written for the movie, and a country standard, "Cindy." Gronsky found solace in that moment of filmed camaraderie. It was a fine way to end the evening, and after the shootout and romantic resolution, he went to bed.

Morning, November 20th

Gronsky woke up Saturday morning and smiled at the memory of the music from *Rio Bravo*. In the shower, he found himself singing a chunk of the song "Cindy." "I wish I was an apple hangin' in a tree and every time my sweetheart passed she'd take a bite off me. She told me that she loved me. She called me sugar plum. She threw her arms around me. I thought my time had come. Get along home, Cindy-Cindy, get along home, Cindy-Cindy Get along home, Cindy-Cindy. I'll marry you sometime."

Stepping out of the shower, dripping wet, he thought Miriam might enjoy it if he serenaded her one night with this ditty. It could almost be a wedding proposal.

He realized that he would have to practice a bit more.

Love, he thought. I guess it's love. Marriage may be pushing it though.

He hoped he hadn't woken Anthea with his warbling. There was no school today, and she did like to sleep in when the opportunity arose.

He ate some yogurt, made coffee, and then went to his appointment with Danny Hawkins.

A quick pre-writing check of the news was worrisome. There were anti-mask, anti-vaccine mandate riots in Rotterdam, and Austria was getting some pushback from the anti-everything forces to the announcement of a total lockdown for the unvaccinated that would start in thew spring. Just as he was preparing to deal with Danny, he got hooked by a brief documentary on the BBC about Tennessee and the former head of Tennessee's vaccine rollout, Dr. Michelle Fiscus. It was depressing and clearly had a message about the world. The world is divided. Angry and divided.

Dr. Fiscus was essentially driven out of Tennessee simply for doing her public health duty. Political opportunists and the like rose up in revolt to good health sense. Gronsky had no doubt that the same ugly forces of selfish political opportunism and the fragmented notions of freedom were simmering in his province, in the whole country. Perhaps not to the same extent, but they were there, the fools who would do whatever they could to demean good public health sense.

He had another thought. Sam. It had been four days since he had used the special number to see if Sam's handlers, if that was the right word – he figured it seemed to be the way the world of espionage and surreptitious activity worked – to see whether there was any news. He could wait, he supposed, but he could see no harm in reaching out. So he dialed the number. It offered the same message as before. He left his name and particulars as asked.

They would either call or they wouldn't.

He opted to get back to the travels of Danny Hawkins. That at least was something he had a modicum of control over.

Chapter Nineteen cont., Scratch an Old Wound

In their silence, Danny and Bobby shared their collective painful memories of war, of that one camp they had been fated to encounter, to witness, where they were compelled to gaze upon the bodies that had been callously piled up by the torturers, the murderers who were carrying out the sick racist actions of the Nazi state.

Bobby told him that he had been hospitalized for months after, slowly helped to accept that he was not to blame, that the memories would always be with him but that he had to find a way to govern his life even with the waves of images that time would barely be able to heal.

"It's challenging work to keep them in check," he said. "But most days, I manage."

Danny nodded and kept his eyes on the road. It amazed him that these eyes of his could have seen such an atrocity and now could see only the winter highway, the long stretch of flatness and white, the simple undeniable fact of the distant prairie horizon.

Sooner than he expected, Danny saw a sign that told him he was on the outskirts of Regina. Bobby had been dozing for the last forty miles and Danny was more than content to let him get some shuteye.

As he entered the city, he rousted Bobby and said, "We've landed in Regina. I plan to stay over. A swanky hotel…the Saskatchewan."

"You're one high roller…"

"Nah, I had enough for a couple of these extravagances. Just wanted a taste of a few luxurious moments before being broke again and having to earn my way."

Bobby smiled and said, "I'm not quite in that bracket at the moment. Drop me wherever and maybe I'll get another lift while there's still light."

"Rosetown…it's quite a ways still, eh?"

"Yeah, sure the heck it. Not a problem, though. I've got a buddy staying in a shack south of Regina, place called Regina Beach. He said lots of vets are parked there getting their lives in order. Said I could bunk in for a couple of days, maybe longer. All I have to do is show up."

"Sounds like a good deal. Look, if you want to spend the night in my hotel room in Regina, on me, and then get a fresh start south in the morning, well…"

"You sure?"

"Yup."

The decision was made, and the two vets checked into to the plush hotel, dined in the hotel restaurant, bought a bootleg bottle of passable scotch, and made a night of it. Both lauded the Saskatchewan government under Tommy Douglas. War had made both of them aware of the inequities in the world. Bobby even said, "You know, Danny, I've heard that something really new and human is happening here in Saskatchewan under the CCF. I hope it lasts."

Danny nodded in agreement, but he had a slightly different take on good things lasting. It boiled down to: Nothing Lasts. Especially if its good.

He hated to think it, and he had the sense not to burden Bobby with his darkness. Bobby had enough gloom of his own.

In the morning, they had a big breakfast and he dropped Bobby at the junction to the road leading to the village of Regina Beach. Bobby gave him his family address in Rosetown, and they promised to write to each other, tell each other how it was all working out.

Back on the highway, Danny re-entered the quiet world of the solo driver. Though he had three hundred and sixty miles to navigate, he'd see if he could manage it in one day. He didn't really expect it could de done. As thoughtful as he was becoming, he decided that the drive would be more achievable by simply taking in the scenery, the passing parade, as it were.

By now he had determined that he would try and find his old buddy, Jigs Wheeler. The odds were that Wheeler had returned home after the war…assuming he had survived. Wheeler would have found a way not only to survive the war but make the war nothing more than a slight annoyance. Their paths had crossed at Camp Aldershot. Danny had completed basic training and was scheduled to leave within days when Wheeler had been a new arrival. Wheeler spoke a patriotic line, but it seemed to Danny and a few others that he was angling for a release of some kind. Even faked a limp one day in.

Danny had no idea if he had succeeded in becoming 4F.

He'd been on the road for hours and sensed the winter sun itching to sink below the distant mountains.

Just after seven, with twilight in full flight, Danny rolled into his hometown. The Wheelers weren't farmers but had a small acreage with an orchard on the outskirts of town. It was possible that Jigs Wheeler had married and set up his own house, but he doubted it. The Wheeler family had always encouraged closeness. Likely due to concern that some family secrets or other embarrassments would pop out. Danny drove through town careful to watch his speed. The town had had their own police force for decades, and Danny had not been a favorite son.

The Wheeler house porch light was on, the veranda welcoming, so he pulled over and parked in front. He opened the picket gate, walked up to the front door and knocked. Ethel Wheeler, Jig's mother, came to the door, her apron dusted with flower, and her face creased with the beginnings of a smile and when she spotted Danny. "Dan Hawkins, is that you? Pete, it's Danny Hawkins. You made it…"

Her husband, ever, as he remembered, a roly-poly fellow, ambled to the door and shook hands with Danny. "Always good to see a local boy come home from over there. Don't know why we bothered anyways. Don't stray far from home…that's what I taught our children."

Danny didn't argue. He had heard Pete Wheeler espouse his jolly isolationist perspective back in the thirties. All too often. His tune hadn't change. "Good advice, Mr. Wheeler. Is Jigs still living here?"

"Yup, we added on. He and his wife…and little Jigs."

"Speak to him?"

"Separate entrance. Close can be too close. Go around the side…and good to see you in one piece."

Danny acknowledged the gesture and went around the side. He saw that they had added a whole new wing. Hardware was still where the money was in this town.

Evening, November 20th

Gronsky checked the time, saw that it was edging close to five p.m. He was disappointed that he hadn't been called back by Sam's contact person. Or persons.

The night was still young, though. Ottawa time would have just turned eight. He wasn't really hungry, so he decided to see what had transpired in the world today. Local news was emphasizing the short-term gas rationing imposed/requested by the provincial government. In Atlanta, Georgia, an airline passenger's gun went off and three people were injured.

"I think I'll avoid Atlanta, maybe even the entire state of Georgia," Gronsky said out loud. Gun lovers.

Strange people.

Dangerous.

A bit more channel hopping, and he chanced upon *Niagara*, an early Marilyn Monroe film. That was always worth his time, sweet decompressing time, a little romance, a mystery, a lot of Marilyn, and the effervescent, down to earth Jean Peters.

He already had his daily word count in the bag. He also had Danny in his hometown. Danny was that much closer to the west coast. There would be some drama in the hometown reunion, and Gronsky was fairly confident that while it would advance the narrative somewhat, add some additional complexity to Danny's story, it ultimately wouldn't halt the movement to the coast. That was still the target.

As *Niagara* progressed, he finally started to get hungry. He scurried out and found Anthea assembling a dish.

"That recipe in the paper. Curried Pasta with Cheese. Okay?" she asked.

"It'll have to be. You *are* a brave young woman."

"And you'll be a brave old man if you eat it. I need about an hour."

"That's okay. I'm visiting Niagara Falls…back in the mid-fifties."

She looked puzzled but got back to her cooking. He returned to the movie.

An hour later, just as *Niagara* was wrapping up, Anthea popped in and told Gronsky that supper was ready.

The pasta was surprisingly good, not Italian, but interesting and very tasty.

Afterwards they asked Miriam if she was up for working on the massive jigsaw puzzle started over a week earlier.

She was.

They did.

Later that evening, Miriam also indicated that Gronsky should come to her bed if he so desired.

He did.

They did.

Morning, November 21ˢᵗ

Well rested the next morning, Gronsky scampered out of Miriam's bed just short of seven thirty. She barely noticed.

Dead to the world.

He went downstairs, had a quick shower, a newer bathing activity that was becoming quite routine, dressed, zipped into the kitchen, got a bowl of yogurt, raisons, strawberries bought a couple of days earlier, and granola, made coffee, ate, poured coffee, and then, reinforced by more coffee, went to his office just in time to watch *Question Period* and more about the current conditions after the great flood.

The Fraser Valley had drowned. British Columbia's transportation infrastructure was devastated. Gas rationing had been implemented. The supply chain was bent out of shape.

And people had died in a cascading, suffocating, death fall of mud, trees, and rock.

Our storms used to be few, he thought. Now we seem to be forever caught in the punishing rage of nature. She is giving us our due, our comeuppance.

Chapter Twenty, Scratch an Old Wound

For Danny, seeing Jigs Wheeler was a mixed blessing. It was grand to see someone from his life before war, someone he had run with, someone who accepted him as is back then, warts and all. And there was always an infestation of warts. Jigs had had more than his share.

Now they mattered more than ever. At least the way Danny thought.

Jigs invited him in and introduced his wife, a girl from Lethbridge and little Jigs, the spitting image of his grandfather.

"The old man added on. Even made a den for me. Let's talk there. You hungry?"

Danny was but said no.

Jigs had a bottle. He poured Danny a jigger of rum. "Prewar. The old man stocked up. Figured there might be shortages."

Settled into Jig's den, Jigs zoomed ahead with more of his story. Jigs had always hogged the airwaves, sucked up much of the breathable air in any room, and really didn't seem interested all that much in Danny's adventures. "So, there I was, basic training. You were in the troop before me. Farm kids, city kids. All going off to do battle. I was ready. Yeah, I was ready, but then I got to thinking, who's staying behind? The country needs young men to do the important work at home. It's unCanadian to leave it to the old farts. Then I heard there were planning to bring in the Japs from the west coast to harvest our sugar beets...because all the farm workers, the white ones, mostly, had signed up. Japs in our town. No one would be safe. What the hell was the damn government thinking? I told the old man in a letter, get me home. Well, let me tell you, he got a hold of Bible Bill and that old man, pity he died so quick, got me home lickety split, sort of overseeing some of the Jap labour. Keeping them in line. Policing like. Let me tell you, they may be hard workers, but some had never been farmers. Fishermen, shopkeepers, yeah, but not all farmers. And, bloody hell, they needed watching. I mean, they were west coast Japs, now weren't they! Well, all water under the bloody bridge now. War's over. The town's ripe for growth. Hell, we have the new War Memorial Pool about to open. A new sugar beet refinery on the books. Built a new twenty-bed hospital just a few years ago. I supplied a lot of the material. We are bloody booming. I'm forgetting my manners, Danny. What about you? What brings you back? Still married to ...what's her name...Ellie?"

Danny nodded, said "Elise."

"Wasn't there a kid? A girl?"

"Yup, a daughter."

"So, you're still married?"

Danny didn't want to tell Jigs much, but he guessed that Jigs might know his marital status anyways and was just playing dumb.. "It was annulled, Jigs. The marriage. She got married again. Catholics frown on remarriages, so annulment was absolutely needed. For her."

"You sure screwed up," Jigs offered.

Danny had to agree. Even if Jigs was the messenger, he was right.

"What's done is done, Jigs. I did screw up. Anyway, I wanted to drop in, see if you were still the same guy I knew. Glad you're doing well. Always thought you would."

He got up, finished his rum, shook Jig's hand, and saw himself out. Jigs tried to say something, but Danny put up his hand to halt any more words. Jigs still spouted, "I don't get you, Hawkins."

He left it at that. Jigs looked confused, both by the sudden visit and the curt departure. He had thought he might tell Jigs that he needed to hear from him about his screw up but he didn't. In an odd way, Jigs was the perfect person to free him from my past. This home town past anyway. Not that he needed that kind of freedom. Maybe it didn't even exist.

Danny surprised himself by not being angry at Jigs. All he felt was a bit of sad nostalgia. And not much else. Except, perhaps, a weight lifted. He knew he could spend additional time here or in Lethbridge and try to find Elise and his daughter, but that would not appease the past.

Leaving it totally behind was the answer for now. Maybe not for always but for now.

He drove into town, saw that the Palace Café was open, dropped in for a sandwich and fries, and then went to the aging Royal Hotel and checked in.

After a couple of snorts in the bar, he went to bed.

It was a twisty turny night.

In the morning, breakfast over at the Palace, and then the road beckoned.

He needed to get to the coast. It was at least five hundred miles of driving and would take him two days, maybe three, maybe even more. It was all new to him. He would be on gravel much of the time and getting through the Rockies would be an adventure. He would just have to grit his teeth, accept the bumps and the grinds of the road, and push on. It was March 18th. Three days since he'd left Winnipeg.

Mid-morning, November 21st

Gronsky had to pause. It was evident to him that his knowledge of the roadways of 1948 between southern Alberta and Vancouver was limited. His googling for facts provided some information, but clearly his research capacity was limited. He had some detail that he could inject, small nodes of truth that might fool the more cursory reader. It was a one-month rush to finish, and facts were just facts,. They had less and less relevance to some. He had done his best, and whatever he provided would have to suffice. Readers would have to accept that.

Then the phone rang. He picked up the receiver.

"You called again, sir."

"I did. I was hoping that there might be an update. We are getting concerned."

"We?"

"The people who live here."

"How many are there of you?"

"Counting Sam. Four."

"We were told only three."

Sam had obviously been obliged to fully disclose who lived in his house. That number had not been updated since Anthea had become a part of their lives. He was not sure if he wanted to share any information about her. If they wanted to find out, they were more than capable of tracking that fact down,. She was registered in school. That was probably available to them. Whoever they were. The government. The Dark Government. Sam's people.

"There is a fourth. My granddaughter. A recent addition."

There was a pause. "Okay. Noted."

Another pause. "Is there news?" Gronsky asked.

"There is. I can only mention it because some information has been posted on the Christian Aid Missionaries website. Two of the recent kidnappees have been released."

It was the longest sentence he had heard the voice connected to Sam's handler say.

"But nothing about Sam?"

Another infuriating pause. Then, "Nothing directly. We are cautiously optimistic."

Gronsky smiled, said, "So are you suggesting we should be as well?"

"If you like," the voice added.

Well of course I'd like to think optimistically, thought Gronsky. Cautiously, perhaps. Maybe even recklessly. So, not a whole lot of facts, but that might be the nature of the Kidnapped in Haiti Beast. He should be thankful they called back.

"Thank you," he said. "Any other news?"

"No. Not at this time."

"Can I call again?"

"We'll call you."

"Good. It's just…we get nervous."

"Being nervous doesn't improve the situation."

"Right!" said Gronsky.

The line then went dead.

Gronsky hung up the receiver. He gave some immediate thought to the conversation just concluded. It was good to hear that at least two of the seventeen abductees had been released. He went to their website and garnered a little more information than he had had before. Of the original abductees, six were men, six were women, and five were categorized as children. One, he remembered, had been a toddler.

In the mix was one Canadian.

He supposed that nationality didn't matter. Not to him, at any rate. Still, it was a factor. And it likely had drawn in the Canadian government. Or their agents, which, he supposed, might include his tenant, his friend, Sam.

Gronsky checked the time again and noted that the day had drifted by yet again almost unnoticed. He wanted to get back to Danny Hawkins and his accelerated journey through the Rockies on his way to the coast. But it was time for the author to eat.

There was a knock at the office door. Anthea and Miriam came in and asked, "We're off to our favourite Greek restaurant, Gilbert. Care to join us?"

"That would be a fine way to end the day," he agreed.

"Oh," said Miriam. "I have an even better way. We'll talk about that later."

Anthea smirked and Miriam laughed out loud.

"Give me five minutes and I'll be ready," he said.

Later, after the walk down the hill, the great dinner, the walk home, the shared moment of puzzle building, he told them about the call he'd received. Not great news, but not deadly.

Soon, they all hoped, as the night disappeared, Sam would be home.

Morning, November 22nd

Gronsky had reached the point – or so he mused Monday morning as he rested in bed, giving serious thought to possibly getting up, an activity with which he had over seventy years of expertise – of thinking that November, for all its ephemeral virtues, was a tiresome month. His NaNoWriMo experience, while enjoyable and creative, had cut into his snooze quotient and those valued moments of plain slackery.

Of course, at that very moment that he was having these thought, he was sharing Miriam's bed. And she had to get up to go to work.

They cuddled for a few minutes, and then both arose.

"Porridge?" he asked.

"It's Monday, right?"

"Yes," he acknowledged.

"Then put on the porridge, Gilbert. I will share your Monday compulsion."

He was so predictable, he realized. At some point a few years earlier, he had created his own little OCD structures. Porridge on Mondays. Pasta on Fridays. Eggs usually on Sundays.

Not rigid. Never rigid. But often the same.

Predictable.

He was creative…but boringly predictable. And, he had to admit to himself, fairly rigid.

By the time he reached the kitchen, an unpredictable event had occurred. Anthea had put on the porridge. "Morning, Grandfather Gronsky," she said. "Beat you to it."

In fifteen minutes, the three of them ate their porridge like a family of bears and drank coffee. Anthea then hugged them both and left for school.

Miriam asked if he thought anyone else might have information about Sam.

"Nobody I can think of. The news is out about the two who were released. We don't even know if Sam is working that file or something else."

They commiserated with each other for ten minutes, small talk, a touching moment between loving companions, and then Miriam left for work.

Gronsky thought about sitting on the porch for a while, but the news of the day and the clarion call of Danny Hawkins overwhelmed him, and he went to his study.

Local news had nothing but small tragedies – a car running down a parade full of people in Wisconsin, the ongoing aftermath of the BC floods, the oddity of the Conservative leader and how he could not fully claim all of his returning MPs were vaccinated.

Gronsky jumped to CNN and caught the closing defence arguments in the Arbery murder trial. Gronsky then remembered that today was the fifty-eighth anniversary of JFK's assassination.

He still felt the import of that awful day. What would the world have been like if Kennedy had not been killed? Probably not much different, he surmised.

Chapter Twenty-one,
Scratch an Old Wound

Danny had never been to British Columbia, but once through the Rockies he embraced every turn, every river, every mountain vista. He expected he would have to hole up in one more town before making it to Vancouver. He hoped to be there no later than the 20th.

From there, as far as he knew, it was a two-hour ferry ride to the city of Nanaimo.

He spent the day weaving his way through the Selkirk and Purcell Mountains, having decided to stay aligned with the southern BC border as much as was possible. At any time, a quick trip to the States might be an option. Not that he needed another diversion. Growing up, he'd crossed over a few times to Butte, Montana to sow a few wild oats. Other than that, America was a mystery to him. This was likely not the time. He had his destination, somewhat vague but soon to be in sight.

Through the late morning and into the afternoon, the trans-provincial highway took him through Trail, on to a late lunch in the farming community of Grand Folks and on to Greenwood..

As the day ended, Danny came down the intriguingly named Anarchist Hill and pulled into Osoyoos. Quite tired, he snagged a bed in a rooming house. It came with a hot meal in the evening and toast and coffee in the morning.

After that simple breakfast, he gassed up and pulled out for the final leg.

He passed through the village of Princeton, veered up the Fraser Canyon to Highway 7 and followed the meandering highway into the Fraser Valley and ultimately the city of Vancouver.

He parked on Granville Street, the heart of the city, it appeared, and went for a stroll. Somewhat later, after six, he found a restaurant, The White Lunch, and grabbed a grilled cheese sandwich and cole slaw. The waitress, an attractive woman in her late twenties, told him that he might be able to catch the CPR evening ferry, but she didn't have the schedule. She thought there might be five or six ferries leaving each day from the downtown terminal.

After eating, he decided to drive down to the terminal and gauge his chances. The late ferry, scheduled to depart at nine, had space so he booked passage.

What a magnificent ferry it was. He wandered around during the two plus hour sail and even ate more than he needed or wanted to, just to enjoy the crowd of late-night travellers. He had confirmed that the ferry docked right in the downtown heart of Nanaimo.

Just before landing, he asked one of the crew where a reasonable hotel might be found. And a good restaurant. "Check out the Plaza for sleeping," the ferry crew member said, "close to the war memorial. Small town. You can walk anywhere. You'll find it. Can't miss it."

"Any good food joints?"

"Plenty. You won't starve there. Down the street from the Plaza, the Modern Café. Top notch. Opened just after the war, less than two years ago. Try the chocolate shakes. Cost a dime, so sublime."

With those last-minute bits of housing and poetic eating advice, Danny drove off the ferry into Nanaimo. In about two minutes he found the Plaza hotel and checked in. It was almost eleven-thirty.

He was both elated and exhausted. It was strange to be at his journey's end, in this new town, the adventure close to completion. He had crossed the entire country in less than a year and a half. Somewhere in or around this hotel, in this city, on this large island, Hubcap lived.

Might live.

Hubcap, the nickname for the vulture who had participated in the murder of his lover.

Danny's plan was simple. Perhaps too undeveloped. He would establish himself as a private detective in this new town. This would allow him all the latitude he hoped he would need to poke and prod and ultimately find the killer.

Evening, November 22nd

Gronsky rolled away from his keyboard. It was just after six p.m. The day had included a fair number of miles as the crow flies, the literary crow, that is, but he had successfully, if a little sloppily, relocated Danny Hawkins to Vancouver Island. There were some facts in question, data that he had not been able to verify, straightforward things, really but his factchecker, Google, had artlessly often been unwilling to tell him what he needed to know. That was on him, of course. His research skills were limited. Additionally, writing a novel in one month was an arduous chore, a daily grind of ferocious word production, and, possibly, his level of creative talent was somewhat limited or gotten lost in the rush.

Yet, even with all of that, he had reached the final tip of the tail of the dramatic tiger he had created, was hanging on to. Now all he had to do was ride it to the end.

With metaphors like the ones he had just thought to himself, he sensed that his novel would be somewhat of a smelly zoo with the animals in revolt. Then he acknowledged that self-criticism was of some value to a writer. Him, at any rate.

Though hungry, Gronsky needed to get Danny settled a little bit more. He watched more of the news just to get his fill. The threat of increased flooding, a new assault by the "atmospheric river," was a daunting concern. He decided to check his basement to see if the recent torrential experience had made entry inside his house.

He should have checked days ago, but he'd been so preoccupied by his novel that it had slipped his mind.

Just to be on the safe side, he entered Sam's penthouse apartment to check for leaks in the roof as well.

Nothing.

With those landlordish tasks done, he returned to the unfinished mission.

Chapter Twenty-one cont., Scratch an Old Wound

Danny slept soundly. In the morning he wandered out into a busy Nanaimo street scene. Heading down the sidewalk to the Modern Café, he could sense a bustling post-war community. In his sight were two Real Estate businesses. Neighbours. Sharing the boom. The Plaza Hotel had its own café right next door. He would have to check that out some other time, but first things first. He entered the Modern.

"Take a booth," the waitress said from behind the counter, "Unless you want up here." That seemed invitation enough, so he sidled up and sat at the counter.

"Coffee?" she asked, already grabbing cup and saucer.

"You read my mind," he remarked.

She placed the cup and saucer in front of him and poured with a flourish.

She had red hair and freckles, a ton of freckles surrounding a wide beautiful smile, and seemed to have an effortless way about her

"Danny," he said.

"Anne," she replied. "You've got the look of someone new I town."

"Fresh off the boat," he answered.

"Fresh to be sure. From Vancouver?"

"A little further east."

"Welcome, Easterner. We tolerate folks from the east. The war has spread us all around, hasn't it?"

"That's been my experience. You from here?"

"Born and bred. So, besides breakfast at the Modern Café, what brings you to Nanaimo?"

Danny smiled, said, "Mostly the breakfast. And I am a newly minted private detective. Thought I would start in a small community, see if my skills were wanted…then maybe move on."

"A private eye. Like Sam Spade?"

"Love Bogart," he said. "Yup. Maybe not as smart as Spade but no dummy."

"And you just landed in town? So how does someone get started in a new town?"

"Well," he stretched it out, "first he gets a mushroom omelette and some bacon and toast. Then he goes looking for an office… and then he advertises."

"Breakfast coming right up," she laughed, and rushed back into the kitchen and yelled, "One mushroom, pig strips, brown toast and throw in some hash browns, Ollie."

In a second she was back. "Home fries on the house. Part of our welcome wagon potato program…."

Danny twirled his seat to look out on the street. It would be a good street to be a part of. He could tell that there was a thriving community here. Even the previous evening, getting the straight goods on the hotel and the Modern Café from the *crewman on the ferry had been an indication of how welcoming the town might prove.*

It made sense to find an office nearby, advertise in the local newspaper. He had to assume there was a local paper. He looked around and saw one on the counter near the door. He walked over and picked it up. It was the Saturday March 20th edition.

He had momentarily lost track of time. "Anne," he asked, "Is it Monday?"

"You are a detective, aren't you!" she laughed. "Yup, all day."

Anne liked to play. He appreciated that. He might need a play companion.

Evening, November 22nd

Gronsky had had enough for the moment. It was after nine p.m. The longest writing day yet, and he had just made the minimum word count. A smart writer would hit the sack. He *was* a smart writer, but he needed some juice. This was the first day in all of November where he had halted, felt trapped by the test of finding the narrative, the test that would move his character along. His factfinding had escaped him.

He needed something, some inspiration. He looked at YouTube. Maybe a movie from 1948, some noir gem that would push him forward. After some minutes of looking, he came across a recent post of a Nicolas Ray crime thriller, *They Live by Night*, starring Farley Grainger and that super villain, Howard Da Silva.

The movie was just what the doctor ordered. Short, punchy, with great characters. Especially the waif, Cathy O'Donnell. She was the spitting image of Anthea.

He knew a little about the film, based on a story, Thieves Like Us. He would have to find the story someday. As he had been watching the film, he wondered what Danny would have thought about it. Though not his story, there were elements that he could relate to. Love, young love, well, not quite the new love he and Monique had had. But they been immersed in a seedy world, struggled to keep afloat, and, eventually, for reasons he might never understand, she had slipped below the waves, gone. Gone.

At eleven he finished the film, tried not to be depressed, failed a bit at that, turned the lights off, went up to bed and was asleep in a flash.

Morning, November 23rd

In the wee hours, Gronsky had a few further thoughts about the movie he had watched the previous evening. As uncomfortable a notion as it now seemed. there was a startling coincidence between the film and the trio of killers who had murdered Danny's girlfriend, Monique. He hadn't notice it until his brain was rested. That coincidence was that there were three killers in his story, and the driver, Hubcap, was the only one left. In Nick Ray's movie, there are three robbers, and only the driver, Bowie, is the last one standing.

It was a small detail, he supposed, barely worth mentioning. He wondered if, when the novel is finished, and someone reads it – hopefully someone reads it – and if he hadn't mentioned the coincidence, would a reader have picked up on that?

He supposed he'd find out.

The brain…it wastes so much time with trivia, Gronsky also thought.

Having wasted a few productive moments on idle speculation, he finally got up and stumbled into the kitchen. It was a wintry morning and he had forgotten his slippers. He opted to get them later, made coffee, poured some granola into a bowl, and went to his den. He heard Anthea showering. That reminded him of the image of Cathy O'Donnell, the waif-actress in the film, who played the character, Keechie. O'Donnell was luminescent in the movie, in many of the films in which she appeared. She died at only forty-seven, a cerebral hemorrhage on her twenty-second wedding anniversary. It could happen so suddenly. You get to a certain age, his age for example, and you had to listen to your body. Of course, it was also possible that your body might keep secrets from you.

These idle thoughts were getting the better of him. Gronsky turned on the television to get side-tracked by the day's tragedies.

Yalda Hakim was reporting from Kabul: the latest dictate from the Ministry of Vices and Virtues. He was always impressed by her, by the whole troupe of BBC journalists. In another life, he might have done that.

Ah, those Taliban. Twenty years the Russians fought them and then twenty years of Allied forces.

Where on earth can peace be found?

Not Afghanistan, that was for sure.

Another sad tale caught his attention: a fatal bus crash in Bulgaria. Forty-six dead, some survivors, a fire, many children, tourists returning from Turkey.

Gronsky drained his cup and went for a refill.

Anthea was having cereal and looked up, smiled, and said, "I'll cook tonight. Tacos, okay?"

Gronsky nodded. "Sounds good. Come fetch me when dinner's ready. I'm getting primed for the final push. Getting distracted easily…"

She smiled again, got up, hugged him, and said, "I've hardly noticed."

Gronsky returned to his computer and buckled down for the ride back to late March 1948.

Chapter Twenty-two, Scratch an Old Wound

The mushroom omelette hit the spot, as did the kibbitzing with Anne. Danny went for more coffee and Anne poured.

"Good?" she asked.

"You know it."

"I do. So, now you look for an office?"

He nodded.

"Know where to go? To find one?"

"This town looks like there are lots of offices. Thought I'd take a walk…find one that way. The shoe leather express."

"There are people you could talk to," Anne said. "The Daily Free Press…drop in there." She wrote an address on a blank bill and added, "Thomas Banks Booth, the owner. Tell him Anne Steele sent you. I babysat his grand nephew a few years ago…"

"Anne Steele, eh!" He took the note from her hand and said, "Danny Hawkins. What time do you get off, Anne? Maybe you could show me around?"

"I could, could, I? Come by at four this afternoon. You can walk me home if you're not too busy."

"Might be on a detective case…could happen."

"Then, fortunately, I know my own way home."

They both laughed. Danny said, "See you at four," paid the bill, left a tip, and departed.

It was a fine March morning and Danny was feeling optimistic. Less than a day in a new town and he had a date. It had been a year and a half since Monique. She would understand. More than that, he was sure that Monique would have liked Anne.

He walked slowly, enjoying the pleasure of strolling, anxious but hesitant as he imagined the newspaper fellow might not yet be at the office. He easily found the Nanaimo Daily Free Press office and entered. He couldn't remember ever being in a newspaper office before. It was a going concern. Typewriters, three of them, clacking away. It was Monday morning and apparently this tiny town had lots of news to report.

He attracted the attention of a fellow on his phone. He put up his hand to keep Danny at bay, finished his call, then looked up. "Help you?"

"Looking for the editor…publisher, a Mr. Booth?"

"Got an appointment?"

"Nope. Was told to look him up."

"Hang on…I'll check and see if he's in."

Danny waited quite patiently. It was a longshot that whoever the publisher was would be of any use for his real purpose, but an office would ground him, give him a base to operate from.

A few minutes later, the receptionist/reporter returned, said, "He can give you five minutes. Name?"

"Danny Hawkins," he said.

"From..?"

"Away…":

"Okay. Mr. Hawkins from away, follow me."

Booth's office was a jungle of papers, boxes, photos on the wall, an ancient desk, and a couple of oak chairs for visitors to park their fannies.

A man in his sixties, portly, medium height, vest, rolled up shirt sleeves, suspenders, and long grey pants, got up from behind the old desk, offered his hand and said, "Tom Booth. What can I do for you Mr.….?

"Hawkins, Danny Hawkins. A friend of yours, Anne Steele, just met her, actually, she dropped your name and suggested you might know of a space I could rent…for an office."

"Fine young woman, Anne. What business are you in, Mr. Hawkins?"

"Private Detection, Mr. Booth. Newly minted. Trained in Winnipeg for the past year."

"Hmmm! Don't believe we have another one of you types in Nanaimo. Have to check, of course. I don't know everything

that goes on locally. Most of it. You really think that there might be a need for folks to hire someone to detect for them, Mr. Hawkins?"

"The world is full of secrets, Mr. Booth. And full of people who want to know those secrets. And there are always the few that will go to any lengths to keep those secrets buried. Even in a small town."

"Sounds mighty cynical, sir."

"It does to me too, Mr. Booth. Still, we have just had a horrible war. Millions dead. Millions on the move. Yeah, detecting is a growth industry. Maybe even like newspapering…"

"Good point. Perhaps your profession and mine are aligned in some way. What brought you to our fair port city? Were you a Winnipeg native son?"

"Nope. Born in Alberta. Southern part. Was also living, if you can call it that, in Europe during the war."

"So, a vet?"

"A survivor of sorts. Anyways, know of any places for rent?

"I might. I just might. I presume you will be advertising your services…in my paper."

"Of course," said Danny.

"Fine. Where you staying?"

"The Plaza since last night. Just arrived," he added.

"So, you'll be there awhile, at the Plaza?"

'Until I can get situated elsewhere."

"Good. Look," Booth said, "Mac MacLennan up the street... he has a couple of buildings he owns. I think he would be your best bet. Let me call him. Why don't you wait out in front. I'll see what he has."

Danny shook Booth's hand and went out to the waiting area.

Five minutes later, Booth came out and said, "Mac is waiting for you. Has a couple of choice deals."

Danny again thanked Booth and went back up the street to meet the realtor

MacLennan was a short bantamweight guy, feisty looking, and quick to move.

"Let's take a walk, Hawkins."

They went halfway down the street to a two-story building. He followed MacLennan in the entrance and up the stairs to the second floor. "Two offices here. One's empty. The other one is spoken for. My son's an appraiser and rents it. The available one is small, just an open room. Water closet is down the hall. Shared. There is a cleaner who comes in once every couple of weeks. Twenty dollars a month. I'll throw in a desk and chair... hell, maybe even a filing cabinet. Do you need a phone?"

Danny thought the whole deal was moving too darn quickly but maybe that was the game."

"Yup, a phone would be useful."

"I'll get the telephone company on it. They will have it up and running by the end of tomorrow."

MacLennan suggested they return to his office and sign the lease. Once that was done, he suggested they go for a drinks.

MacLennan was a man full of suggestions.

It was still the morning, but a drink seemed just the ticket.

He took Danny back to the Plaza Hotel and into the lounge.

They had brandy and pickled eggs, and MacLennan waxed on about business growth and his son who was a 'bloody war hero' and came back with not a scratch.

Danny allowed that he had been in the war but wasn't much for talking.

MacLennan gave him the keys to the building and his office.

Tired of chatty realtors, Danny returned to his new office and sat in his new chair and pondered next moves. He remembered that in The Maltese Falcon, after Miles Archer was killed, Spade redid the signage. Signs were important. He would have to get a painted sign that said something like D. Hawkins, Private Investigations.

Or maybe Daniel Hawkins, Confidential Investigations.

But that was for tomorrow.

For the rest of the morning and early afternoon, Danny walked the streets of Nanaimo. It was a compact community, laid out almost in a wheel shape. It seemed prosperous. There were new cars in the street, hundreds of shoppers, a range of businesses, a store owned by Singer, several cafes, a hardware store, taverns, movie houses, and not far from the Modern Café, a dance hall, The Pygmy. He seemed to be spending more time than ever being attracted to dance halls. He hoped Anne would go with him when he explored the Pygmy.

At 4:00 he stood outside the Modern Café and waited for her.

She was out the door in a jiffy.

"So, Detective Hawkins, rent an office?"

He told her he had and asked, "Want to see it?"

"Darn tootin'," she said. So he showed her.

"Pretty plain," she commented.

"It'll do. I'm pretty plain looking, myself. The work is what impresses," he offered with just a swagger of modesty tinged with bravado. "So, where do you live? You did want me to walk you home, right?"

"I did say that didn't I? Well, Mr. Hawkins, we'll have to go up Bastion to the two hundred block Milton That's where I live. That's my street. It's not an awfully long walk."

"You live alone?"

"With my parents. Moved back home when the war began."

"Back from where?

"Jimmy, my husband, we had a small apartment. He signed up…"

Danny could sense where the conversation was heading.

"He didn't make it back?"

She nodded.

He could see her sorrow. She had loved the guy. Another war victim.

Her playfulness let him think she might have finally accepted the loss of the man she loved.

He'd find out. What else could you do with the death of a loved one but accept it and eventually move on. Death always sets its own terms. That was a cold hard fact.

Late Afternoon, November 23rd

Gronsky was further ahead of schedule than he often was at this time, so he decided around three-thirty, to focus on research, gather more facts, tidbits of local lore that would aid him as he moved towards the end of the story.

About six p.m., Anthea knocked on the door and said, "Tacos are ready."

The shells full of refried pinto beans salted with cooked onion, covered in cheese, sauce, sour cream, avocado, green onions, and lettuce were excellent.

He ate two fully locked and loaded tacos and gave some serious thought to shooting for a third but held off. He could always have a third curtain call.

He was feeling worded out, realizing how close worded out sounded to weirded out, and said, "That puzzle needs some work, don't you think?"

Of course she did, and she went to see if Miriam was also up for it. While he waited, Gronsky reflected on the progress he had made today in Danny's sojourn. He would, in the next chapter have, in fact, moved Danny six weeks along in his resettlement in Nanaimo. His new career would be taking off…and he had a girl…All in all, a reason for Gronsky to spend time with the women in his life, work on the giant jigsaw puzzle, and then get a good night's sleep.

Morning, November 24th

Gronsky knew that today was not a good day for the earth. At least he was quite sure because the east coast of his country was being deluged with buckets of tears from the wrathful gods of nature, and his own side of the country was swimming, floundering under water, in mud slides, in drowned cattle, chickens, goats, and God knows what else. A few humans had been swept away as well.

It was always his compulsion to watch the morning news, to adjudicate for himself precisely where the world was, where he was in relationship to the state of the globe. He realized he was just one man, one now aging man, and his existence meant so little to the survival of mankind, the joys, the pleasures of the planet.

With catastrophic disaster seeming to be everywhere, with his worry about Sam in Haiti, with thoughts that he might never see his son Robert, again, he jumped out of bed, showered, dressed, made coffee, toasted some bread, reminded himself to buy a new loaf, and rushed to his den.

He then turned on the television and landed on a Swedish / German Women's Olympic trials curling event coming from Switzerland. Gruyere was painted all over the ice, and he wondered idly when the last time was that he had tasted Gruyere.

He had never curled, but he enjoyed the lithe forms of women playing the game. These women in particular were pleasing to his end-of-the-world eyes. For some reason, it gave him hope.

It was an extra end...a tie score. The chatter of Swedish and German tongues overlayed by English commentary was becoming slightly annoying. He turned off the sound and returned to 1948.

Chapter Twenty-three,
Scratch an Old Wound

A month and a half later, Danny was a recognized sight in the downtown core. Almost from the get-go, he had a client. He was still resident in the Plaza Hotel but had taken two rooms in a boarding house effective the first of June, less than two weeks away. And he had a case. Mac MacLennan took a chance on him, if only, perhaps. to ensure that his new tenant had the rent money. It was quickly clear to Danny, however, that MacLennan had some serious concerns

"My kid, Mickey, Mick, I told you he was an assessor."

Danny nodded. "What does he do? What does he assess?"

"He works mostly for me at the moment. I've done well. My son…well, you know you go to war, and when you come back, you're a few steps behinds the ones who stayed home."

Danny understood that quite well.

"Anyways," MacLennan continued, "Dolly, Mickey's wife… they married weeks before he shipped out, and from day one, she, she needed reassurance from men that she was fun, still …whaddayoucallit…attractive. I don't know how to put it any other way. Once Mick got back, she settled down, became the wife Mick needed. But I think that dam has burst."

"So, what needs doing?" Danny asked, trying to pin down the sad and shabby story.

"Proof that she's fooling around, I suppose. If I get that, if it's there, I'll deal with it."

He gave Danny the details, addresses, schedules as far as he knew them. The younger MacLennan lived in a house owned by the elder. Danny was told there were no children yet. Mac regretted that. He had another child, a daughter, who had produced two grandchildren and who appeared to have a happy marriage. She was older, and her husband had not gone to war.

The first order of business was to tail Dolly MacLennan. That was not an unpleasant task. Dolly was tall, five-eight or -nine, with a busty figure, a Rita Hayworth-like face, short brown hair. She was efficient looking, with big eyes with dark-framed glasses, which added to her beauty. From Danny's perspective, she looked like she was on the ball, that she had a lot going on upstairs, as well as down.

The first day he followed her, Tuesday, May 25th, Dolly spent much of her time shopping. At noon, she met a woman at the restaurant in the Malaspina Hotel. Mid lunch, a man Danny later verified was the hotel manager, Fred Fall, stopped by and chatted with the two women. They all looked like friends, and the conversation was animated. After lunch, the women parted, and Dolly visited a beauty parlour a few blocks away. Danny stayed in his car but had an unobstructed view inside the establishment. Dolly was very social and seemed to have a lot of friends who frequented this particular beauty shop. The women working there also looked like they enjoyed her company.

After two hours of hair business, she drove home.

The next day Danny had a sense that he should get in position early. It was barely light when Dolly and her husband left home, and the younger MacLennan dropped his spouse at a ferry terminal. She appeared to be heading for a nearby Island, Gabriola.

As she was a foot passenger, Danny opted to take the ride as well in that fashion. It was about a twenty-five-minute journey aboard the Atrevida. Upon arrival at the smaller island, he was disappointed to see that someone in a car, and it was unclear whether the driver was male or female, picked up the errant housewife and drove her away.

Disappointed that he was unable to follow, he had two options: catch the next ferry back or loiter at the terminal and twiddle his thumbs, doing nothing much but watch waves lapping. He took the next ferry back to the Nanaimo terminal.

The next morning, Dolly left early, but this time she drove her husband to his office and then headed south to a community called Cedar.

Half an hour later, she pulled into a driveway out in the country, a driveway that led to a two-story house of uncertain vintage. He noted the address and waited. There was no opportunity to get close in and determine who she was meeting. She spent much of the day there and departed at about three. She returned to her husband's office, went in, and soon the two of them came out and returned home.

Danny then drove to his office, called his client and asked to meet. MacLennan said he was heading out to work on his boat and asked Danny to meet him at the Nanaimo Yacht Club. Danny agreed, and in fifteen minutes he and his client were sitting on the dock next to a sizable motorboat.

"My baby," MacLennan boasted. "A 1939 Chris Craft. Thought about getting a vessel with sails, but the hum of a motor is thrilling to me…and one fellow can manage it nicely. You cruise?"

"No," said Danny. "Never had a boat. First one I was ever on was the one that took me to Europe. Second one…the return trip. Third one, Ferry to Nanaimo. Fourth one, yesterday to… Gab…Gabriola. This would be number five were we to go anywhere, but the dock suits me fine."

"Takes lots of care, a beauty like this. Could pay someone. But for now, I'm the one."

Danny was thrilled that MacLennan loved his boat, but he wanted to make his report, a report that he didn't have much to work with. He gave MacLennan the straight goods and waited for a response.

"Gabriola, huh. Doing Mickey's job."

Danny waited for his client to explain. MacLennan didn't seem to want to hold back. "There's a property I picked up on Gabriola. Used to belong to a Japanese family. I bought it for peanuts when they were removed after Pearl. You know about that?"

"Some of it," Danny said, preferring others to share what they knew about whatever the topic was.

"Well, these folks were hustled off to Empire Stadium for a bit of time and then up to Greenwood, I heard. Bad business all around, but good for me and mine, if you get my meaning."

Danny nodded. He got it.

"Anyways, been sitting on it. I wanted my son to appraise the land. House is a shack. I guess he sent Dolly. We'll see what the appraisal says. Dolly knows her stuff too, but Mickey knows I wanted his assessment."

MacLennan didn't recognize the address Dolly had gone to out in Cedar. He said he could easily check. His boat had a phone. He ducked into the cabin and made a call.

In three minutes, he was back. "A friend of my son's. Haven't seen Lewis in years."

"He owns the Cedar property?"

"Parent's do…or did. Hadn't heard anything in a while about them. Come to think of it, I did bid on it. Japs owned it as well. Fisherman Japs. Never lived there. Lived on their boat. Bought it way back in the middle of the depression, I think. They had money when no one else had much. Except for me and a few others. Neighbours out that way made a fuss. at the time, I recollect. Can't blame 'em. Anyways, Lewis's family outbid me. Don't often lose out to many folks that way."

Danny was feeling that the case had pretty much concluded. His client had other ideas.

"Lewis was never a young man on the beam. Always something off about him. Knew his cars, though. Loved to race them. Be damned if he tolerated speed limits or the safety of others. Good driver, though. Lasted one year in infantry and then they cut him loose. Just not a soldier. Never did make it overseas. Least ways, that was what I heard."

He stopped for a while, then started pacing on the dock. "I can't figure why Dolly would be visiting him. If that was him. If he is living there...out in Cedar. I wonder what's going on?"

MacLennan continued his pacing and then stopped. He looked like a man who had resolved what direction to take. "Keep following her. If she heads out to Cedar again, to that house, I'd really like to know what's going on."

Danny reminded him that she had spent a number of hours in the house. It didn't take much imagination to figure out what she was likely doing.

He went for it. It wasn't exactly a hit for hire like in Winnipeg, but it had some of the colouring. "Would you deal with it? I mean, talk to the guy? To Lewis. If it is Lewis. Could be a tenant, I suppose. Just talk. Maybe he'll tell you, man to man..."

Danny kicked imaginary dust on the ground, on the dock, and then said, "If there's an opportunity. There may not be."

"Sure. If you can. All things are usually possible. That's my motto. There's aways a deal somewhere. Everyone's on the prowl, even them that don't know it."

Danny smiled at MacLennan's philosophical underpinnings but didn't comment. Instead he asked, "What's his full name? This Cedar fast car guy?"

"Lewis Capra. He was born Luigi, but when he was a kid, he insisted that we call him Lew...Lewis. Capra, like the movie guy. Wanted to sound Canadian. Couldn't blame him for that."

It hadn't escape Danny's ken that there existed a long-shot chance that Lewis, aka Luigi, Capra was the driver he was *looking for. Could it be that easy, he wondered? Nanaimo was a small town. Maybe it was.*

He was sure he would find an opportunity to have a talk with Lew Capra.

Evening, November 24th

Gronsky had had a very productive day. He could almost see the end of the story, and even though it was just over the horizon's line of sight, it felt in reach.

It was almost seven in the evening. He was hungry but wasn't in the mood to cook. In an hour, Survivor would be on. He found Anthea in her room doing homework, and she confirmed that Miriam would be ready at eight. With Popcorn, chips, and dip.

"And wine," she added.

"I can hardly wait," said Gronsky.

At eight, Gronsky settled onto Miriam's couch in between Miriam and Anthea and the games began.

After the initial angst, the plotting, the deception, the conspiracies, the racial factor and the like, the first challenge unfolded. The physical test and then one of perception. Gronsky hadn't noticed it before, but in this episode it was evident that few of the survivors were actually good swimmers. A number relied on dogpaddling.

It made no sense to him that a poor swimmer would think they could participate on this show. In any case, the reward was pizza and a comfy bed for the winner.

And more intrigue, of course.

In the end, it was a round of deliciously duplicitous backstabbing. The devious pastor, Shan, bought the biscuit and went to the jury which would ultimately decide who gets the million dollars. He would miss her conniving, though Miriam and Anthea were not so inclined, were in fact happy to see her depart.

After the show ended, Gronsky felt the need to get his forty winks. He kissed Miriam goodnight, and he and Anthea left for their separate rooms.

As he was about to enter his room, he remembered that *The Mask of Dimitrios* was on.

Smyrna, Sofia, Belgrade, murder, treason, and betrayal. A book, a wonderful character for a novel.... Sydney Greenstreet and Peter Lorre were superb. And there was a great line from a policeman, Colonel Hak, who said: "But to me the most important thing to know about an assassination is not who fired a shot - but who paid for the bullet!"

The film proved to be raw, rich with intrigue, death, and deception...a little more exciting and exotic than *Survivor,* Gronsky deemed. The ending, dark and deadly, tied the fictional author-character, Cornelius Leyden, in with the title character, Dimitrios in a somewhat slam-bang way. That sort of uniting of fiction and reality, book and film reality at least, Gronsky could well do without. He preferred to keep his fictional and real world wholly separate.

He went to bed at eleven and was asleep in seconds.

Morning, November 25th

Gronsky was up at seven to watch the beginning of the Davis Cup from Madrid. Canada versus Sweden. The major Canadian players were not present. It would be a tennis miracle if the journeymen Canucks could carry off a win. In the first match, Steven Diaz, the Canadian was up 4-1 in the first set before taking a momentum break and losing 4-6 to the Swede, Elias Ymer. Both players were unknown to Gronsky, and that affected his interest in the game.

Just before starting his time-travel back to 1948, he noted that a Catholic order, The Oblates of Mary Immaculate, were in hot water for hording monies that they were supposed to distribute to Residential School survivors. The sins of the holy fathers, mused Gronsky, aware that there was clearly a sad pun in the mix somewhere, but he was too enthralled with NaNoWriMo and its imminent completion to spend much time mining puns. On the other hand, the painful irony of this failure of justice towards those who miraculously 'survived' Residential Schools stuck in his craw. He had to admit that he had taken his time coming to understand the need, the absolute need for reconciliation. Not just in Canada but in all those countries of the world where indigenous people had been abused. It was enough to make even a cold-hearted author weep. Not that he thought he was all that callous.

After these quite sobering thoughts, he did remember to have some toast, coffee, and an orange. After getting all that organized, he started writing.

Chapter Twenty-four,
Scratch an Old Wound

On Friday, the day after his meeting with MacLennan at the yacht club, Danny was surveilling Dolly MacLennan by seven a.m. Mickey had left in their car around eight. The first sign of Dolly was towards noon when she went for a walk to a neighbour's house, spent a couple of hours there and then returned. She was in for the rest of the day.

The next day, Saturday, Mickey and Dolly left together around nine a.m. and, just like a couple of days earlier, she dropped him off at his office and then proceeded to drive out into the country south of Nanaimo…to the same house she had visited on Thursday.

Danny had to admit that the situation confused him. Observing from afar offered no satisfaction. Unlike the previous Thursday, his investigative curiosity got the better of him. There seemed to be no other choice but to drive up to the house in the country and stir the pot. Close to ten a.m., about half an hour after Dolly had arrived, Danny drove up the lane, stopped in front of the house, got out, knocked on the front door, and waited.

The door was opened by a handsome fellow, late twenties or early thirties, wearing brown slacks, blue corduroy shirt, socks, and moccasin slippers.

"Help you?" he said to Danny, not in a rushed way but with an edgy tone tinged with a touch of fake polish.

"Lew Capra?"

"Yeah! Who are you?"

"Dan Hawkins. private dick."

"Really," he sniggered, ever so lightly. "You lost?"

"No. I'm not lost," Danny answered. "Maybe Mrs. MacLennan is. I'd like to ask her about that."

That threw Capra. Frontal assaults were like that. In war. In peace. Capra wouldn't know a good deal, if anything, about war. Or maybe even frontal assaults. Danny figured that gave him an edge. He could see Capra thinking that he could deny that Dolly MacLennan was there, but that would just stretch the whole uncomfortable enchilada out too much.

"Maybe you better come in."

Danny accepted the invitation.

The house was in rather decent shape. It had the feel of someone living there. Capra led Danny into the living room. There were a couple of leather sofa chairs, a leather couch, and a scattering of coffee tables.

The whole room seemed…serviceable.

Dolly MacLennan was sitting in one of the sofa chairs.

"We have a visitor, Dolly. Seems he thinks you're lost. Are you?"

Up close, she was even more Rita Hayworth-like then he had imagined. She had soft glowing skin and bright blue eyes. Her lips were about as red as one could get them.

She let out a laugh that some men would pay good money for. Not Danny, but some men. "Hah," she laughed, "well If I'm lost, then it's the end of the world." She moved quickly to serious mode and demanded, "Who the hell's asking?"

Before Danny could answer, Capra tossed in, "Says he's a private eye, Dolly. Someone must have hired him. Mickey, you think?"

That garnered another laugh from Dolly MacLennan. "Why would Mickey care where I go. I tell him everything."

Danny quickly processed that response. The situation was indeed more confusing than when he had started.

"Must have been Mac. Fuck! No one else would care..." screamed Capra

That guesswork seemed to concern Dolly more than if it had been her husband who had hired him.

"Don't spew your guts out, Luigi," Dolly spat out to Capra.

"Fuck you, Dolly," he rebutted.

She softened her tone and rephrased with, "Lewis."

Capra regrouped and told Danny, "I think we're done. Dolly's fine. You can see for yourself. And I'm fine, should anyone care. The whole fucking world is fine. You fine, Mr. Private Dick?"

Danny was pondering that question just as the front door was busted in and Mickey MacLennan rushed in loaded for bear and armed with a luger.

He had the attention of all three.

Afternoon, November 25th

Gronsky was listening to the wild whistle of the escalating wind, the unrepentant rain, the sounds that were there and the ones he was imagining. He knew he needed a diversion. He had reached a critical moment in Danny's story. Now it was more than just Danny's story. Other forces, almost beyond a writer's control – Gronsky's at any rate –were at play.

He turned up the sound on the television and watched some of the doubles match. He had googled the Davis Cup scores and saw that Canada had dropped the second singles match between Vasek Pospisil and Mikael Ymer, Elias's brother, by the same 4-6, 4-6 score as the first match. Canada was up against it.

As was Danny Hawkins.

Now Pospisil was playing doubles. It did not turn out well. Canada could not catch a break.

Gronsky was overdue to have a bite of lunch when the phone rang.

"Hello," he said, expecting perhaps a telephone survey or a request to donate to the BC flood victims, something he had been meaning to do.

"Mr. Gronsky?"

It was Sam's contact.

"Yes."

"We have news."

"I'm listening," said Gronsky. He reminded himself that he had heard nothing new about the kidnappees since the last report four or five days earlier.

"Sam Simmons is on his way home."

"That is excellent news," Gronsky effused. "Now? When can we expect him?

"Likely on the weekend. We'll see."

"That's fine. Thank you. Is there anything else you can tell me?"

"No, sir, that's it."

And the connection ended.

He was still hungry.

Though not an exceptionally proficient cook, Gronsky liked to dabble with what he called recipe rescue. He would find a stray recipe on the internet, test it, and then make improvements. Occasionally it worked. He had found a tasty sounding Asian rice noodle recipe that seemed to be not only simple but potentially adequate. He grated some carrots, sliced a few mushrooms, found some not quite composting greens in the fridge, garlic, and cilantro (totally composted), made a quickie sauce of hoisin, rice vinegar, sesame oil, and soy sauce and mixed it with cold cooked rice noodles, added a few other items laying around and bob was suddenly his uncle from somewhere in the orient.

Anthea didn't turn her nose up at the concoction, so the evening meal was a relative success. Later they enticed Miriam into working on the puzzle for an hour and he shared with both of them the news that Sam was on his way home.

"That's wonderful," Miriam said, and Anthea started weeping with what they both assumed was joy. They all hugged.

"Then, he's okay, nothing wrong…?" Miriam asked.

"Nothing was mentioned. It was quite cryptic…just that he'd be home sometime on the weekend."

"We'll have to celebrate," Anthea glowed… "Something…"

"We will," Gronsky reassured them both. "We will."

As he'd stayed up quite late the previous evening, and the news about Sam was somehow invigorating and draining at the same time, Gronsky went to bed shortly after nine.

Morning, November 26th

The radio announced that it was Friday, and that British Columbia was between storms. Two more gales were still expected within the next few days. Saturday would be a soaker, but nothing compared to the whopper expected the following Tuesday, a tempest that was currently forming in the Philippines.

The province's infrastructure was in disarray. Miles of highway and bridges had been washed away. Provinces on the east coast were similarly awash.

Death and destruction were happening all over the world. An as yet unknown number of miners were killed in Siberia. So much more.

And there was, surprise, surprise, a new Covid variant, or so the news reported. Out of South Africa. *The B11529*. Catchy name, thought Gronsky. He would have named it Debola. Something that might at last frighten the anti-vaxxers into submission.

Then the radio said it was also called Omicron which sounded to Gronsky like an invading force from the planet, Omicron.

With all of that atmospheric swirling poised to volley down, Gronsky reluctantly crawled out of bed at seven and peered out the window. With luck, Sam would be home by the weekend. He wondered if he'd found any trace of *the* Robert Clapson. It was foolish to suppose that the Robert Clapson who was thought to be in Haiti was his son. There were likely dozens with the same name. Gronsky hated getting his hopes up about anything.

His son was lost to him. His daughter was dead. Those pungent aspects of his past were over. His future was likely all too short as well.

That was the way of life, then, death.

There was only the present, what he made of it. He showered quickly, dressed in sweats, and headed for the kitchen to feast on yogurt mixed with raisins and granola. After eating and making coffee, he woke Anthea and reminded her that it was

Friday laundry day and that she had best get up and strip her bed. She looked sadder than usual. Noting her glum look, he took the time to ask if something was the matter. "Nothing," she whispered.

"Nothing something or nothing nothing?" he asked rather clumsily.

"I don't know, Gronsky. It's so hard just not thinking about my grandmother, all of this, Sam. I really like Sam…you…I love… Miriam has …"

"It's all quite new to you," he said. "New to me…to us. We'll keep figuring it out. Talk about it. There aren't many other ways to live; we have to talk. I forget that sometimes. And this November writing thing. It was bad timing."

She smiled and said, "I'm fine. I'll get up."

They hugged, and he left her to her next steps and went to his office to get on with Danny's story.

Chapter Twenty-five,
Scratch an Old Wound

Mickey MacLennan had their attention. Danny immediately thought that the gun, the luger, must be a piece of memorabilia from the war. Useless information but something to note. He waited to see who said what next. His bet was on Dolly.

He was right.

"What the hell, Mickey? What are you doing? How'd you get here?"

MacLennan stared her down, then said, "Borrowed the old man's car. And you two! Behind my bloody back. You both were trying to screw me out of…everything."

At that point, Capra interjected, "Mickey, my dear, dear friend, nobody's trying to screw anybody out of anything. We're all in this…"

"Shut up, Luigi," Dolly interrupted, "My God, you two…spitting and spatting at each other. Grow up. And we've got this guy here," she said, pointing an exceptionally long finger in Danny's direction, "So be careful about what you say. And Mickey, put that damn gun away."

"What if I…" Mickey started to say, and then, "Fine. Okay. What about him? Who's he?" Mickey whined.

"You don't know?" Capra asked.

"Why would I know? Who is he? Wait a minute. Yeah, I have seen him."

"He's a private detective someone hired to follow Dolly, lover," said Capra to Mickey, who then probed further with, "Who the fuck do you think would do that if it wasn't you?"

Mickey MacLennan put two and two together as fast as anyone Danny had ever seen. "That meddling old bastard. He must suspect something. Jesus, this joker's been parked in the office next to me for weeks. It WAS the old man! Musta been!"

"Shut up, Mickey. You…" she said, pointing to Danny, "GO!"

"Don't be so hasty, Dolly. Maybe our private eye friend needs to stay and get acquainted. You sure you want him to leave?"

Dolly started fuming and again emphasized her intentions. "YOU!. GO! Before we change our minds."

It was an effective request. Before the trio worked their way up to a less palatable scenario, Danny quickly made his exit. He rushed to his car, got in, and drove away at a healthy clip. Five minutes later he pulled into a tavern perched above the Nanaimo River. He went in, found a table in the back, and ordered a beer.

Given a moment to rest and gather his thoughts, it seemed to Danny that there had been enough verbal spillage from the three people in the house. He now had a sense that the three of them were entwined in something quite shady. He had no idea what it was but the first thing that came to mind was that they were trying to divest Mac MacLennan of property, and if not that, something equally valuable. He didn't quite grasp why

MacLennan's son would be part of that sort of scam, but he knew that humans were capable of almost anything. The recent war had proven that horrendous point.

And he was certain that Dolly was the ringleader.

She was clearly directing their duplicitous traffic.

Whatever they were up to, and that might include some interesting sexual shenanigans, though he was only guessing there, his job was done. He needed to do two things. Notify his client with facts and maybe a smidgen of speculation. That and seriously consider moving offices. It didn't make a ton of sense to continue being neighbours with the gun-toting hothead, Mickey MacLennan. It had been serendipitous that they hadn't really run into each other until today, but obviously Mickey now knew with certainty that he was a threat as well as a neighbour. As for Lewis Capra, aka Luigi Capra, Danny still knew diddly squat about him other than that he seemed uncomfortably familiar with both Dolly and Mickey. Danny reflected that he might be reading too much into the brief interlude. Still, it was a strange collaboration and getting stranger by the moment.

The beer was cold. He finished one and decided to go for another. He also bought a pack of Export A and lit one up. He'd quit the day he met Monique, but there was no reason now not to return to the pleasures of a good smoke. The bar was fairly empty, and he revelled in the smell and the quiet.

In that quiet, the familiar cigarette smoke swirling in the late morning tavern air, he knew that he needed to go back to the house and tackle Lewis Capra. Capra might not be his quarry, Hubcap, but there were no other immediate candidates.

Half an hour later, he drove back to the Cedar property. Dolly and Mickey's car was gone, as was the one Mickey had borrowed from his father. The only way to determine if Capra was there was to sneak in and take a peek. Danny grabbed his revolver from the glove compartment.

He darted towards the house and squirreled along the side to the rear. He peered in a window and caught a glimpse of movement. Capra was sitting at a desk making notes. Danny went to the back door, tested it, found it unlocked, and entered, gun drawn. He inched through the kitchen and came up to Capra hunched over his desk.

"Don't move. You're covered." It was a much-used movie line but apparently effective in real life. Capra immediately froze. Smart guy, Danny thought. Not easily rattled.

"Do we have more business?" Capra calmly asked.

"I think we might," Danny replied.

"Mind if I turn around. I'd hate to be shot in the back. Always like to see the end coming. I'm funny that way."

"Carefully," Danny advised.

"Oh, baby, I am always careful."

Danny was impressed. Capra was as cool as the most bitterly chilled cucumber.

"Move over there," Danny ordered. He wanted access to the desk Capra had been working at. His thinking was that there might be some documentation, rail ticket stubs, something that placed Capra in or near Montreal on April 9th, 1946.

Capra did as directed. "Face the wall, hands on it," ordered Danny.

"You gonna frisk me, friend? I don't mind," Capra cooed. "You look like you have gentle hands. You'd be gentle with me, wouldn't you?"

Danny decided he had better frisk Capra and did so smoothly and quickly. Capra was weaponless.

With one eye on Capra, he rummaged through the various drawers of the desk. There wasn't much and certainly no financial records or ticket stubs. There was a small red book that drew Danny's attention. It was barely three inches by four inches and had a series of short poems in it.

"You're a poet?" he asked Capra.

"Why friend, yes, I dabble. Don't you?"

The poems were tiny. Modest. Three lines each. He thumbed through the little book, trying to make some sense of them. There were thirteen of them.

One of them struck an odd, improbably personal note:

> *April, cruel month,*
>
> *your die is cast, her blood flows,*
>
> *whimpers on her knees.*

Danny knew nothing about poetry. Couldn't stand it in school. He had tried, certainly in his early teens, to make sense of it, but poetry had nothing to offer a farm boy. At least the farm kid he once was. Was this poem, this seventeen-syllable rendition, proof of anything?

Evening, November 26th

Gronsky had to stop. He was so immersed in Danny's moment that he was almost hyperventilating and needed a breather.

In no time, as with all time, the day had disappeared. It was after five, and he needed a distraction. Something silly would do. He hunted down Althea and Miriam and asked them if they wanted to go to a movie. Both were game. Althea said, "The new *Ghostbusters* sounds like fun." She admitted she had never watched the old one, but both Gronsky and Miriam had.

"Silly will about cover it," Miriam announced, "but let's go. Nothing wrong with silly every so often." They made it to the 6:30 show down the hill. Gronsky appreciated that the film portrayed a family dynamic to which he could almost relate. The past coming to the fore, memories revived. Still, it turned out to be a totally inane movie but a shared silliness that they all enjoyed and one Gronsky, though he slightly cringed at the stupidity, found it surprisingly cathartic.

Afterward they went to an excellent Mexican restaurant on the lower main street. Miriam had the tofu-simulated Fraser Valley faux-chicken, avocado, tortilla strips, crema, chili tomato broth, and Oaxaca cheese. Anthea had the grilled romaine hearts, chili-dusted chicharrón, charred lemon vinaigrette, pumpkin seeds, and Manchego cheese. Gronsky enjoyed the fried brussel sprouts, sikil pak, and charred jalapeño vinaigrette. They all shared their tasty morsels with the others.

It was a fun evening all around and they were home by eleven. Gronsky wanted to sleep with Miriam and though she was willing, he said, "I'll be getting up early so I could wake you."

"You are a charming fool, Gronsky. I'll survive."

Anthea seemed to enjoy their banter, and once they had settled on their evening's activities, she said, "Goodnight, you two."

All were aware and thrilled that Sam might be home sometime tomorrow.

Morning, November 27th

The night was exceptionally stormy and wet. Gronsky and Miriam had cuddled more closely for longer periods than each had remembered doing before.

There was some comfort to be had in the wake of the atmospheric river onslaught.

Resting in bed just before eight a.m., Miriam said, "He won't want to go out and celebrate. I'll fix us a fine dinner. Lasagna. Sam loves that."

"So do I," said Gronsky. "Good idea."

"You want to get going, am I right?"

Gronsky nodded, kissed her, and said, "November is about to expire. I am running out of time."

"Then go, Gil Shakespeare. Write."

Gronsky went downstairs, showered, dressed in sweats, made coffee and toast, grabbed a fading banana, and adjourned to his den.

He quickly scanned the world news. This new variant, Omicron, was worrying. Already it seemed to be spreading and countries were locking down again. He decided to watch Al Jazeera, which offered an excellent streaming news service with an edge he appreciated. One story, brand new to him, was about the French islands of Guadeloupe and the battle between anti-vaxxers and the government. Nothing like the deteriorating unimaginable chaos that existed in Haiti, but just another example of a world that was, is, in near irredeemable pain.

Gronsky turned the television off and gave some moments of reflection to his Danny Hawkins narrative. He knew he was at that point where a resolution had to happen. It was fiction. That was evident. He had laced his story with a number of truth touchstones, facts, elements of that long ago time that gave a sense that the period he was documenting was being accurately portrayed.

Still, it was fiction, and required a fictional ending.

Chapter Twenty-six,
Scratch an Old Wound

Danny plowed through Capra's little book of odd poetry. Another one drew him in.

You old greedy man,

son of the father rebels,

laughs over his grave.

And, just before it, in the little book of dark haiku:

Motor on, old man,

set sail in your oily sea:,

gasoline delight.

"You seem to be very interested in my poetry, friend," Capra commented, face to the wall, clearly anxious about his fate but seeming the sort to bluff away and trust that his usual survival skills would serve him well. Danny still hadn't formed a plan that would conclude his quest. He was fairly sure now that Capra was Hubcap but needed something conclusive. He kept thumbing through the notebook and finally it was there, as clear as it might ever be.

They will not see me,

I am but the messenger,

and they will be capped.

Would Capra be so obvious, he wondered?. Maybe he would. The man seemed almost unfazed by his presence, his gun, his curiosity.

"Not particularly," Danny replied. "I mean, they seem so easily written. Not much thought. Little meaning."

"Everyone's a critic," Capra said. "You know, as I stand here, facing the wall, I've been wondering what's your game. No doubt you're working for Mickey's old man. That was pretty obvious. Most days, Mickey wouldn't blow a fuse if someone were hot to trot with Dolly. So, maybe something set him off. His old man? He never did understand his son, me, Dolly. Stuck in the past. Can't get beyond the world he used to know. That's it, isn't it? Christ, she's a dish, I'll give you that, but cracked… cracked. That old man probably wants a piece of her too."

Danny stayed silent. Capra might be a wise guy, but he liked to yammer. That could be useful.

"Come on, Gumshoe, I'm getting tired of this. So we have a scam going to buy up Jap land under Mac's nose. Big deal. He thinks he's such a bigtime hotshot. He's done well, the old crook. Greedy as hell, if you haven't noticed, and tight with money. Mickey wants more. And sooner. That's what this is about. I just don't get you. Aren't you tired of the rich bastards hogging it all?"

"Take off your shoelaces," Danny ordered.

"What game you playing now?"

"Do it."

Capra did as he was ordered. Once Danny had the shoelaces in his hand, he told Capra to put his hands behind his back. Awkwardly, Danny made a loop and wrapped it around Capra's hands. He did the same with the second lace. Once he had Capra secured, he said, "Let's take a little walk."

"What the!!!" sputtered Capra.

"Out to your back forty. Out of sight of any snoopy neighbours, assuming you have any..." And Capra did as he was told. Beyond the garden area, Danny whispered, "It looks like the previous owner was quite the farmer. Japanese, you say. Let's toddle off beyond that fertile chunk of land, then we'll stop in the woods...Maybe I'd better gag you." With that Danny yanked Capra's shirt down his back, tightening his hold on the man. He then tore a strip from the shirt and gagged him.

"Keep going..."

If Capra wasn't quaking in his boots by these manoeuvres, he must have ice water in his veins, thought Danny. They made their way through the remains of the large garden and shortly entered a copse of trees. Ten feet in, Danny told Capra to stop. He undid Capra's pants and pushed him down on the ground. He removed Capra's unlaced shoes, socks, pants, and underwear. He let his shirt dangle where it hung low down on his tied hands and back.

"What the hell are you about?" Capra tried to yell; his panicked voice muffled by the gag.

He looked at the mostly naked man on the cold, tree shrouded earth. Danny's anger was as palpable as Capra's fear. Though convinced that Capra was the driver of the car that carried the other two gunsels who had killed Monique, he still had an iota of doubt. What he didn't doubt was that the man before him, squirming near-naked on the ground, had likely committed other crimes. Or sins of some wretched sort.

He didn't care about any of that.

He had reached a semblance of catharsis by stripping Capra of his clothes, his bravado. Killing him would be doing him a favour and likely eat away at whatever passed for Danny's soul. It had come down to this. As focussed on revenge as he had been, as prepared as he thought he was, by war, by lost love, by the fiery furnace of retribution, it was beyond him.

Now, at any rate. At this moment.

And there was that iota of doubt.

He turned and left the pigeon crawling in the soil.

Danny returned to his car and drove straight to the Modern Café. It was about a half hour drive. Time well used to decompress. Anne was working. He sat down and ordered lunch. "I don't get off until four, remember?"

He smiled, said, "Of course. I know that. I was hungry. But mostly though, I wanted to see you. Just see you."

"Well, take a good look, buster. I have a busy lunch crowd. Eat and then scram. Pick me up at four. I can't have you glaring at me all afternoon. It could cut into my tips. And my concentration."

Danny ate and then went to see Mac MacLennan. His secretary said he was at the yacht club. Danny drove to the yacht club and met up with his client.

"You have a report for me?" MacLennan demanded.

"That I do." He then told MacLennan that while he had no actual evidence, it looked very much like there was no affair between Dolly and anyone that Mickey was not aware of. "Very European approach to fidelity," Danny added, somewhat unsure if he was precisely conveying the right information. "Also, if you haven't been buying properties that Mickey has assessed because the cost was too high, it's possible that he was inflating the value and scooping them himself. With his two partners."

"Partners?" MacLennan asked.

"His wife and their lover."

Danny had made it as clear as he could.

MacLennan looked like he didn't appreciate the bluntness.

"You're nuts!"

"Probably am," Danny acknowledged.

"I've never heard such a load of cock-eyed crap in my life." MacLennan added.

"I imagine you haven't," Danny said. "Anyways, it's yours to do with what you want. Oh, and I am giving notice. The office doesn't suit me."

With that Danny went office hunting. By four, he had found a new space down the street in the Hall Block.

Later, he picked Anne up and took her to dinner at Dot's on the Island Highway. Anne had previously raved about the roadside café, and it didn't disappoint. That evening they went to the Pygmy dance hall and cut more than a few rugs.

On the way back to drop her off, he told her that he was falling for her and wondered what she thought of that.

"So you're not moving on," she asked. "I thought you were a bit of a tumbleweed."

"Not anymore," he said as he walked her to her door. "Not anymore. Apparently I have a good reason to grow roots."

"A bit of a gardener, my friend," she said.

"Victory gardens are still in vogue," he added.

Early Afternoon, November 27th

Shortly after one p.m., Miriam knocked on Gronsky's den door and entered. "Sam just called from the airport. He's arrived and will grab a cab. Should be here by two. Once he's settled in, I think we should have a gathering, maybe some wine, a prelude to the dinner I'm preparing. Are you progressing well enough to do that?"

Gronsky wasn't progressing at the clip he had hoped to, but there was no way he would miss a sit-down with Sam.

"It'll be as far along as it will be," joshed Gronsky, not particularly feeling lighthearted but aware that his writing project was nothing much more than a frivolity. He knew with certainty that storms, refugees, political upheavals, and the host of tragedies that were consuming the world were the matters serious people were concerned with.

Gronsky kept working on researching Danny's story, and around three, felt that he had achieved a likely conclusion. There were still loose ends but that was life. Loose ends dangling like a bandage slipping off an old wound. Sometimes you scratch the wound and inflame it bit but mostly you need to let it heel.

At three-thirty, the four of them gathered in the living room where the jigsaw puzzle was still slowly being assembled. Sam looked weary. He was close to forty years old, Gronsky knew, but today he looked fifty. And inching towards ninety.

Government work! That's could age you.

"Its good to be back," Sam said, once the wine had been poured and they were seated together.

Gronsky sensed that Sam was in a sort of shock. He had that look, that woken in the middle of the night and thinking you might never sleep again look. Maybe the deer in the headlights look…one hundred-fold.

"It's good to have you back safe, Sam. The news reports from Haiti were, still are frightening," Gronsky said.

Sam nodded, knowing intimately what the others could only talk about. The truth was that much of the world's horrors had escaped Gronsky. He was thankful for that. He hated horrors.

"Look," Sam said, "Before I begin, I want you to know that I took a lot of Covid-smart precautions on this foray. Masks and such. Let's just keep a little space between us now…okay?"

They all nodded.

Sam sat there, shaking his head, began speaking words the group could have found by googling: "Almost half of the Haitian population is starving. Nothing much there is working. Food can't get to the people. Fuel is scarce, and when they try to deliver what they have, it gets stolen. The gangs are everywhere. The Police are immobilized. Saying they are ineffective doesn't even get close to describing how it really is. As for government, if you think we have problems here, well, its smooth sailing in Canada compared to Haiti. And the kidnappings…the awful theft of people…"

Sam's words came out in slow motion, and the exhaustion of his foray into Haiti seemed overwhelming.

"The key members of our delegation were engaged in trying to coordinate the rescue of the one Canadian caught up in that large Missionary kidnapping you know about. My job, and the job of my small team, was to source out missing Canadians, ex-pats and the like, who might be in country and findable." Sam paused and then addressed Gronsky and Anthea. "We did have the name Robert Clapson, the name of your son," and to Anthea, "Your uncle, on our list. There was little information about him to start with, but we scoured Port-Au-Prince first and then headed out into the countryside. Many of the names on our list were charity volunteers and such. Some easily traceable. A number were simply not interested in their own safety. Courageous…I guess. And there were places we, candidly, just couldn't, wouldn't go. Too damn chaotic. Dangerous as hell."

"So, no word?" Gronsky asked, just as Anthea put her arm around him.

"Oh, there was word. We made it as far as Jacmel. Other Haitian cities, a number of them, are still pretty much rubble. Jacmel is a heritage site. There is an international effort to rescue it. Time will tell."

He fell silent and then resumed his soliloquy. "In Jacmel, we found the man who had the papers identifying himself as Robert Clapson. There was a faint resemblance, the man in Jacmel and the passport photo. It was easy to see how it had fooled immigration officials."

"So he wasn't my uncle?" Anthea asked. "Not Robert?"

"No," Sam said. "He admitted that he had lifted the passport in Honduras a couple of years earlier. In 2019 to be precise, a place called San Pedro Sula. From near a body that was charred beyond recognition. He scooped the passport that was nearby, close to the body. Passports have value, but not to dead bodies. He said he was sorry."

"So he came back with you?"

"No, a Brit…"

"He stayed?"

"His choice. The fear of the known. In Haiti, there's much that is unknown. Death always…but not when. He stayed. His business. We had no mandate to remove him. We pleaded, but he was pretty firm. Stupid maybe. Then we left."

"And the passport?"

"He wouldn't give it up. I suppose we could have used force. Didn't blame him. It'll expire. Won't be all that much use to him. I've advised our people about his scam. Kind of guy he is, he'll scrounge up a replacement in any event. No doubt still has his own if he has one."

After a time, the wine was gone and the four of them worked on the puzzle of the Perfect Dawn.

The night slowly moved along, each comforted by the presence of the other three. At ten, they threw kisses instead of hugging. Sam would isolate for the next two weeks. Fully vaccinated and tested a number of times, he was a cautious man, especially in the home where he lived with the loved ones he lived with.

Eventually, sleep called them all to their beds.

Morning, November 28th

Gronsky slept well considering the rainfall. In the morning, listening to the CBC, he was consoled by the knowledge that the three people he most cared about in the world were in the house, his house, and that they were safe from the harm that seemed to permeate the rest of the world. He knew it was a fleeting comfort. That did not lessen it for him.

He was also closing in on the end of this month-long epic NaNoWriMo experience. In the grand scheme of things, writing fifty thousand words was no huge feat. Authors since time immemorial had been jotting down hundreds of thousands of words by hand, pen, quill, their very blood. He had the benefit of a convenient technology. Writing words was a breeze these days. Making those words, those captured thoughts, meaningful was another thing entirely. Of course, his words carried some meaning for him, and that might be as far as it went. That didn't concern him. At the moment, he wanted to end the narrative and prepare himself for his next challenge, whatever that might be.

He was also painfully cognizant that the last image he would have of his two children was more than fifty years old, the day before their mother absconded with them. Dawn, his youngest, was dead. He had held out hope that Robert was alive somewhere in the world. Robert seemed to have become a wanderer, though Gronsky had no specific detail of his life. Now it seemed he had died a murder victim in Central America, his corpse burned, his identity – always a question mark in Gronsky's mind anyways – stolen.

Gronsky got up, dressed, went to the kitchen, boiled a couple of eggs, made toast and coffee, ate, went to the porch, saw the deluge, knew that there must be flooding out in the valley and elsewhere, went to his study, turned on the television, confirmed that Abbotsford was under partial evacuation, saw that Covid was spreading, with the new Omicron variant identified in thirteen travellers to Holland.

Would it ever end, he wondered?

What would end would be his story about Danny Hawkins. That he could control.

At least marginally, for it had a version of life all of its own as well.

Chapter Twenty-seven,
Scratch an Old Wound

Sunday morning Danny had breakfast at the Plaza Café, attached to his hotel. The paper had a story about the heat wave and melting high mountain snow flooding farmland in the Fraser Valley. It sounded like it could get much worse. He spent the rest of the day moving his office to its new location. The new phone connection would take a few days. Like the old office, he had little in the way of furnishings. That didn't matter in the least. He was out of sight of the MacLennan family and, with a little luck, would not have any future dealings with them.

His luck didn't hold. Shortly before two in the afternoon, he heard an explosion. It was some distance away but drew quite a few people out on the street. They had heard sirens after the loud noise and had wondered. They would learn about it later, he figured. Explosions of any kind were worrisome. Certainly, war vets and those who had been caught in the blitz over England would suffer some residual agony.

Danny returned to his new office and made some notes about the MacLennan case. That evening he went to Anne's parents' house to have dinner and meet them for the first time. Anne's father, George English, was a carpenter, and her mother was a housewife. As Anne had told him shortly after they had met, she had moved home temporarily after her husband had been shipped out. When he died, she decided to make that return to the nest permanent. Until a better offer came along.

Danny hoped to be that better offer.

Over the roast beef dinner, conversation turned to the explosion earlier in the day. "I heard it," Danny said. "Around two o'clock?"

Anne's father nodded, "Yup. Look like Mac MacLennan is gone…"

"MacLennan?" Danny asked.

"Yup. Local businessman. All that wealth and he won't get to spend it. Boat blew up. Son, you look like you might know him?"

Danny gave the Anne's family the short version – MacLennan as landlord. The rest seemed best kept under wraps. He expected the police would contact him if needed. At that point, he would decide what to share.

The next couple of weeks were quiet. Danny had one case come his way. A teenage couple who may have run away because their Romeo and Juliet moments were being interfered with by concerned parents. It took a couple of days to locate them in the district of Harewood, adjacent to Nanaimo. They were holed up in a barn on a rural property, being fed and protected by teen friends who absolutely loved a true love story.

On June 8th, all flooding hell broke loose in the Fraser Valley.

On June 9th, two members of the BC Provincial Police visited Danny in his office. He was as prepared as he could be.

The lead cop, Sergeant Weems, did the talking. "We have a few questions, Mr. Hawkins."

"Been expecting you," Danny replied.

"Could have contacted us earlier, I suppose. Why didn't you?"

"Been busy… starting a new business can keep you occupied."

"I suppose. And moving…in fact you moved the day Mac MacLennan perished. You weren't his tenant for very long?"

"No. It was quite a brief relationship."

"You saw him on the Saturday before the Sunday of the explosion?"

"I did. At the yacht club."

"You were more than a tenant? He paid you. We have a cheque stub. A retainer?"

"Still owes me. His sudden demise has interfered with that, I imagine."

"I'm sure his estate will make good. Son's handling that. Mickey's a good lad"

Danny remained noncommittal. He wasn't expecting compensation from Junior MacLennan. As for him being a 'good lad,' that was open to debate in Danny's book.

"What were you doing for Mac MacLennan? What private detective work, that is?" the sergeant asked

"Confidential, I'm afraid."

"Won't matter to him now. And we understand that you are new to the gumshoe game. Where did you come by this profession?"

"I worked for the Vincent Brass Agency. Back in Winnipeg."

"We'll check. But back to what work you were doing for Mac MacLennan…why not help us out?

Danny had given considerable thought to this question. He was expecting it. "Sergeant Weems, you get a release from the estate, from Mickey MacLennan or their lawyer, and I'd be more than pleased to share what I was doing. It had ended the day before he blew up. Can't see where it would matter."

"Everything matters," Weems countered, "Until it doesn't. And even after that, it might. Okay, keep in touch, stay in town, and we'll get that release."

"Oh, I'm staying in town," Danny smiled. "Might even settle down, get married. By the way, do you know what caused the explosion. It was a fine-looking boat. I have to think that Mac went to extra trouble to care for it."

Danny hoped he hadn't given too much information about the boat. He needn't have worried.

"Not much left of it. Or MacLennan."

And with that they left. He had no expectation that Mickey MacLennan would want to talk about what his father had hired Danny to do. The explosion was much too coincidental for Danny's liking. He doubted that he was also a target, but Hubcap, who was maybe Lew Capra, was a force to be reckoned with. He had made an enemy, and that was always alarming. Maybe even two enemies. Or three.

Afternoon, November 28ᵗʰ

Gronsky was thrilled that he had reached his target. Fifty thousand words and counting. He posted the final day's number on the NaNoWriMo site. A certificate appeared.

He was a winner. Of a sort

The story, alas, needed more narrative.

Winning did not end the race.

It was Sunday night, and he had two full days to add to the total, not to add words for words sake but because the story, both stories, his story and Danny Hawkins's, might need further elaboration. Gronsky was not yet skilled at endings. He knew that about himself. Perhaps no one really was all that skilled. They arrived, endings, did. They happened all the time, in fiction and in life. Sometimes they were planned. Other times, they were most unexpected.

He made polenta and a tomato onion mixture with Indian spices.

It was experimental and not half bad.

Next time, he would find a recipe.

Morning, November 29ᵗʰ

Gronsky tried to get up a little after seven. Alas, his motivation was weak. Having achieved fifty thousand words the day before, the need to pound out word after word for these final two days was noticeably less.

He had never been much of a social man, and that was becoming evident in his relationship with Miriam. After Stella Fishbine – who was still clearly not, nor would she ever be, Stella Fishbine – had absconded fifty years earlier, he had very few liaisons with the fairer sex. Women, that is. Some were not as fair as he would have preferred. Fairer than he, to be sure. None of these dalliances stuck. He wondered if he was starting or continuing his romantic feelings for Miriam a tad too late in life.

He had lived much of his life in his mind and stepping out of that mindset – a mind trap he supposed he should call it – was difficult. Only in the past couple of years had he taken to pen and paper, of the computer keyboard sort, and begun to document all of the images that appeared in his brain. He had found so much pleasure in this late-in-life creative outlet. If there were a way to marry this obsession, if that was what it was, with the companionship of Miriam, not to exclude Anthea, for she was integral to his remaining future…. if there was a way to have it all, as he had heard women express their collective desires on more than one afternoon talk show, then he would be fully satisfied. He expected it was pretty much up to him and Miriam to discuss it and decide.

With that, he stepped back into Danny's future. He owed his character something equivalent to his own desires. Not forcing his elderly ambitions on a thirty-something fictional man in 1948 but letting the narrative flow, a peaceful river seeking its own way to grace on its way to the sea.

Chapter Twenty-eight, Scratch an Old Wound

The summer of 1948 had ended. So had the Fraser Valley flooding. That tragedy, however, was still reverberating. Families had been dislocated. Some had yet to be reunited.

September had yet to show her true colours, and the winter of '48 was poised to be similarly climactic.

And Daniel Hawkins and Anne English Steele were wed in a quiet ceremony at noon on an autumn Saturday in her parent's backyard. A few of Anne's friends attended as well as close card playing companions of her parents. Minister Harry Gates officiated.

With financial help from Anne's parents, they bought a small, partially completed house on 7th Street and would take possession at the beginning of October. Becoming a married homeowner told Danny that this indeed was his destiny. This town, this woman, and this house had grounded him, reassured him that not taking his grief, his revenge on Lewis Capra had been the right decision. And if not right decision, at least a tolerable one.

No honeymoon was planned. That would come later. Instead, after the ceremony and the afternoon celebration, they went to the Capitol Theater and watched the new Humphrey Bogart and Lauren Bacall film, Key Largo. *It had everything they wanted in a film: romance, bad guys, a drunken moll, torrential weather, and a favourable if somewhat cataclysmic ending. Later, they went to the Pygmy dance hall just around the corner from the movie house, met friends, Anne's friends, danced on the great dance floor, closely, tightly, memorably.*

They then went to their honeymoon suite at the Plaza Hotel.

Sunday morning they returned to Anne's parents house, where they would live for a further few days.

Anne planned to continue working at the Modern Café for the next while. Danny's detective business was treading water quite well. There were enough small, manageable cases, mostly of a domestic nature, to keep him afloat.

As for Mac MacLennan's death, it remained an open case, and Danny expected that eventually, whoever caused the explosion – Mickey, Capra, even Dolly, some combination, or someone/something else entirely – would be found out.

Or wouldn't.

He wasn't all that concerned.

He was still waiting for his final payment from the MacLennan estate.

That expectation fell into the gurgling vat of 'fat chance.' Not so the tenacity of Provincial Police Sergeant Theodore Weems. Weems kept coming back, week after week, not so much with new questions but with a constant and unwavering curiosity about work notes and about any lessening of Danny's resolve not to disclose his deceased client's reason for hiring him. Danny insisted over and over that if Mickey or the lawyer gave a release, he would be delighted to share.

He actually wanted to give Weems that information, with some self-protection parameters, of course. He doubted that Capra would want to ever describe his brief moment of captivity.

The thought of his retribution still amused Danny. It wasn't enough retribution of course. More might still be required. He acknowledged that to himself. Anne was aware of much of his history, but he had kept a few pertinent facts from her. Out of love, mostly. For now, his own life, his marriage, their marriage, were the key factors he cared about.

Capra kept his distance.

As far as Danny knew.

Morning, November 30th

It was the last day of NaNoWriMo. The storm had arrived and, reportedly, was lashing the west coast. Weather prognosticators anticipated it would be a force to be reckoned with for at least a day and a half.

Gronsky had been restless all night.

The previous evening, he had noticed that TCM would be showing *The White Tower* the following morning at seven thirty. He had never seen the 1950 Claude Rains, Glenn Ford movie, made a couple of years after the novel had been released. He was surprised to read that the movie had been planned to be filmed in 1947 with a different director and actors. The director they wanted, the excellent Edward Dmytryk, became a victim, for a time, of the House Un-American Activities Committee.

Gronsky would begin his day watching that film. After all, early in Danny's journey, he had Danny read the book. It seemed serendipitous that TCM would play it on the last day of November, a title he had referenced weeks earlier.

And then he thought: I am reaching, aren't I?

Gronsky quickly arose, dressed, ate, made coffee, and started to watch *The White Tower.*

It had been colourized and was immaculate from the beginning, including Glenn Ford's character playing "Red River Valley" on his harmonica...another serendipitous moment, to be sure.

Early in the film, the tragic chronicle of the mountain, the White Tower, is told to a group in the bar of the inn below the mountain. Carla's father, the most famous mountain climber in the world, had died in his last attempt some years earlier..

Glenn Ford's character says, when asked to help Carla climb the unclaimable mountain,

"What's the point. What have you got when you get up there?"

"Nothing," is her reply.

Later towards the end of the film, Rains' character – a French novelist left behind by the climbing party because his energy is tapped out –finds himself trapped in an alcoholic daze and a blinding storm. He finally finishes the book he had said "cannot be dashed off," steps out into storm and knocks over a lantern that sets his tent ablaze. Standing in the blizzard, he goes mad, tosses the sheaves of paper, his book into the ferocious night and wanders off to his death.

Gronsky didn't want to belabour the metaphor. The film was set in a post war world. A residue of the antipathy generated by the Nazis lingers in the character, Heim.

Mountain climbing requires collaboration, he supposed. Writing is most often a singular effort, but NaNoWriMo espouses collaboration. Heim seeks to be a Superman. It proves to be his undoing.

As the films ends, love, rather then sheer will, conquers all. The mountain will always be there. As will the unwritten novel, or the novel thrust into the hungry storm..

Enough said, Gronsky decided. He needed to wrap up Danny's quest. It is mostly done. A little final tidying and that would be that.

For Danny, and for Gronsky's world.

Chapter Twenty-nine,
Scratch an Old Wound

On October 1ˢᵗ, Danny and Anne, with the help of her parents and a few of her friends, took occupancy of their new home. Both family and friends had provided furniture and kitchen ware, and Anne had stored some furniture from her previous marriage.

The future was uncertain for them, for many of those impacted by World War 2. It would always be so.

Anne and Danny had agreed on some ground rules. Children were important. Two seemed a respectable number. The house was perfect for a family of four.

In bed that first evening, he told her his full story. He had thought about keeping it bottled in but realized that they had now started on their own marital journey. Honesty was really the only option. Her first marriage had ended in loss. Things had been left unsaid. The price of war and of death and their respective journeys had to be put aside, left off in the distance. But first they had to be spoken.

As they shared their pasts and their future plans in bed that night, the radio in the living room. left on, began to play the "12ᵗʰ Street Rag," the number one song of the day.

"A little too noisy," Ann said, and Danny got up and turned it off.

And the night ended in embrace, in the quiet of the lovers' arms.

Afternoon, November 30th

It would have to do, thought Gronsky. But before this narrative was ended, he needed to give some final thought to what should happen next. He mostly knew. There were obligations, not only to Miriam, for he now felt strongly that they needed to come together in something more permanent, more committed than landlord-lover, tenant-lover.

She might demure, say that the status quo really was sufficient, that she didn't want to disrupt his trajectory.

Or she might surprise him and say she was moving to Kenya to run a rural library. Or take a female lover and then run away to Kenya to open a gay library.

Gronsky felt a little silly writing these thoughts. All he really knew was that he was the one who had to state his intentions. If she agreed, all well and good. If not.

If not, what?

There would be some sorrow, he guessed.

He wanted to see if Sam thought that there was a possibility of finding Robert's remains in Honduras. Even as he thought this he knew the answer. He wondered about Sam though. Worried about him. He had proven to be a great friend, and Gronsky needed to tell Sam how much he valued him, what he had done for him – risking his life to seek out a truth, even though he ended up finding an impersonator.

He would do that soon. Thank Sam in some special way.

Then there was and is Anthea. Thus far, she had melded smoothly into his life, the life of the people who lived in his house. She seemed to have managed going to school quite well. He suspected that there were many things she wasn't fully able to talk about.

Next spring they would have to go on a road trip. She had seen much of his life. He wanted to see where she had once lived, how she had lived, understand all of the parameters of her pre-Gronsky world. He hadn't approached the idea with her thus far. He had come close a few times, but as with many aspects of life, Gronsky was hesitant.

Afraid, perhaps.

But a journey to the Kootenays had to happen.

They could do that. For both their sakes.

They would do that.

In the spring.

Definitely in the spring.

The End

About The Author

Bill Engleson is a writer, retired child protection social worker, community volunteer and an avid Pickleball player. He was born in Powell River, raised in Nanaimo, and spent his first year of life trapped aboard his parents leaky fishboat. He resided in New Westminster for most of his adult years, retiring to Denman Island in 2004.

He writes fiction, essays, poetry, reviews for the British Columbia Review, and letters to the editor. He has been writing most of his life and his first couple of poetic efforts were printed in his mid-teens in the, now, sadly defunct Nanaimo Daily Free Press.

He self-published his first novel, *Like a Child to Home* in 2013. Silver Bow Publishing released his second book, a collection of humorous literary essays titled *Confessions of an Inadvertently Gentrifying Soul*, in October 2016. He is working on several projects including a prequel to his first novel, *Drawn Towards the Sun*, and a long simmering mystery, *A Short Rope on a Nasty Night.*

While many of his longer projects are taking their own good time, his story, *Fidelity*, recently took second place in Geist's short long-distance writing contest.

Until recently, he was poised *(he often uses the word, poised)* to publish his latest novel, *The Life of Gronsky.*

Now it is done.

And he hopes you enjoy it.

His website/blog is www.engleson.ca

CPSIA information can be obtained
at www.ICGtesting.com
Printed in the USA
BVHW040711090323
659778BV00004B/5

9 780228 888413